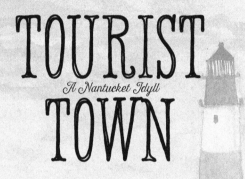

TOURIST
A Nantucket Idyll
TOWN

Also by Steve Sheppard

NANTUCKET YACHT CLUB: 1906 – 2006
A history

TOURIST TOWN

A Nantucket Idyll

by STEVE SHEPPARD

Tourist Town, A Nantucket Idyll

Capaum Pond Publishing
First edition

Cover art: Karin Ganga Sheppard

Book design: Kimberly White

ISBN-13: 978-0692512661 (Custom Universal)
ISBN-10: 0692512667

For Karina
Island Girl

There is no world without Verona walls,
But purgatory, torture, hell itself.
Hence-banished is banish'd from the world,
And world's exile is death.

— William Shakespeare
Romeo and Juliet, Act III, Scene III

The future is murky, and at least it's pleasant to
know you had a past.

— Paul Newman

It took me years, to get those souvenirs,
And I don't know how they slipped away from me.

— John Prine

"And now, who am I?"

— Alice, *Through the Looking Glass*

It happened several years ago …

Prologue

THE LIGHT stung, and she closed her eyes. The sunlight, how-ever, was insistent, turning the inside of her eyelids purplish red, no matter which way she turned her head to make every-thing go black again.

Or had it been black? She couldn't remember.

She opened her eyes again, slowly, but still the light was awful. Perhaps, she thought, if she opened one eye … but the attempt seemed to focus the sunbeam into a shaft that zeroed in on her partially opened, winking eye. She covered her face with her hands. That was better, but she couldn't stay like that all day. No, she would just have to adjust; her mind was urging her to see, as if her eyelids were a curtain that her consciousness needed opened.

She brought her fingers away from her face, let the flicker-ing purplish red behind her eyelids linger for a moment before she at last looked down and slowly opened both eyes.

The light was softer looking down, but she didn't know what she was seeing. Everything was hazy, strange.

Where was she?

But no sooner had that thought entered her mind when another made her heart skip and she covered her face with her hands once more.

Who was she?

The realization made her shiver.

Who was she?

She had no inkling who was peering into the harsh sunshine, who it was who was looking through her eyes. It was as if she had been born that instant, a fully realized newborn with awareness of her surroundings but not of herself. Like a baby, she had no memories, nothing. She didn't even know her name.

She would sit for a while until something came to her. She would sit wherever she was and watch the little blue buses across the way come and go, their steady movement and rolling wheels calming her as an infant is calmed by a slowly rotating crib mobile.

And as her eyes adjusted she thought this, too: wherever she was it was pretty. At least there was that.

———

"Pretty freaking awful if you ask me."

Although this was said in a whisper from somewhere near the back of the bus, Sandy Bronson heard the comment still. Hell, if she had been a passenger she'd probably be saying the same thing.

This was not good, not good at all. Summer hadn't even started and here she was, not a mile into her tour, when her microphone craps out and she can barely speak because of this damned spring cold that's given her laryngitis and all she can do is point.

"What's she pointing at?" someone else calls out, this time not in a whisper.

"The Oldest House," Sandy tried to say, but because of her

raspy throat it came out sounding like, "the coldest mouse."

"This is awful, just awful," the stage whisperer repeated. "The worst tour I've ever been on."

And it was then Sandy knew she had no alternative but to turn around and head back to the wharf.

"Screw it," she told herself as she raced through town, giving up on even pointing at anything. If she could, she'd be anywhere but here right now, anywhere but Nantucket.

She shouldn't even have attempted giving a tour that day, but she'd missed several days of work and thought the distraction of driving again would do her good. Besides, she could use the tips. "Fat chance of that," she said hoarsely under her breath.

"Did you hear that?" one passenger told another. "She called someone a fat ass."

And as Sandy pulled her bus onto the wharf, resigned that there would be no tips from this misbegotten tour, the sunlight hit her windshield at such an angle that she was temporarily blinded. "That's all I need," she thought, "to hit some tourist."

She didn't see the woman on the bench across the way, the woman who covered her face with her hands as Sandy maneuvered past the people and the delivery trucks that filled the wharf at this hour. She wished she'd brought her sunglasses. The sun seemed brighter than usual, piercing almost. She couldn't remember such a strong sun in spring before.

Get hold of yourself, Sandy, she thought, it's still early May. It's another two months anyway before summer fully unfolds.

Which was good.

Summer was a pain in the ass.

Chapter One

THREE MONTHS later:

Based on what she had heard he was a lucky guy, the kind who had good things happen to him, like making good tips after a rotten tour. But that was probably just sour grapes from the other drivers — as far as she could tell he was a pretty decent guy; a wise guy, perhaps, a little full of himself at times, but not an asshole; certainly not an asshole.

Not like that guy today (or was it a woman?) who tried passing her on the Polpis Road with a landscaping pickup coming right at her. Fortunately there was no guardrail at that point in the road, and Sandy was able to get off onto the shoulder without too much disruption to her tour.

Asshole.

And that was it, she knew; more than half the tour to go, and no matter how entertaining, how charming, how frigging soothing she was from there on out it wouldn't make any difference. The trip was ruined. She may as well have just turned around right there and gone back to base, but she didn't — she continued on with the tour, out to the beach, back past the cranberry bog and the airport, explaining everything, telling the people in the rearview mirror, who weren't listening to her at all, but mumbling to each other about the close call they'd had on this winding country road, going about 30 miles an hour, on a perfect day with no rain, no ice, on this little freaking island they'd heard about but now wanted to get off of as soon as possible, no matter that Jackie Kennedy used to live here — or was it that other overpriced island? — who gave a shit now? They weren't even seeing how beautiful the place was; she knew it was over. And then …

And then she got stuck in a major, major traffic jam just outside of base. She had miscalculated and not taken a right behind the old gas tanks because she couldn't see the backup — she wasn't thinking, that was the problem, she hadn't kept her focus on the tour, a rookie mistake — and now it was too late and there was nowhere she could go — they were lined up from the boat all the way back through two stop signs and nobody was moving. She had stopped talking a while ago anyway; she was sick of everybody on the bus and they were sick of her. So when a man stood up and began walking down the aisle she was ready. *No, there is no way you are getting off this bus now, I don't care how much you say you have to go to the bathroom.* Once you let one off, they'll all want to get off, and there was something about it, something psychological, that if they get off before getting back to base, back to the place they started from, back to the beginning like a ride at Disney World, it was as if the tour had malfunctioned and they did not have to tip! It was one of the first things she was taught when she took this job and it was one of the first things she taught new drivers, including whatshisname, who everybody thought was so lucky because he always seemed to make great tips, no matter how rotten the tour. No, this wouldn't be happening to Addie McDaniel, Sandy thought as she leaned her elbows onto the steering wheel and her passengers begged to be let off. He's probably back at base right now, counting his money.

———————

Addie McDaniel at that moment, the one everyone thought was so lucky, was not, by any means, back at base and counting his money. Instead, he was counting his passengers, making sure they were all right while his bus supported itself on three wheels. If not for the rabbit that darted from out of nowhere, a white rabbit, he thought, which was strange (was it somebody's pet?) that he braked for, hard, the tour would have been over and may have been great. To top it off, he was just a mile from the wharf where the buses lined up, his last tour of the day.

Things had started out so well. He was "on" — he had the passengers laughing before the wheels were rolling. That was important, to get them laughing early, to make them feel you were their friend.

He forgot now what he'd said, he'd been doing it so long most of his tours were improvisational, his comments off the cuff. He may have talked about the poor slobs who weren't lucky enough to be on his bus, the ones standing outside the bus windows lighting cigarettes or looking around for a bathroom, but it didn't matter now.

Because now his bus was listing off to the side of the road and his passengers were either staring at the bus's collapsed wheel, wondering what in God's name had ever compelled them to get on this tour in the first place, or were walking in stunned pairs back towards town. There was no way to keep everybody on the bus, even though his first instinct after he swerved to miss the rabbit and the ball joint broke and the bus made that horrible grinding racket and everyone started screaming was to yell out, "Everybody stay on the bus," it was no use. They were at the door as soon as the bus screeched to a stop. There'd be no tips from this tour.

It could have been a hundred dollar day, too.

"Summer is a pain in the ass," he said under his breath as he waited for the tow truck to arrive and the passing traffic slowed to gawk.

Chapter Two

RELISHING SUMMER at that instant a woman turns to the warming sun as it slowly drops behind the buildings on the wharf, the low sunlight lending a rich glow to the sky, turning the harbor water a navy blue. To Verona, summer was a kaleidoscope of colors, with each new flower that bloomed a reminder of all that was good about the island. How lucky she was, she thinks, how fortunate that it had been Irene who'd plucked her off that bench on Straight Wharf and taken her home.

At the time, she would have followed anyone who asked her.

Now, as Verona sits on the same bench where her awakening began three months before, for that is how she thinks of it, as her awakening, her rebirth, she marvels at the people swarming around her — the tourists in all different sizes and colors waddling onto the tour buses; the tanned young men and women hurrying to their summer jobs or huddled at the gazebo at the center of the wharf, drinking and talking and showing off for each other.

It had been different when Irene had found her, when it was like waking from a dream, a dream that left her mind a blank slate, a tabula rasa, if you will. Nothing was familiar. A haze clouded her vision at first, a fog that made the colors and buildings and people blur into an incomprehensible mass. She paid no attention that day (as she wondrously does now) to the people passing by: the overweight men wearing T-shirts that proclaimed, "I Am the Man from Nantucket," or the ones in sweatshirts with an arrow pointing sideways that said, "I'm with stupid;" the blue-haired women licking ice cream cones; the teenagers who poked and prodded each other. She sat confused in the blinding sunshine as the people paraded by and streamed around her. Some boarded the little blue buses she saw across the way; she could only watch them, the thought of getting on one never entered her mind. Leaving the safety of the bench was too frightening to consider.

She was visibly distressed, she must have been, because a girl came up to her — Irene, it turned out, Irish Irene from Cork — to ask if she was all right. A boat docked in a nearby slip bobbed peaceably, the name "Verona" stenciled on its stern. It soothed her to realize she could read it, that she understood something, the recognized letters an anchor of sorts. "Ver-o-na," she said to herself, mouthing the name silently, the syllables from her lips formed separately and deliberately.

"Are you staying somewhere?" the girl asked. Verona, she found it easy to call herself that, her vision focused now, marveled at the different shades of color: the bright blue sky, the subtle green-blue of the harbor, the dark and light green of the leaves on the trees like fingers filtering the sunlight.

The girl asked again if she was staying anywhere. Verona looked, saw this person moving her lips while the rest of her face remained curiously out of focus. Verona's attention shifted to something beyond the girl, to a white rabbit sitting amidst a rhododendron. The haze that moments before had obscured her sight had lifted; her vision was now intensely acute — she was able to zoom in on the rabbit, almost see its individual hairs, count its whiskers. It seemed, too, as if the rabbit was looking back at her, as though it somehow recognized her.

As she wondered whether the rabbit was indeed looking at her, she heard a voice, as if from a different world. "Do you need a place to stay?"

Stay? What? Is somebody speaking? Verona looked towards the voice, shifted her focus in that direction. The girl had a kind face, but what was she asking? Finally, the question registered, and Verona said, at last, "I don't even know where I am."

"Right, then. You're coming home with me," the girl said without hesitation. "Where's your bag?"

"Bag?"

"Suitcase; knapsack; paper bag. Do you have any clothes?"

Verona looked down at the clothes she was wearing. Were there others she needed? She looked bemusedly at the girl who was walking around the bench she was sitting on. Funny, Irene thought, looking under the bench, looking beyond it, usually these summer workers have one large suitcase and a knapsack. Funny, too, that there wasn't anyone to meet her at the boat.

This woman, Irene thought as well, was older than the other workers who were coming from Bulgaria, Russia, Belarus, Brazil, not to mention the now-established workers from El Salvador and Jamaica. Some Irish still came, but the days when Nantucket represented Ireland west were over. This woman on the bench was not Irish that was for sure — she obviously had a tough time with English — and the way she was dressed, in a skirt and blouse and short, button-up sweater, suggested an Eastern Bloc country.

Whatever; she'd get her home and get things sorted out. It was a small island — someone would be looking for her.

———

Irene lived with six other Irish girls in a three-bedroom house in the southeastern corner of Nantucket, an area of the island called Tom Nevers.

"So, you've a name have you?" Irene asked, plugging in an electric tea kettle.

The image of the boat reappeared in her mind. "Verona," she said.

"Your parents must have read Shakespeare."

Verona had no idea what she was taking about.

She should have been frightened, Verona thought later, waking up not from a dream but into a dream where she had no sense of who she was, where she was, or how she'd gotten there. She could have been frantic, needing to know what had happened to her, broken down in tears, but Irene's calm ways were soothing. It had been easy to follow her home, to let someone else think for her. As she sipped the tea Irene had made for her, a wave of resignation poured into her body. It was easier not to know than to think about knowing. Yes, that was better — her mind was clearer now, her body more relaxed. Things would reveal themselves in time. She didn't know where she was but she was somewhere, she was safe. She was tired. On Irene's insistence, she stayed in Irene's room that night and, mercifully, slept a dreamless sleep.

———

The woman was strange, Irene thought as she made up the couch into a temporary bed for herself, but she figured what the heck, if no one else wants to claim her for work, I will. A couple of girls didn't work out, and she could use the extra hand cleaning houses. Someone had obviously arranged for her to come to the island to work for the summer; she had the dazed look of others she'd met at the boat, the girls from foreign countries who were a bit overwhelmed at first. That was all right, like the others she'd adapt soon enough.

Yet Irene couldn't help thinking that this woman, after she'd loosened up a bit, spoke English so well, yet didn't seem to understand a thing. Oh, well. That, too, would get sorted out.

The next morning, Irene asked Verona if she wanted to work with her for a while, and it would be no problem because "yer man" could always use an extra hand and it was an added plus that she spoke English. "Oh, we have some Dominican girls in the summer who are quite nice, but some of our clients prefer girls who speak English, if you know what I mean."

Verona did not know what she meant, but if Irene felt she should work with her, why not? She could always figure things out later.

"You can stay here if you like," Irene proposed. "There was supposed to be another girl coming over, but her visa fell through. You can share the room she was going to have."

Verona had slipped from sleep easily that morning, her eyes taking in the bedroom as she yawned herself awake. She was content at first, comfortable, until the slow realization came that she was in a strange room. She sat up in bed — she didn't know where she was! An adrenaline surge shot through her so quickly she felt she was shrinking. But wait — she remembered it now — this woman, Irene, had taken her home, given her her bed. Yes, that was better, she was calmer now, no longer shrinking, eyes adjusting as she dangled her legs off the side of the bed and gazed idly at her flexing toes.

As for who she was, however, she still had no clue. It was as if that part of her brain had been disconnected.

When Verona met "yer man," who called himself Harold Starbuck and filled his positions at Ahab House Cleaning Service primarily with illegal immigrants, he was standing outside one of the old homes on Main Street, a two-story white clapboard sea captain's house, complete with roof walk. Sure he had work for her, Irene could train her, and there'd be no forms to fill out he assured her because "you'll be paid in cash, it's easier that way." He assumed Verona was Irish and most likely didn't have working papers. Why else would Irene have brought her to him?

"So, Verona, is it? Unusual name. And your last name?"

Verona was too busy noticing the mole on his cheek to absorb what he'd just said.

"Your last name?" he asked again.

He was standing next to a parked Ryder Electric truck. She almost said Ryder but immediately another truck drove by: Smith Siding and Shingling.

"Smith," she said. It popped into her head and slipped off her tongue.

That she hadn't said Ryder was fortunate, she realized later, because there were so many Ryders on the island that at some point one of the family, had they met her or even heard of her, would probably wonder how they were related, and that would raise all sorts of questions. There was no glut of Smiths on the island, however. And what Verona hadn't known was that the Smith Siding and Shingling truck was on the island for just that one day, it being a mainland company that previously, or since, had no other business on Nantucket.

Her anonymity seemed destined.

Chapter Three

IN THE three months since Irene had found her, Verona had had no revelations, no insights to her identity. As one day folded into the next she accepted more and more her state of not knowing, embraced it even. She was comfortable with who she was, she liked her life. She loved the blankness of her mind, her uncluttered consciousness.

Oh, she'd had her trepidations, her moments of fear. She'd fingered the fabric of her clothes that first morning at Irene's, hoping the tactile sensation would be a trigger to her past. But as the hours went by, it was easier to take things as they came. Thinking about it only confused her.

Why am I here? she asked herself soon after she'd moved in with Irene.

Nothing came to her. She concentrated: still nothing. Rather than squeeze her mind around nothing, she let the matter drop. She busied herself by walking outside, allowed the summer breeze to blow her thoughts away.

As one day ceded to the next, the prospect of encountering her past made her apprehensive. There had to be a reason she couldn't remember. Who knew what secrets the past held?

A thought then entered her mind, a notion that arrived with the same suddenness as when consciousness first came to her on the wharf: she didn't want to know.

Yes, that was it, she would simply stop wondering. And as she let herself accept this, she reflexively released a deep exhale.

In her heart she knew she'd been given a second chance at life. For whatever reason, she was granted the serenity of an unencumbered existence.

She took solace in what she did know — that she understood language, for instance, that she could identify the things around her: trees, birds, the moon, the stars. Things could be worse, she told herself, things could be much worse.

"I could have woken up in prison," she thought, "or in a hospital bed."

At first, Verona hadn't contemplated where she was, other than knowing she was living with Irene and a cluster of other girls in some place called Tom Nevers. Within a week or so, picking up on smatterings of banter within the household, it was evident she was living on an island, removed from the rest of the world, surrounded by the cradling ocean. She did not know how or when she'd arrived on this island, but if she was fated to be anywhere, she was glad it was here, where everything was so beautiful. Irene was curious how she'd gotten to Nantucket, but was gracious and didn't press when Verona was circumspect in their conversations.

The limits of the island appealed to Verona, seemed to hold her in place. That she was restricted in her travels to where she could get by bicycle, or on foot, was fine with her. She enjoyed roaming the streets of the old town. She was particularly taken by the cemeteries and found she could wander the worn paths amid the tombstones for hours without being seen or questioned.

She understood she had to be careful in her journeys

through town, however; that her walks couldn't become habitual — people would notice: that strange, new woman who walked the streets alone.

She was glad now that she'd taken that job with Irene; it gave her a purpose, something mindless to focus on, a way to fill the empty day.

She had learned much about the island on her daily drives to clean houses with Irene. Although Irene had only been on the island about two years herself, she knew, or knew about, pretty much everyone they passed.

"There's old Sarah," she recalled Irene saying on her second or third day of work. "Walks every day to Mass, then to the A&P."

"Oh, hi, Jimmy," Irene waved through the windshield on another day. "Surprised Jimmy's out and about, he had quite a night of it last night."

After a few days of Irene's pointing out the comings and goings of various people, Verona realized that she could never allow herself to be someone who could be so readily identified. Even if no one knew who she was, they'd wonder after a time what she was doing here, what her story was.

She came to understand that it was better to know a few people and not be such a mystery around town that people would make it their business to know hers.

She had all that she needed: a bed to sleep in at night, a job where no one asked questions (and paid her in cash), a bicycle to get around on. She did not want or need anything else and she had no desire to ruin everything by asking too many questions. She was happy where she was and she wanted it to stay that way.

She felt good; the sun was shining. Why wreck it?

That no one had come looking for her was good; if she understood one thing it was that she never wanted to leave the island. As long as she stayed on Nantucket she was safe.

She just knew it.

Chapter Four

To ADDIE McDaniel, summer was once a glorious ride, the sun-filled payoff after the long, cold, grey, windy winter. Now it seemed more and more a season to be gotten through, to endure. The shops on Main Street were closing — they had just lost one of the old drugstores and its vintage soda fountain last summer — the town's former identity was fading. The mega-rich had arrived, and with their coming the soda fountains and hardware stores and camera shops were beyond quaint, they were unnecessary; they offered nothing the new wealthy needed. It was lucky there was still a small supermarket downtown, but, hey, it was convenient for the yachters. The island was changing, all right; there was no doubt about it.

On his way to the bus lot that evening, Addie posed the question to Digit Hathaway:

"Don't you think summer's turned into one big pain in the ass?" he asked him.

Digit wasn't paying attention. He was too busy affixing a bumper sticker to his truck. "Re-elect Sheriff Shank," it said.

"Hey, Digit, the election was last week. Shank got back in."

"Exactly," Digit said. "Why do you think I'm putting his bumper sticker on? It pays to back a winner."

"But he's already won."

"Now you're catching on," Digit said sarcastically. "I've got stickers for his two opponents in the house. Whoever wins goes on my truck. Take a look: see any losers here?"

Addie inspected Digit's rear bumper, his tailgate, and even his back window, where the previous "Re-elect Sheriff Shank" sticker resided from the last campaign, right alongside his "Endangered Species: Nantucket Native" bumper sticker. Everyone represented on Digit's truck was in office, including Jason Bonere, the new chairman of the Board of Selectmen.

"Why take chances?" Digit explained. "I don't care who's in office, but the people who win obviously do. If I stick my neck out and the sheriff or selectman I backed doesn't get in, what do you think the odds will be that the boys in blue will give me a break the next time I get pulled over, or if I've parked an hour over on Main Street? This way, they'll see I'm on the side of law and order, especially if Shank's in a rotten mood, which he usually is."

"Planning on getting pulled over?" Addie asked.

"Of course not, but you never can be too careful. It's a small island, my friend."

Digit was not Digit's real name. Like a lot of natives, "Digit" was a nickname, a moniker given him in first grade when some wiseguy caught him counting on his fingers — once. It didn't matter that Digit went on to be a whiz in math, and that he studied agriculture at Cornell, the name stuck and he was forever branded "Digit." In truth, he didn't mind; his real name was Clarence.

"Who'd name a boy Clarence?" his Uncle Bob asked his mother when he was born.

"I named him after our father," she reminded him.

"I always thought Dad's name was Skip."

Addie met Digit soon after he'd arrived on the island, coming, he thought, for a short summer stint to paint houses. Digit had recently inherited his aunt's home, an aunt who had never married, never had kids, and Digit was taking in boarders. Addie had come with his girlfriend at the time, and the couple struck up a conversation with Digit at the Brotherhood, a restaurant located in the basement of a nineteenth century house that had been refashioned into an 1800s whaling bar. Nantucket was different in those days. Even though Addie and his girlfriend had just met Digit that afternoon, and even though they had accommodation of sorts — sleeping in cots in the houses he was painting — the next thing Addie knew they were both living with Digit.

"Sleeping on cots sucks," Digit had told them. "I've got real beds. You're staying with me. Don't worry, I'm cheap."

Addie and his girlfriend parted ways after that summer, but Addie, with no place else to go, no plans, decided to stay on for a while, hang out for the winter, try out island life in the off-season. The change would do him good, he thought. He'd regroup, get his act together, find himself.

Despite his penchant for sarcasm, Digit was, Addie would find, a compassionate kind of guy; he didn't up Addie's rent after his girlfriend left, letting him pay the half-room rate he'd been accustomed to. Winter gave way to summer, summer to fall, and Addie stayed. There was no pressing need to leave, the pace of island life agreed with him. In time he and Digit grew close, they shared a common outlook, and Addie was Digit's best man when Digit finally married his girlfriend of fifteen years, Marsha. Digit said Addie could stay in the house, but Addie knew better. "If we stayed living together after you got married people might get the wrong idea," he said.

———

And so began Addie's odyssey of moving from winter rentals to summer shackups — the "Nantucket Shuffle" it was called. Because Digit got married in the fall, Addie was able to find a winter rental that first year, a small cottage — a converted chicken coop really — that included a bed, a bathroom, a tiny kitchen, and Addie supposed you could call it a living room although it only had room for a couch. But it had cable TV, and hot water, and was cheap to heat.

But when the rents went up in the summer, Addie was forced to move; first, back to Digit's, luckily, since Digit and Marsha had had the winter alone and why not make some money in the summer? Marsha was all for that. Addie even got his old room back.

When fall arrived, Digit again said Addie could stay, but the chicken coop rental was available.

After that winter, however, summer housing was scarce. Marsha had family from the mainland visiting that year (the first surprise of their married life — Digit had assumed all of her family, like his, was from the island), so that option was gone. Addie wound up sharing an attic bedroom with some kid who was a waiter. He wasn't a bad kid, but he came in late and was tanked most of the time. His feet stunk. Everyone in the house shared the kitchen and there were always arguments about some housemate or other eating someone else's food.

The next summer he lived in a retired couple's basement. No one disturbed him at night, but he could hear their every movement on the creaky floors upstairs, even when they went to the bathroom. They were both hard of hearing and yelled at each other a lot. His room had no windows and was always dark. His landlords also thought it would be nice if he'd mow the lawn once a week and take their trash to the dump to repay them for the largesse of letting him live with them, never mind that he was paying rent.

The summer after that he lived with a baker, a babysitter, and a Buddhist. The baker was up and out by 4 a.m., which wasn't bad except that he had to pass through Addie's bedroom in order to go downstairs. If Addie got lucky, and a girl slept over, the baker's early and abrupt appearance, especially if they were *in flagrante delicto*, ensured she wouldn't be coming back.

The babysitter, for her part, often had her charges sleep over — their parents, on vacation, needing some alone time, even if it meant having their kids staying with a questionable bunch of nomads — and they'd be up hollering and jumping around soon after the baker left. The Buddhist was quiet most of the time, unless she got angry about something, for which the prescribed remedy suggested by her therapist was to blow the whistle hanging around her neck. If she detected that someone had eaten one of her tofu burgers, she'd start to blow, and would continue blowing until everyone left the house. If Addie pulled into the driveway and heard the whistle, he'd go to the beach for an hour.

All this time, he was doing a variety of jobs that, like his housing, were seasonal. He liked that. If a job was terrible, it'd be over in a couple of months. The summer after his girlfriend left he worked for the public works department, picking up rubbish off the side of the road and driving around with an old Nantucketer named Cy who called everybody "boy" and never had a kind word for anybody. "There goes another guy who never worked a day in his life," Cy would say as he drove the DPW pickup around town. Cy also liked pointing out that Addie wasn't an islander. "Is that how they do things in America, boy?" he'd ask whenever Addie did something even slightly wrong, like emptying a trash barrel before it was full. "Why do they keep giving me help from round-the-Point?" meaning Brant Point, the little lighthouse that the ferries coming to and from the island passed by. If someone was from 'round-the-Point,' he was either incompetent, or stupid, and always not to be trusted. "No one from round-the-Point's going to tell me how things should be done on Nantucket," was another of his favorite sayings. Cy wasn't a bad guy, although he could be a bit harsh. In later years, Addie mentioned to someone that he'd once worked with Cy.

"That guy," was the response. "I used to cross the street whenever I saw him coming."

Addie learned that Cy was just kidding most of the time and he learned to kid him right back. Thinking back on it now, he had to admit he kind of missed Cy. There was never any question where you stood with him. No bullshit. Nantucket needed characters like Cy, people who indoctrinated new arrivals to the Nantucket way.

But, like everything else, the characters, and the Nantucket way, were fading, seemingly swallowed by the fog, or, more likely, stampeded into submission by the arriving hordes.

The job with Cy wasn't bad, but it wasn't great either, and Addie wasn't unhappy when he got laid off at the end of that summer.

From there he found work landscaping; he delivered the morning papers for a while; at one point he answered phones at the Chamber of Commerce. In the winter he opened scallops, the sweet seafood delicacy that kept Nantucketers tied to the sea. (Although there were rumblings after each fishing season that the scallop beds were dying out and the industry was in danger of extinction.)

If his jobs were temporary, that was all right. He wasn't going to live on the island forever.

But the years had a way of piling up quickly. Before he knew it, ten of them had come and gone.

For lack of anything better to do, and on the suggestion of a co-worker at the Chamber of Commerce, he got the job driving the tour bus. He liked the boss, Ken, immediately, and the hours were pretty loose, arriving around 9:30 and done before 5. The pace was good and he knew the island well enough by then to have fun with his monologue. The best thing was that if he was broke in the morning, he'd have some money from tips after the first tour.

"That must be a helluva job to do hungover," Digit said after Addie had been at it for a couple of months.

"You've got that right."

After his first summer driving the bus, and as he considered getting a real job on the mainland, Addie lucked into a coveted year-round rental. It was a small cottage, but much larger than the chicken coop. It had a fireplace, a good-size kitchen, and a decent living room. The people who owned it were Nantucketers who'd retired to Florida and simply wanted someone in there who'd cover the mortgage payment, which was affordable, even for a bus driver who got laid off every fall.

Life was good for Addie, and that's perhaps why his fellow drivers considered him lucky, because he chanced into year-round housing during his first year on the job. Like Digit and his nickname, once Addie was branded lucky he remained so in everyone's eyes, even people he didn't work with. He once found a five dollar bill outside the A&P, and as he stooped to pick it up he heard someone say: "Sure enough, Mr. Lucky. Who else would find five dollars on the street?"

Now, after twenty-odd years of island living, his luck appeared to be running out. With the island changing into a full-blown, upscale resort, real estate prices spiked, so that even his old chicken coop dwelling was worth over a million dollars. The couple from Florida put their cottage on the market. When it sold, for 2.5 mil, they weren't heartless; Addie had until October first to pack up his things and leave.

That gave him less than two months.

———————

"Hey, Digit," he asked before hopping back onto his bus, "that selectman's sticker, Jason Bonere; isn't he the one who wants to put up a traffic light?"

"It'll never happen," Digit said.

"It could — everything else is changing around here."

"There'll never be a traffic light on this island," Digit insisted. "I'll know it's time to leave when that happens."

———————

Heading home as well was Sandy Bronson, who'd trained Addie when he'd first started driving the bus, before he was known as Mr. Lucky.

It had been a lousy day. She'd only gone out on two tours. Addie, that jerk, had pulled a fast one and shortened up his second tour so he was first in line — and the only bus required — for the 3 o'clock.

All she wanted now was to get home. She was tired. She stole a glance at herself in the rearview mirror, wondered where the years had gone.

She was raised in Little Compton, Rhode Island, and was one of the prettiest girls in Newport County. She grew into her figure early, and the boys from middle school through high school had been too intimidated to approach her. That was all right with her; she had no intention of going out with anyone from Little Compton. As soon as high school was over, she was gone.

She'd come to the island with Mack, a boy she'd met on the Cape who had gotten a job as a barback for the summer. She figured if he could get a job, she could, too.

She took a waitressing job, but soon she was bartending with Mack — poor Mack who never had a chance with her — as *her* barback. The manager wanted her where she'd be seen and where she could chat up the men. The tips were fabulous. She had an easy way about her, as do those who are comfortable in their skins, and her skin, too, was gorgeous.

She'd landed on the island when everything was more casual, when livelihoods still in many ways revolved around the surrounding ocean. Her black hair and green eyes made her seem mermaid-like to men who ogled her at the bar. She loved the looseness of the life and lived, over the years, with three handsome men: a musician, a fisherman, and a carpenter.

There were those who yearned for her during her eventual down times from each of these relationships — serious, college-educated boys who'd watch her walk up Main Street, or who sat nursing beers when she bartended, staring at her dopily, who dreamed of sharing a bottle of wine and pouring out their secrets, for they were sure she was a serious beauty. And intellectual. And, of course, wonderful in bed.

She was great in bed, there was no doubt about that, but she was attracted to men who were older than she, and more mature than the boys her age, boys like Mack. In the end she married an artist, a man eighteen years her senior.

She hadn't thought of him in years now. When they divorced, ten years after their marriage and twenty years ago now, she had to support herself again and newer pretty girls had taken her place behind the bar. She waitressed for a time, worked summers at some of the art galleries, for she'd learned a great deal about art from her husband (he was good for something after all), and finally, because she knew so much about the island after years of living on it, was a true islander now, she thought giving tours might be fun. It beat standing for eight hours a shift, dealing with developing varicose veins, and clearing dishes and handling people's chewed and unchewed food and getting home after midnight.

Now, driving home after that last, rotten tour — no tips at all, not even a dollar — she recalled worse times; the talk that had almost driven her from the island. Although the hurt had lingered, lingered somewhat still, it was not the constant ache that had once absorbed her. She had put those memories behind her, like war wounds; nothing anyone could say could hurt her anymore.

But the rumors had been out there. Like snowflakes on the wind they swirled around at first, melting as they made contact, but they soon began to accumulate, pile up, and take form.

No one ever said anything to her face, of course, but she had heard the lies; heard them as if they had become part of the atmosphere surrounding the island.

That the lies were so ridiculous didn't matter, they persisted, so that in time people took them as fact, believed them as surely as they knew — just knew — that old Doc Forester sometimes sampled the diet pills he prescribed, although there was never any evidence to support it. The good doctor was just naturally hyper yet somehow reserved at the same time.

Why she was selected she could never understand. Perhaps people were jealous of her beauty, or her carefree attitude; her confident demeanor after her divorce that some may have viewed as arrogance. There was no sense to any of it. Still, the rumors started. And they grew.

How she coped, how she even stayed on the island when every day the whispers were there, following her, trailing her, filling the space around her if she even went to the post office, had her wondering now how she had gotten by. She remembers wishing she could become somebody else — let the rumors happen to the identity she'd leave behind.

But to do that, she reasoned, she'd have to leave the island, and they'd win. She resolved to outlast them, or, if need be, outlive them.

She persevered, as she had since she'd moved to the island. And after the rumors thinned, as people moved on to other tidbits and as she held on, the thoughts directed toward her dissipated so that at last she could breathe freely again and leave the house without feeling watchful eyes following her.

They said she'd killed her father, that's what they'd said — that's why she'd moved to the island in the first place. Her father had been ill, the story went, and the two of them had agreed, without ever having discussed it, that if he got bad enough she wouldn't let him go to the hospital, but shoot him. It was true, her father had died, but she hadn't shot him. Wasn't it bad enough that he had shot himself, and that she had found him? Wasn't that enough?

It's true what they say about friends, she thought now. Her old ones stood by her, buoyed her up, helped her ignore the steady and unpleasant vibes.

One misthought led to another. The gossipers said her husband took her in to protect her, to shelter her with a new last name. They weren't really married, the rumors went, but had some kind of phony ceremony staged by a performance artist or something.

They weren't married by a minister or priest, that much was true, but by his old friend who was, in fact, a boat captain who received a special license for the occasion, but still it didn't count in the eyes of the gossipers. That her husband had taken up with an even younger woman and moved to Maine never seemed to factor into anyone's stories either.

Other rumblings were uttered. Wasn't that house she lived in haunted? Why, sure it was, everybody knew that. There were plenty of haunted houses on the island. Well, isn't that strange. First she doesn't get married by a minister and then she decides to live in a haunted house. And what do we really know about her, she's not from here. She could be some kind of voodoo queen for all we know. And on and on it went.

Perhaps it was then her hair began turning grey.

Time had passed since those awful days. Her beauty had faded, the sun through the years had added lines to her face and she had let her body go its own way. Someone who'd known her when she'd first arrived on the island would still see the beauty that had been there, but young men would only see what she'd become.

Yes, she had outlasted the searing gossip and was as comfortable in her skin as she'd always been. And if any of those serious boys from way back when still cared to bother, they'd find she'd be willing to share a bottle of wine, and, at 60, a thing or two about love.

A strand of her hair hung past her eye as she steered the bus toward home, the house she'd kept after the divorce. It was an old home, an antique in town, and she loved living there, happy that she shared in its history simply by being there. It was a large house and she'd done well enough renting out rooms in the years after her divorce, although she'd eventually tired of the partying and the hormones and had given up taking in boarders.

A prospective tenant was coming tonight, however, someone older than the college girls or, more recently, the waves of young immigrants who inquired about rooms. It would be nice to have someone with a little maturity in the house; she could use some stability for a change.

Although it was August the wind was picking up for some reason — from the north, unusual for summer. Summer, with its traffic backups and invasion of cell phones, was enough to be gotten through without the threat of a storm on the horizon.

Chapter Five

EVERYONE ADDIE worked with was manic-depressive.
There was Rudy, nonstop Rudy, who said he'd been an executive with IBM or something and was now retired. Rudy, however, seemed younger than retirement age, unless, of course, he was secretly rich. Rudy talked a lot, always wore his blue button-down short-sleeved uniform shirt with his name tag appropriately pinned above the pocket (which nobody else ever wore), smelled like a barber shop, and wanted to know what everybody had done the night before.

"Nothing, Rudy."

"Ah, come on. Me and 'Cille went out and dug some clams and she knows how to steam them just right and make a broth that'll knock your socks off. Clams are good for you, you know, puts lead in your pencil." And then, without pausing, "Man, I feel good today." He'd hold out his arm. "Here, feel. See how good I feel."

By this time, anybody who was just hanging around the office was finding things to do: checking their radiator water and oil, washing their windshields, kicking their tires; in effect, doing the circle check of their buses that they were supposed to be doing every morning but never did unless Rudy was working and talking everyone out of the office.

And then there was Margaret, who had worked on the island summers through college and now that she'd graduated was back for a second post-graduate summer of driving. She did something in the winter, but nobody was sure what it was and nobody really cared. Margaret was young, Margaret was perky, Margaret always gave a by-the-book perfect tour, with the jokes always coming at the same places, and the inflection in her voice rising at precisely the same time in every tour. If you'd taken a tour with Margaret three years ago, it would be exactly the same tour today and Margaret would be just as bubbly and glad to see ya now as she was then.

"I consider this another one of my skills," Addie overheard her saying one day.

Between tours, however, Margaret could be sullen, Margaret could be quiet. Addie had seen Margaret be quiet for a week. She'd be upbeat on her tours, but as soon as the last customer had filed off the bus, down came the veil of sadness. When the week had passed, Margaret was again as animated off the bus as she was on it.

There was Frankie, too, a native, whose glasses hung at an angle so that one lens covered one eye completely while the other lens kind of hung up in the air. Although Frankie regularly wore glasses, he always lifted them onto his forehead when he was reading, and he read all the time — one hand holding up his glasses and the other holding his book.

There was Sandy, of course, and Reggie Barney, the man with two first names. Addie could never figure out why Reggie drove because his tours were terrible and nobody could understand him anyway. Reggie, according to Ken, slipped on ice outside the Atlantic Café one winter night and was hurt pretty badly. He was out cold in the hospital for several days and no one was sure if he was going to come out of it. He did, eventually, and although he'd never studied a foreign language in his life, had hardly been off the island — ever — and was about as sophisticated as a turtle, Reggie woke up speaking with a French accent.

" 'Foreign Accent Syndrome' they call it," Ken said. "It took the doctors up in Boston weeks to tell his mother that."

So Reggie, who had grown a thin mustache to accommodate his new accent, welcomed passengers thusly: "Bonjour mes amis, welcome to Nantuck-et. Bienvenue."

"I think he's full of shit," Addie said to Ken one day. "He's only doing it because he thinks he's going to get better tips."

"I thought that, too," Ken replied, "but he never falters. He's still got that accent even when he's shitfaced. Although he says, 'Le visage de shit,' which I don't think is right."

And then there was Chuck. Smiling Chuck Finley.

Chuck came back from the first tour of the day cursing his passengers. "Stupid moron," he said. "Screwed my whole tour. Kept on talking over me so I grabbed the microphone and told her to shut up. Of course no one would tip me after that." Chuck, blonde-haired, handsome Chuck, in his early 40s, built like a cowboy, perfect teeth, let out a half-snort/half-cackle as he took off his sunglasses. "Man, you should have seen them. Not a peep. It was worth it."

Chuck gave the best tours, Chuck gave the worst tours, depending on his mood, his hangover, or the kind of passengers he had, although Chuck didn't care what blend of humanity he had with him. He could be packed with Lithuanian tourists, a few Mormons, or huddled masses of blue-haired senior citizens, and he'd have them all roaring before he even closed the doors. Chuck was cool, a genuine charmer who could coax little nips of liquor from stewardesses during a plane's final approach, after the plastic cups had long been collected and people advised to return their seats to their full and upright positions. It didn't matter that he was gay; women loved him anyway. Everyone loved him.

That was the secret to the tour, Addie knew. People didn't want to hear about history — they wanted to be entertained, and Chuck was always entertaining.

Part of Chuck's charm was that he sincerely did not give a hoot if he made any money on a tour or not. Perhaps it was because he made so much in tips most of the time that he had a cushion, or perhaps he, like Rudy, was secretly rich.

He could have been rich. You couldn't fall over on the island without falling into a rich person. A lot of the people on the island that Addie knew who he thought were like him — that is, living paycheck to paycheck — were instead from families who were well off. They had trust funds or inheritances, some bigger than others.

"How do you think I came to Nantucket in the first place?" Joel Schuster, who built houses only when he felt like it Addie later found out, said to him one day: "We summered here."

"Summered." It was a word Addie had never heard until he moved to Nantucket. Nobody "summered" where he came from; in his neighborhood, kids were lucky if they spent a week in some rental on the Cape. Summer had never been a verb in Addie's vocabulary.

For Chuck, on the other hand, it wouldn't have surprised Addie if he not only "summered" as a kid, but "wintered" as well.

Chuck was so relaxed he relaxed everybody on his bus, especially the people who had no idea why they ever got on a boat to Nantucket in the first place except that it was somewhere off Cape Cod, and it had been hot in Hyannis, and perhaps they'd see some rich or famous people. "Welcome to the island," he'd say, as if it was Jamaica. He wore Hawaiian shirts most of the time, and sunglasses all the time. Chuck was also a great gossip and he didn't mind telling his passengers — if they were good — everything he'd heard about every shop owner on Main Street. What the hell, he'd never see them again and the people on the bus didn't know the people he was talking about. He'd tease them, telling them he'd get back to what Mr. Hooper's wife didn't know, but first he did have to tell them about the Three Bricks — the three identical Georgian-style mansions built next to each other at 93, 95, and 97 Main Street in 1837 by whaling merchant Joseph Starbuck for his three sons — because, he'd say, you never could tell when the tour company had an incognito quality control officer on board (which, of course, everybody on board knew wasn't true). All of Chuck's gossip was true, however, most of it from personal knowledge, and it did not matter one iota because everyone on the bus was leaving on the 4 o'clock boat.

"That's why he gives the tours, so he can gossip," Ken told Addie. Ken didn't give a shit what people said as long as the tours were done on time. "I need you back in an hour," he'd say.

"But Ken, there's tons of traffic out there."

"I don't give a shit."

The people on Chuck's tours got their twenty dollars worth — after an hour with Chuck they knew more about who was screwing whom than most summer people did. "Oh, this is rich," he'd say driving up Main Street, lowering his voice and cupping his hand over his microphone, letting them all in on another secret. "Do you see those two talking?" It was a man and a woman, and Chuck slowed down so everyone could get a good look at them. "They own the businesses next to each other, isn't that cute? The only thing is his wife doesn't know he's been seeing her on the sly for the past six months." (Chuck's tour was not geared to children, even though children were usually on board. On Chuck's tours mothers put their hands over their kids' ears, just like in the old movies. 'Why are you laughing, Mommy?' the children would inevitably ask. 'What's so funny?').

And, as his bus creeped forward, Chuck would continue: "I think there's a door from one building to the other in the basement, like the tunnel between the rectory and the convent in the town where I grew up." He'd give them some history of the island, sometimes, but it wasn't the version written up as the official tour monologue. "And now we're passing lower Main Street, home to one helluva gay bar in its day. If you want to know where the gay bar is today, see me after the tour and we'll make arrangements, if you know what I mean."

Although he wasn't supposed to, Chuck let everyone off the bus for ice cream in 'Sconset, the summer colony at the east end of the island. If he lost a couple of people who wandered off into the village he didn't care. He made up for the lost time by driving back to base at 60 miles per hour, even though the buses were thirty years old and in terrible shape.

"He's got a deal worked out with the guy in 'Sconset," Ken was telling Addie one day. "Chuck gets ten percent of every ice cream cone."

"Don't you care that he's doing that?"

"I don't give a shit as long as he gets back here in time."

It was amazing the buses made it back at all. Some engine parts were held together with hairpins. They were little buses that held twenty-three passengers, twenty-five if everybody liked each other, and were pretty easy to maneuver around the island's narrow streets. They were painted blue and white and were "cute." Those who called the buses cute tended to call the island "quaint."

But the buses were made to drive around airports, not cobblestones. The bus company owner got them cheap after they'd already put in ten years of service. It was no wonder, no wonder at all, that Addie's front wheel had collapsed.

"Just take it easy on the cobblestones," Ken had taken to advising the drivers after that.

Chapter Six

Plugged into the island vibe, it was Irene who told Verona about the room at Sandy's.

"It would be perfect for you," she said to her. "It's in town, and you wouldn't have to be biking in on days that I'm not working."

Verona wasn't sure she wanted to leave the protective cocoon of living with Irene, and Irene sensed her misgivings. "You can stay here as long as you like," she said, "but who knows how long this rental will last? I wouldn't be able to guarantee your accommodation if we all had to move."

Irene knew, too, that Verona was suited for living with Sandy; she wasn't as young as the other girls in the house and could use a place that was a little quieter. Besides, some of the girls thought Verona a tad strange. Oh, Verona was nice and all, and gladly chipped in with the chores, but she kept to herself a little too much. She was cheerful enough, but she often didn't seem to know why.

"I've already spoken to Sandy for you. She's expecting you this afternoon."

Irene hadn't steered her wrong yet, Verona had to admit, and if Irene thought she should see about the room, she would. In her short time on the island she had taken the opportunities as they came, and everything had worked out so far. Go with the flow. She didn't know where she had heard that expression before, but she liked it: Go with the flow.

Before biking into town, she rode out to the lighthouse at Sankaty. She was drawn to the old structure ever since she'd moved in with Irene and first saw its beacon sweeping across the moors. The light seemed to beckon her. She'd sit at its base at night, the distant darkness illuminated at intervals as the light circled the horizon. There was something mystical about being on the high windy cliff where the light resided, and when the wind was quiet the steady sound of the waves pulsing on the shore beneath the bluff called to her.

In the recent decades, the constant beating of the ocean against the bluff threatened the lighthouse's existence. Every year, especially in winter when the winds were fierce and constant, chunks of the bluff — up to ten feet at a time — were carried off by the wind and water, so that over time, inevitably, the light was less than thirty yards from the edge.

Verona became uneasy when one day workers appeared and roped off the area around the lighthouse. Soon, more workers arrived and she watched from a distance as they first wrapped a giant girdle of wire and wood around the middle of the light. Trucks came next, followed by more construction equipment. With no one else to ask, for she would not approach the workers, never in a million years, she asked Irene if she knew what was going on.

"Oh, they're moving it," she said. "They're moving the lighthouse away from the bluff to save it."

"To save it?"

"Move it back so it doesn't fall over the bluff."

This pleased Verona. She watched as workers dug deep around the light, pushed I-beams through its base, and eventually hoisted it up on giant machinery to move it, inch by inch, inland, to safer ground.

She kept her distance as the work went on; the construction, and the fascination of moving such a towering object drawing scores of onlookers. But when the work was finished, and the light safely ensconced in its new foundation, the inquisitive were sated, the curious stopped coming, and Verona was able to visit the light alone once more.

There was something puzzling about the hole that had previously housed the lighthouse, however. Verona could feel something, a presence, which seemed to emanate from the ground. It was as if something was pulling her toward the old foundation, and she'd stand by the edge at night and let the feeling envelop her.

Her visits to the light became more frequent, and it was one of the reasons her roommates felt it was time for her to go.

"She must be meeting somebody out there," one of them said one night.

"I don't think so," Irene said. "I think she just likes being alone."

"I think she's pretty weird."

———

Verona didn't think about the strange attraction she felt at the light as she bicycled back into town. It seemed vital to be there, as though she was being bathed in some kind of energy.

And as she straddled her bike in the twilight outside the address Irene had given her, she had a similar feeling. Before she even knocked on the door, she knew Irene's suggestion was a good one.

The house was on the edge of town, away from Main Street,

fronting what Verona would learn was the Lily Pond, a park-like place with trees and shrubs and open meadows. The story Sandy told her bus passengers was that it was indeed a pond three hundred years before, complete with a working mill, but that a young girl playing on its banks with a clamshell in the early 1700s had inadvertently created an opening that began as a trickle but developed overnight into a steady stream of rushing water. The next morning the Lily Pond was gone, totally drained, and the girl said nothing about it until she was an old lady and confessed to it on her deathbed.

The house was old, and its grey shingles and odd angles appealed to Verona. Sandy liked that she could park her bus out back in the Lily Pond's parking lot. She was at the door before Verona could ring the doorbell.

Because of the lousy day she'd had she must have looked frazzled when she first saw Verona, Sandy thought later. She couldn't wait to get home and was perhaps driving a bit too fast because a cop had pulled her over. "Just what I need," she said to herself, but the cop, young enough to be her son, was kind and let her go. He must have suspected that she was in no mood to be messed with. When Sandy was in such a mood, no one wanted to mess with her, not even Ken. "Just do what you need to do, Sandy," he'd say.

The front door creaked when she opened it. "Come in," Sandy said to the woman standing by her bike on the sidewalk, the woman with chin-length, light brown hair wearing a black skirt and a knit jacket.

"Thank you," Verona said demurely as she walked up the front steps. "Irene said I should come."

Sandy opened her mouth as if to say something, but instead swept her arm to motion her inside. Stairs in the front hall led to the second floor. Across from the steps was the parlor, beyond that a large dining room and, finally, the kitchen. "The room's upstairs," Sandy said. "You can enter and leave by this door. My room's way down the hall, so you pretty much have the upstairs to yourself. There's a full bath up there, too."

When Verona saw her room overlooking the Lily Pond, with its two windows revealing the wooded scenery, she knew she had to stay. The house, this room, had a welcoming feel to it, almost as if she'd been in it before, but she was too shy to say this to Sandy. Sandy, after showing Verona the bathroom and how the shower worked, stood there awkwardly for a time before saying, "Interested? It's a hundred dollars a week." Sandy did not like to gouge her boarders — living on the island, in her opinion, wasn't always about money.

Verona had the money in her pocket and tried handing it to her. "Why don't you wait a week, see if you like it, and then you can pay," Sandy said to her.

Verona was back the next day with her things, all of which fit into her backpack. Sandy was on her way to work and handed her a key. "Not that you'll need it," she said. "The house is always open, but some of my tenants felt the need for a key."

It was Verona's day off, and she had time to get acclimated.

There was a mirror in her room and she glanced at her reflection as she passed by. She put her backpack down on the bed and returned to the mirror. She hadn't really looked at herself since Irene had found her.

She approached the mirror tentatively, as if it might speak to her. She looked, looked away, and stared at the face that looked quizzically back. She studied the creases at the corners of her eyes that she saw were brown, with hazel-like dabs of color in the irises. Her nose was not large, nor was it sleek, but it was a woman's nose all the same, although she thought it seemed pretty plain. There were the beginnings of lines in the center of her forehead and, now that she looked, at the corners of her mouth, a mouth marked by what she supposed were standard-sized lips.

Who is this person, she wondered as she pondered her reflection, how old is she? She knew she wasn't as young as Irene, but she didn't think she was as old as Sandy, either. How do you gauge such things you don't know?

The mirror also reflected the room behind her, and as she stared she lost herself in the image, looking beyond herself and letting the wallpaper colors blur so that what she saw was a wash of colors. It was like looking into another world.

She did not know how long she'd stared, she was only conscious of time when she needed to be, but something seemed to pass between her reflection and the room beyond — like a shadow, but more than a shadow, something with depth. The disruption brought her out of her reverie and she caught her breath — not for what she had seen but for losing herself and letting her mind wander. It startled her, she felt as if she could have gone someplace else. Can't do that, she told herself. She did not want to open any secrets the recesses of her mind might hold.

Chapter Seven

"Ever wonder about the thousands of people you've come in contact with?" Digit asked Addie that afternoon at the Atlantic Café, the in-town, year-round watering hole that summer day-trippers also frequented because the prices were reasonable. "What's their story? Take that guy over there," and he pointed to a man sitting at one of the finger bars in the corner looking perplexedly at his cell phone. "Maybe you notice him for one second, and then he's gone, you'll never see him again. Now imagine what his life is like: is he happy, is he rich? Did kids poke fun at him in middle school, but he's now more successful than any of them?

"Think of it: here we are sharing space with him, breathing the same air, but in the next moment he'll be out of our lives forever. Even though we live on this tiny island, you and I have had these same little contacts with thousands of people over the years, people we pass on the sidewalk, people who'll never influence our lives."

"And your point?" Addie asked.

"That's the thing, there is no point — it's pointless. You think about crap like that too long it'll drive you crazy.

"But," Digit continued, "sometimes these random people that you never think you'll ever see again do come into our lives. Maybe they were just walking off the boat with you a couple of years ago, and then, wham, you're invited to the same party. You meet them, you have a few laughs, and the next thing you know you're seeing them all the time downtown. Pretty weird, don't you think?"

"You know what I think?" Addie said as his Coke with a wedge of lime arrived. "You're pretty weird."

"Weirder than you know."

And yet Digit's words strangely made sense. Addie remembered back to when he'd first moved to the island and how at different times of the year, spring and fall mostly, the so-called "shoulder" seasons, he'd see women with bandaged faces on Main Street; not many, but several sometimes, always wearing low, slouch hats and dark glasses, going in and out of the shops like a legion of Greta Garbos.

"There's a famous plastic surgeon from New York who also has an office here," Digit had told him. "The women come here to get their facelifts done because they don't know anybody and they don't care if anybody sees them."

Addie thought back to others, who, like the bandaged women on Main Street, passed in and out of his vision and out of his life.

One guy said he was a writer, but Addie mostly saw him drinking. There were plenty of people who called themselves writers, but if they stayed, most were soon driving cab, or banging nails, or bartending.

There were others, now that he thought about it, like the guy who bought the guest house over on India Street and said he was coming here to escape the rat race and seemed like a nice guy, but turns out he was wanted for embezzlement or something, a huge rap, and it was his wife who turned him in, at least that's what the paper had said. Addie had only waved 'hi' to him a couple of times, didn't even know his name.

He thought of those he'd known casually, people whose names he did know. He wasn't friends with any of them, and yet their passing pleasantries made those fleeting moments when he was in their company enjoyable. Many had left the island; in the end, they weren't islanders but island sojourners.

"Hey, what are you guys talking about?"

It was Fred. Fred had been working at the Steamship Authority for a few months and regularly stopped in at the Atlantic Café when his shift was over. He was friendly enough, and Digit and Addie humored him as a bar mate. Usually, though, when Fred came in, it was time to go.

"So what are you guys up to this weekend? Getting laid, getting high?"

"Actually, Fred," Digit said, "we were planning on robbing the bank — until you busted in on us. Do us a favor, don't tell anyone. Hey, don't put your drink on that napkin, you just ruined our plans."

"That's why I like you guys: you're always busting my balls."

"With friends like us, who needs enemies, right, Fred?"

"You got that right."

———

"He thought that was a compliment," Digit said to Addie when they got outside.

"What?"

"With friends like us who needs enemies."

"He's not the brightest bulb in the deck, or whatever that saying is."

"Wonder where he came from?"

"Who knows, the Vineyard?"

"Yeah, who cares, right? Probably the Vineyard. This is

where they send them when they screw up over there."

Addie noticed a bit of white behind Digit's ear and he told him about it. Digit dabbed at it.

"Shaving cream," he said. "Funny, Marsha usually tells me about stuff like that; I guess she missed it."

Addie wished he had someone to tell him about traces of shaving cream that had eluded his glance, but the thought lingered only for a second. The last thing he needed right now was complications in his life; he was leaving the island and he wanted to be as unfettered as possible when he did.

He was leaving. As tough as that would be, he was leaving.

But how do you leave a place after so many years, a place that had become home, the place he had lived nearly half his life?

Just the other day he was having coffee and the waitress was saying the same thing. She was moving to Florida. "Look, I'm 39," she said, "and what are my prospects here? Besides, I can always come back. … Can't I?"

Addie supposed the only way to find out was to go.

The decision hadn't been easy, and he wasn't leaving because his rental was up. He wasn't leaving because of the traffic, the traffic that had devolved in summer into vehicular stampedes along the slim, driveway-wide byways of town, with the luxury SUVs of the summer people joined by the over-wide trucks of the builders and contractors who rushed from job to job, from one rising trophy house to another with a "gedoudamyway" attitude that made driving a tour bus hell. People saw a tour bus and had to get by it, just had to pass, no matter if the bus was traveling the speed limit or not. For most of the summer Addie drove with someone constantly riding his ass.

He wasn't leaving like so many islanders because they simply could not afford it any longer, because the island they loved and its laid-back atmosphere was eroding, as slowly and relentlessly as the bluff was wearing away in 'Sconset.

The once welcoming flophouses in town were long gone — converted into restaurants or upscale inns, and the network of sharing they represented was gone with them. People had once been able to get off the boat, get a cheap room, find a job, all word of mouth, all passed along by those living in these communal quarters. Because of economics, really, because the island had become just so damn expensive and land so scarce, with only the rich, the super rich, able to afford it, the attitude was now, "I've got mine, and I'm hanging on to it — my job, my house, my car — gedoudamyway." And while there were more houses, lots more houses, there were fewer places to stay. The old ladies who rented out rooms and the rows of guest houses around town gone to history, as archaic as the times when everyone came to the island on a three hour boat ride from Woods Hole.

He wasn't leaving either because the sounds of the island had grown harsh: the incessant, pulsing whelps of police sirens; the steady attack of hammer hitting nail; the sleep-jarring start-up of lawn mowers, weed whackers, hedge trimmers, leaf blowers all combining in a mind-numbing cascade of noise.

In truth, he didn't know why he was leaving. He certainly hadn't gotten his act together yet. He'd been driving a bus for fourteen years; if he was going to be a bus driver he should move to the Cape and drive for Greyhound, but he knew he couldn't do that. He was leaving, he supposed, because he didn't want to drive a bus anymore, and he didn't want to bang nails, and he didn't want to be a checkout person at the A&P.

He also didn't relish the thought of seeing what brand of roommate had evolved over the last ten years. He was 47 — 47! — and too old to share housing with bartenders or whistle blowers anymore.

His housing was up, his options were exhausted, and he needed a change. After all these years of calling Nantucket home, he, too, would become a sojourner.

Chapter Eight

"I'VE BEEN swimming in the cesspool," Digit said to Addie.

"What?" Addie had known Digit to be outlandish at times, like the time he drove a moped naked up Main Street one summer night, for which he was arrested, of course, but that was before he had gotten married.

"You know, been on that chat room website, Island Breezes."

Addie couldn't figure out when people found the time to give their opinions on the website dedicated to all things Nantucket. Was everybody doing it at work? All it did, it seemed to him, was give gossiping a license. Digit was right, it was a cesspool — everything everyone wrote was conjecture, and the negative spread through the computer cables and into the island air with unerring speed. "Why are you wasting your time?" Addie asked him. The Web. Good name for it, he thought, like something a black widow would spin.

"It's something to do when I'm bored. You can only play so much solitaire. There's a new rumor floating around — that selectman, Bonere, he wants to abolish the tour buses, says the rich people don't want them; they're clogging up the streets, ruining people's 'Nantucket' experience."

Addie had heard the rumors. It didn't matter, now that he was leaving. They could get rid of all the buses and all the cars, too, for all he cared. "But, Digit, you've got his bumper sticker plastered on your car."

"I scraped it off," Digit said. "And I told everybody on the website to do the same. I don't use any fake name, either, like Labradorgirl or ACKman (ACK was the airport's official identifier, like JFK in New York, and it had been showing up for years on baseball caps, T-shirts and license plates, becoming as overused as 'I am the man from Nantucket.') I sign everything, 'Clarence,' Digit said.

"How many people know your real name's Clarence?"

"Not many. And those who do aren't checking out that website, either."

"Why don't you just give it up?"

"I will, tomorrow."

That was Digit's answer to everything. When his wife asked him when he was going to cut the grass he'd say, "Tomorrow." If Addie asked him if he'd like to go to the movies Digit would say, "Tomorrow."

Addie figured that would be a good time to tell his old friend he was leaving — tomorrow.

————

Sandy had heard the rumors about the buses, too. No one needed a website for rumors to spread, she knew that all too well. As rumors went, this one was pretty benign. If they wanted to get rid of the buses it wouldn't be happening this year, or the next. There was a contract between the wharf owner and the tour company that ran through the next season. Rumors didn't need facts to feed on; all they needed were willing participants.

Sandy was convinced that some people moved to the island

simply to gossip. The island was fertile ground for those looking to sow trouble. They could get to know their neighbors quickly, and seem interested, and to care. One of her roomers had barely been on the island two months before she began spouting untruths about people she didn't know. She came off as wanting to fit in, to be involved, but what she was really about was spreading gossip. She was a nice girl on the outside, and presented a cute face to the world, as if she couldn't care less about anything outside her own sphere, but on the inside, Sandy quickly learned, she was controlling, manipulative.

"Everybody knows about Tom Gordon," she heard the girl say loudly into her cell phone one day. "You know he had relations with his neighbor's horse; he was put on trial for it."

Sandy knew all about Tom Gordon, all right, and how the rumors about the horse had ruined his life. It had been over twenty years ago and still the talk persisted. He had been the town tax collector, but the stories and the whispers resulted in his quick and efficient termination, and he lived the rest of his life as a pariah, shunned by all but his closest friends, something Sandy was quite familiar with. Sandy knew Tom Gordon to be a gentle man, a kind and decent man, and had even tried getting him to drive the bus one summer. "Screw everybody, Tom," she had told him. "Ken would love to have you. You know the island, that's for sure." And Ken would have had him, too, he didn't give a shit, but it was too late; Tom was worn down, and his body and being wore out the next year. Sandy was one of the few at his funeral.

She kicked the gossip out of her house the day after that cell phone conversation. Who knows what lies she began spreading about Sandy after that, but Sandy didn't care anymore.

Which was why she liked Verona, who didn't concern herself with other people's business — hell, she hardly spoke. Sandy had to insist that it was all right for her to store some food in her refrigerator and that kitchen privileges were part of the rental agreement. Verona was hesitant about it at first, but was soon in the kitchen more often than not, getting acclimated to where Sandy kept her pots and pans, the silverware, the cutlery and spices. If Verona wasn't in her room, or out on the Lily Pond or on a bike ride somewhere, she was in the kitchen.

"Where did you learn to cook like this?" Sandy asked her one afternoon as she sampled a simple, yet delicious tomato soup Verona had prepared. "I'm not sure," Verona said truthfully. "It just seems to come to me."

As she said this, however, Verona had a feeling that she'd had this conversation before, not with Sandy, but with someone. If she thought about it for a while, maybe it'd come to her.

Instead she closed her eyes and told herself: *Don't think. Don't go inward. Don't go back.*

"Are you all right?" Sandy's voice shook her from her introspections. Verona gave a weak smile and nodded, trying to stay in the moment, trying hard not to think.

"You looked like you were having a panic attack or something," Sandy said, blowing on a spoonful of soup.

———

Driving to base one day, to where the buses lined up on the wharf, Sandy decided to do something she hadn't done since she was still married to that asshole artist. Yes, she thought as she effortlessly turned her bus and took her usual parking spot — first in line — I'll have a dinner party. And she'd invite those who'd stood by her during that awful time, the friends she hadn't had to her home in years, the old hippies who were still on island but who now kept mainly to themselves. She would celebrate old times and new beginnings, and even — why not? — the future demise of the bus tours. It was time to start over, and she couldn't help but credit Verona for her new outlook. There was something about Verona that gave her a renewed appreciation for the island.

And she liked the feeling.

Hopping off the bus, Sandy breathed deeply the clean island air. Cotton-grey clouds made the sky a muted, metal blue; a mix of robins and cardinals and swallows flitted and floated above. Sandy noticed these things as she had when she'd first arrived on-island, and for the first time in a while, she paused to marvel.

Nantucket shared its secrets freely to those who stopped to look, to listen, to savor them. No matter how overrun the island seemed in summer, it was still an oasis in the ocean, still unspoiled when compared to the world of highways and sprawl and night-piercing lights a mere twenty-eight miles away.

In her busy-ness, in her absorption with the day-to-day, Sandy had forgotten why she had moved to the island in the first place. She hoped she'd never forget again.

———

Addie didn't know why he'd agreed to go to dinner at Sandy's. In all their time working together they'd never socialized. And yet he was charmed by her invitation and asked what he could bring.

"You can bring Digit if you'd like," she told him. She also asked Ken, who didn't go because he never went anywhere, and Chuck. Chuck drove her crazy but she loved him anyway.

Addie and Digit arrived together at Sandy's funky old house, one Addie remembered was a remnant from the post-whaling era, a house that seemed to show its age with pride; not like one of the nearby makeovers whose paint shone like bright plastic and whose backyards were sculpted with precision. "I haven't been here since I was a kid," Digit said. "This was one of my aunt's houses," the "a" in aunt pronounced in the broad way of a coastal New Englander.

"I thought you lived in your aunt's house."

"This was another aunt."

Although he'd driven by it many times, pointed it out on his tours as a classic example of mid-Victorian architecture, Addie had never been inside Sandy's house before. Also invited to the dinner were people he hadn't seen in years, people who'd been living on the island since long before he'd arrived. In his early years they were out and about more frequently but lately he'd seen them around town less and less, as if they'd found some secret place in the moors to reside.

Some of them were natives, some were the original hippies who'd come to the island when it was looser, freer, when everything wasn't so damned upscale, when you could go barefoot in the bars around town. He was happy to see these people again, happy he'd come.

So here was Gus, the former selectman who, years before, had hosted the hippies and flower people at his acreage in the Badlands — gentrified to 'Gladlands' in recent years — where island bands showed up on Sunday afternoons for outside jam sessions and everyone danced their cares away. There was George, the obsessive-compulsive landscaper who would cut an entire lawn twice if he finished mowing from a different spot than the place he'd finished the week before. And here was Susie, the flower child who was now a taxi dispatcher, a job she liked because her interactions with people were confined to conversations over a microphone. ("I can't work with people anymore," Addie overheard her telling Gus. "Not face to face, anyway.")

One face, however, Addie couldn't place.

"Hey, Digit, you know most everybody here."

"Isn't it great? I haven't seen Adam Cartwright in years. I thought everybody on the island was a Republican now."

"Who was that girl sitting next to you?"

"Girl?"

"Girl, woman. Who is she?"

"Not sure. I thought she was somebody's girlfriend. Never seen her around, I don't think. Cute, though."

That's what Addie had been thinking. She wasn't a girl by any means, but still she was cute. He had been looking at her without trying to stare. There was something about her, some mystery.

He was going to ask Digit to switch seats with him but changed his mind. He didn't want to go to the trouble of making small talk. Besides, he was sitting next to Chuck, who was a riot and kept asking everyone, "Are you enjoying the wine?" Maybe he'd get to talk to her after dinner was over.

But that wasn't going to happen. The girl/woman had moved into the kitchen to help Sandy and Irene with the dishes and never reappeared.

Nobody stayed much longer. They'd all had too much wine and cabs were called (unlike the old days when people would weave home, it left less to think about with a cab; perhaps with age came responsibility, although Addie doubted that; there were so many cops now that no one wanted to risk getting arrested). The girl/woman never left that Addie saw. "She lives with Sandy," Digit told him in the cab. "You know what? She looks familiar, but I can't place her."

———

When Sandy had told her about her plans for a dinner party, Verona quavered. It was all right cooking for Sandy, but she didn't want to cook for a bunch of people she didn't know, and she didn't want anybody else knowing about her newfound abilities. She wanted to keep her cooking private, and she told Sandy so; she had grown comfortable enough with Sandy in the short time she'd been living with her that she felt able to speak freely to her.

"I can't do it," she had said. "I don't want to cook for anybody other than you."

Sandy understood. Verona had a delicate nature and she didn't want to push her. "All right," she said, "You plan the menu. I'll buy the groceries and help you with the meal, but we'll tell everybody that I cooked it."

Verona was still unsure. Couldn't she just cook that evening and then leave the house? She didn't want to meet new people.

"Now, Verona, stop being ridiculous. These are my old friends, the least judgmental people I know. I want them to meet you. I'll invite Irene, too, and don't worry, I won't even tell her about your cooking."

"All right," Verona said, even though she was against it.

She had bicycled out to the lighthouse early that afternoon to get her bearings. She was calmed when she finally saw the light in the distance, looking like a red-striped candle on the horizon. "Why is she doing this?" Verona thought when she reached the light at last and approached the old foundation. "Doesn't she know I just want to be left alone?"

Verona sat by the hole that once housed the light, feeling the same strange pull she'd felt before. As she lingered and watched a couple of rabbits approach the hole cautiously before scampering off, it became clearer to her that the feelings conjured there were the same as those she felt at Sandy's house. Somehow the two had to be connected.

Looking at the lighthouse's sweeping beacon made her feel better. She remembered the piercing sunlight on the afternoon she awakened, how invasive it was. The lighthouse, however, with its revolving eye, calmed her. It was if the light was seeking her out, drawing her to its soft presence.

It was better at night, when the light defiantly swept the sky, but still, in mid-afternoon, the reassuring, if muted, blink of the eye let her know it was watching out for her, ever vigilant.

To Verona, the lighthouse was a 'she,' a feminine presence on the island's edge. She called it Sheila.

"Thanks for being here, Sheila," she thought as she bicycled away.

On the bicycle path that led from town to 'Sconset and back, the bike path built in the late-1950s and the first of its kind in Massachusetts, Verona noticed an old boat residing far from the water in a meadow. On its bow was a wooden quarterboard with the name 'Memories' neatly painted on it. She pictured the boat sailing away from Nantucket, taking her own memories with it.

———

The afternoon was bright and warm and Verona veered off the bike path and onto the dirt trails of the moors on her way back to town. As Addie and Sandy both pointed out on their tours, Nantucket was home to some of the only true moorlands in the United States, short rolling hills with low-lying vegetation that traversed the center of the island, vestiges of the Ice Age that created Nantucket. The farsightedness of a few in the early 1960s, fortunately, had prompted conservation efforts years before the moors could be threatened by development, and so the bulk of this distinct acreage remained pristine. In the fall, the moors turned various shades of reds and greys but on this summer day, the scrub oak and runt pines lent their muted green to the underbrush.

Verona bicycled on through the sandy trails, wandering aimlessly as one dirt road branched into another, taking forks without any sense of direction. She noticed the rabbits as they skittered undercover, the pheasants that quick-stepped away, the voles that scurried into the grasses and the occasional hawk soaring majestically overhead. She had no inclination of encountering a wolf, or a coyote, or a fox on her travels, nor should she have, since none of these predators lived on the island.

The landscape slowly changed, the scrub pines shifted shape and evolved into pine forest. The trail continued, however; narrower, covered now with dense needles. She had no feeling of being lost; she simply marveled at the diversity that surrounded her.

A flight of dragonflies appeared from nowhere, encircling her, flitting here and there, helicoptering up and down, guiding her along the path. *They all seem so earnest,* she thought. *It's as if they're protecting me.* Finally, as the path widened, they flew off, disappearing as quickly as they appeared.

She got off her bike after a time and walked it through the woods, listening to the calls of the finches and chickadees and sparrows overhead.

And then a man popped out of a hole.

She saw it from a bit of a distance, a section of the leaf and needle-covered ground lift up, an arm pushing the square of earth to the side, and then a head, a body, climbing up and out of the ground. Once on the surface, the man pulled the square back over the opening, covered it with surrounding brush and leaf scatterings, looked around once or twice, and then calmly walked off through the woods.

Verona began to call after him, but thought better of it. She waited until he disappeared into the forest and then she slowly, cautiously, walked her bike to where he had first appeared.

If she hadn't seen it, hadn't seen him exiting from beneath the ground, she would never have noticed the covered-over opening.

"Curious," she thought, and her curiosity getting the better of her, she leaned her bike against a tree and walked over to the covering. She looked up, the man was gone, and without hesitation pushed the covering to the side.

A ladder-like stair descended into the ground. Verona peered down, but it was dark. She looked around, there was no one she could see, and she quickly climbed down the rungs and into the hole.

Although it wasn't a hole at all, but a room, a room she saw when her eyes adjusted to the dim light offered from the opening above, with a pot-bellied stove, a sink, and wood paneling covering the walls.

Surprisingly, she could stand upright in this subterranean dwelling. Who lived here, she wondered?

Not wanting to disturb anything, not wanting the man to suddenly return and discover her invasion, Verona quickly climbed the ladder. She thought she heard someone approaching as she reached the top step, and her heart raced, but it was only the wind rustling overhead. Quickly, she covered the hole, scattered leaves and twigs around it, hopped on her bike and rode away. Civilization was unexpectedly close, as she soon heard the cars along the Polpis Road and spied the bike path through the trees.

The island was full of wonders, she thought as she pedaled back to Sandy's, the dinner she bemoaned inconsequential to her now.

It was just as well, Addie reflected as he went to bed that night, that he hadn't spoken to that woman at Sandy's. He'd had too much wine (thanks to Chuck continually filling his glass) and he didn't want to meet anybody new, not when he was leaving the island. He had to prepare himself for that, he told himself as he fell off to sleep; he had to get serious about packing — and he had to tell Digit.

He dreamed that night that he was in church, which surprised him even in his dream because he rarely went to church, unless it was a wedding or a funeral. The church had high, stained glass windows. A light shone onto the pews from the top of one of the windows. The light was bright, and as he looked at it, someone seemed to be walking out of it towards him. It was a silhouette at first, but as the person got closer he began to make out who it was, and it was the woman he'd been eyeing at Sandy's. Although she was walking towards him, she didn't seem to recognize him, but kept coming closer, and closer, until he thought she was going to walk right through him.

But then she was peering down into a well and Addie was afraid she'd fall in. He tried reaching her but he couldn't get close enough. Then, suddenly, she tumbled in.

He woke with a start. "Weird," he said.

Verona was falling. She saw the sky above her, and what appeared to be mud below, although the mud had a motion to it like waves along the shore. That she was descending at an unusually slow rate didn't seem surprising; perhaps she was buoyed by the wind. She saw the edge of a high bank and then, an arm, reaching for her.

She extended her own arm and almost touched the fingertips of the hand reaching out to her. She stretched and stretched as far as she could but she now was falling faster and the saving arm was beyond her grasp.

But before she hit the ground her mind spun her awake. "Weird," she said softly.

Chapter Nine

ADDIE MET Verona the next day, sort of.

He was last in line. After all the wine the night before he didn't feel like driving and he arrived at the wharf intentionally late. Thankfully, it was a slow day. He went out on the second round of tours and dogged it, hoping it would be the only tour he'd have to give.

Knowing he wasn't going to push it when he began, he was relaxed, and he incorporated all the short tours he gave on days he wanted to get back quickly to base into one big tour extravaganza.

"I hope you really want to see the island today," he said to his passengers as he closed the door and the wheels started rolling. Ken wouldn't like it, but Ken would just have to get over it.

He'd give the tour by the book, with some extra-added material he'd picked up over the years thrown in. He knew most of the other drivers' routines and, from time to time, selected some of their stuff for his tour. Today, he'd give them everything. Hell, he'd even take them out to the lighthouse, even though he wasn't supposed to — the summer people who lived near the light didn't like the buses with their cargoes of hoi polloi.

"Well, screw them," Addie thought. "It's time they saw some regular people for a change."

And so he turned down Easy Street and talked about the old Nantucket Railroad that operated around the turn of the last century, the little steam-powered engine with yellow passenger cars that chugged along through town, out to Surfside, across to Tom Nevers and out to the village of 'Sconset. It had been a sightseeing-cum-real estate promotion train, real estate values of the time minuscule compared to today. *(Minuscule,* Addie said to himself. *How about microscopic?)* Addie sometimes fantasized about being the conductor of the train instead of the driver of the bus. Riding the rails — how cool would that be? A few of the old railroad beds still remained, hidden berms that meandered through the dense underbrush on the way to 'Sconset.

He told his passengers that cars were outlawed on the island at first, and how the postmaster in the early 1900s hitched his automobile to a horse for trips through town only to untie the horse when they hit the state road and drive the six miles to 'Sconset because the town had no jurisdiction over the state road. That small defiance, combined with an increasing summer populace that was becoming acclimated to the relative ease of automobile transportation on the mainland, helped spell the end of a car-less island.

The demise of the Nantucket Railroad didn't help.

During World War I, with the island willing to sacrifice for the war effort, most of the little Nantucket railroad was shipped away to France. The railroad car that still served as the bar of the Club Car restaurant was all that remained as a visible souvenir of the era.

Addie pointed out the milestones along the state road on the way out to 'Sconset, the stone markers that had been placed by Peter F. Ewer in 1824 to mark progress to and from town. On his way to the light at Sankaty, he talked about the Broadway actors who summered in 'Sconset from the late-1800s into the early twentieth century. There were still places in 'Sconset that had that old-time feel, he told them, where the ghosts of summer denizens could still be imagined; places like the old tennis club, named the Casino as tennis clubs were in the early-1900s, and the post office, even though it had been recently refurbished.

Before heading out to the light, he even let them off for ice cream at the little market in the village square. Addie stood outside his bus and enjoyed the late summer sun. A woman walked in near lockstep in his direction. Did he know her? "You're not supposed to do this, you know." She was angry.

"Do what?"

"Let people off in the village. You have definite routes you have to take."

"Somebody had to go to the bathroom."

"But they're all buying ice cream."

"Hey, lady, I can't stop them if they want to buy ice cream."

He was getting annoyed by this woman's attitude. The first bus tours ever, he knew, stopped for ice cream in 'Sconset all the time; Chuck hadn't invented that part of the tour, he'd stolen it from Ken, who'd told him about the old routes that he used to drive. This woman was like the others who didn't like seeing the buses in their neighborhoods, as if they were a blight, as if they were carrying a disease instead of sightseers. How did she know what the routes were? Just another busybody with way too much time on her hands.

"Everybody back on the bus," he called out loudly. As the last person got on, and before he closed the door, he said just as loudly, "And now we're off to the lighthouse," and he snapped the door shut before the woman could say anything to him. "I'm calling the police," she yelled, as Addie pulled away.

"What did she say?" a passenger asked him.

"She said she hopes we'll stop by her house."

At the lighthouse, Addie was amazed by how far they'd moved it from the bluff; he hadn't been out to see it yet. He'd followed the progress of the move in the newspapers; how they'd jacked it up and caressed it to its new location, inch by painstaking inch. He let his passengers walk around the old site, advising them to watch out for the hole in the ground.

He looked up at the light and its bold red stripe, one of three lighthouses strategically placed around the island when the world's highway was the ocean and Nantucket was in the midst of the major shipping lanes. To Addie, the light was a 'he.'

"How could it not be?" he thought, as he stared skyward at the massive granite shaft.

The passengers sang songs on the way back into town, as though they were kids in summer camp. The trip took two hours by the time he got back to base. Ken would be ripping, but Addie didn't care. He had to keep the good times rolling right up until he parked the bus so that the tips might— just might — match the tour. You could give the greatest tour in the world, but if they weren't laughing when the bus stopped, the tips would be the same as any other tour, a buck a person if he was lucky. He and Chuck talked about it all the time. "Jokes, jokes, jokes," Chuck told him. "They don't want to know about history, they want to forget their troubles."

The passengers had stopped singing, but that was all right: Addie simply had to get them laughing before the wheels stopped rolling. "I've got to tell you about my nephew," he said as he approached the wharf. "He's my sister's kid and her husband's parents were visiting." He checked his rearview mirror to make sure they were paying attention. He continued: " 'Grandpa, talk like a frog,' my nephew said to his grandfather when he arrived. Now the old man smiled but he didn't know what the kid was talking about. A little while later my nephew asked him again: 'Grandpa, talk like a frog.' This time my sister shooed him away. After dinner, when his grandfather was relaxing in the living room, my nephew snuck up on him again: 'Grandpa, please talk like a frog.'

"What are you talking about?" he finally said back to him. "Why do you want me to talk like a frog?"

"Because grandma says we're going to go to Disney World when you croak!"

The bus was back in line, the wheels had stopped rolling, and everybody was roaring. Perfect. No one was trying to rush off the bus before he could thank them — and before they had to tip. No, they were all taking their time, rising slowly as if they had just watched a movie. Taking their time was good: it meant they just might be reaching for their wallets.

Utilizing French-speaking Reggie's method, he'd ratcheted up the size of his tip jar. No longer did Addie use a plain old coffee can. Thanks to Reggie, who would do anything to squeeze every penny he could from his passengers, Addie had upgraded to a motel room ice bucket — not too big, and definitely not too small; didn't want anybody hurting his hand on a coffee can rim. "Thank you," he said to each of them as they exited with a smile and a bill deposited in the ice bucket. "Thank you very much. Watch your step. Please come back soon. Restrooms are at the end of the wharf."

When they'd gone, all twenty-two of them, he counted out his loot: fifty bucks, a bonanza! More than two bucks each. The joke had worked!

As planned, he'd gotten back too late to go out on the day's last tour. Now all he had to do was placate Kenny. He walked back to the office where Margaret sat behind the ticket counter. Where was Ken?

"He had to go," Margaret told him. "There was some meeting on the mainland. He left right after you went out on that tour … which took a little time, by the way."

"Fifty bucks," he said to her.

"Awesome!" Margaret was in an up mood today. "Have a great night."

What a day. Everything was falling into place: one tour, fifty bucks, no Ken, and now he got to go home, and …

She sat licking an ice cream cone on the bench across from his bus. He knew she didn't notice him because she was looking off blankly into space. She wasn't young, but the way the afternoon sun lit her features made her seem almost angelic. Her hair appeared lighter than it had last night by candlelight; her face shone like starlight on the water.

He was standing on the other side of his bus and watched her through the open bus windows. She had to be married, he thought. No one that cute — and, let's face it, no one her age — would still be unattached. She was older, but had a look of innocence about her that intrigued him.

On an ordinary day he would have gotten in his bus and gone. On an ordinary day he wouldn't notice anybody sitting on the wharf — man, woman or child. But this wasn't an ordinary day, not after making fifty bucks on a single tour. Perhaps this was his lucky day.

He walked out from behind his bus and, pretending he wasn't noticing a thing, sat near her on the bench.

"Haven't you seen me somewhere before?" he said casually, thinking he was being funny.

She turned with a start. She looked at him as though she'd truly never seen him before, as though he was a total stranger. The calm, placid appearance she'd had as she casually licked her ice cream was gone; in its place was a look of surprise, of panic. Her stare froze both of them.

"Wait a minute, I'm sorry, I didn't mean to … "

But she turned and walked quickly away from him, off the wharf, not looking back.

"Don't think, don't think," she said to herself as she hurried back to Sandy's and the Lily Pond, the houses and cobblestones blurring together along the way.

Back at her room she fell onto her bed, her heart racing. Who was that, why would someone do that to her? She hadn't been so frightened since, well, ever — that she could remember.

But she knew who it was, now that she was home. It was that man who'd been looking at her last night, the man who'd caused her to go into the kitchen and stay there until everyone had gone. Why did he keep looking at her? It was as though he knew something about her, and while it made her uneasy last night, the feeling turned threatening today. "Haven't you seen me somewhere before?" That's what he'd said. Was she supposed to know him? Oh, please, no.

That dinner party was a bad idea — why had she agreed to it? If this man knew about her, knew the secret she didn't want to know, her life, her simple, unthinking life, would be over. She stared at the ceiling, hoping, praying, he wasn't here to take her away to some unimaginable place. Why couldn't she be left alone, she said to herself one, two, three times. Why couldn't she be left alone?

Maybe she'd find that man in the woods and ask him to build an underground room for her. But that thought dissolved as quickly as it was conjured: she liked it here at the Lily Pond, she was at home here.

Maybe it was time to talk to Sandy, tell her about herself, what she knew and, more importantly, didn't know. Could she confide in her, could she trust her? All she wanted to do was live the life she was living, remain in the present, ignore whatever the past may have been.

Perhaps it wasn't too late. If she didn't think about it anymore, maybe it would all go away. And, to stop the thoughts that raced through her head, she willed herself to sleep.

———

Addie pounded the steering wheel as he drove his bus back to the lot. "Stupid, stupid, stupid," he said out loud. He was only trying to be funny, using a line he'd heard once in an old '60s movie, *What's New, Pussycat?* Richard Burton had said it in a cameo appearance, he remembered. Why that line popped into his head he didn't know. He was trying to be slick, but instead he'd frightened her, scared her off. Scared her? She'd practically run away from him.

Who was he kidding? Who did he think he was — Romeo? What an idiot. If only he could see her again, make it up to her. He had only wanted to be friendly, but he was too full of himself, emboldened by his self-perceived perfect day. "What an asshole," he said.

That was it; he was packing tonight. The sooner he got off the island the better.

———

Verona didn't cook that night, and didn't come down to eat either. Knowing Verona was in the house because her bicycle was by the back door, Sandy, concerned, went up to her room. When Verona didn't answer she opened the door and saw her staring into her mirror. Verona appeared to be in a trance. Sandy said nothing, fearing she might startle her. Verona turned. Her expression was blank, as though she'd experienced some deep sorrow.

"What's wrong, Verona?" Sandy asked, and Verona fell into her arms and sobbed.

They sat on the edge of the bed, saying nothing for a long time. "Did something happen to you?" Sandy said when she felt the time was right. Verona shook her head. "Is it someone in your family?"

Family? She didn't have a family, not in this existence. Before the conversation could continue in that direction, Verona finally spoke.

"Who was that man who was here last night?" she said haltingly.

"Man?" Sandy asked. "There were several. None of them did anything to you, did they?"

"No. No one did anything to me."

Sandy exhaled, relieved. "What man are you talking about?"

"He was sitting next to that funny one, the one you like, the one who kept trying to give me wine."

"Oh, Chuck. Do you mean Chuck?"

"No, the one who sat next to him."

Addie? She couldn't mean Addie McDaniel. Addie was many things but he wasn't the type to upset someone, he wasn't an asshole. "That was Addie McDaniel. He drives with me."

Verona looked at her curiously. "Have you known him long?" she said.

"Long enough. As long as he's been driving. About ten years or so, I guess."

"Has he been living on the island that long?"

"Oh, longer than that. I'd say Addie's been on the island more than twenty years. Why? Did he say something to you last night?"

"No, today. I saw him on the wharf."

So, he finally showed up for work, Sandy thought. "And what did he say?"

"I can't remember," although she could. She'd feel embarrassed saying what he'd said. "He sat next to me."

That shit, Sandy thought. Trying to hit on her. Of course Mr. Sensitive wouldn't realize how delicate Verona was, how she had to be approached carefully, tenderly. If he was interested in Verona, why hadn't he asked her?

Because he shows up for work when he feels like it, that's why, she thought.

"I'll talk to Addie," Sandy said.

"No, please, don't," Verona implored, and seeing her expression, Sandy promised she wouldn't. The color had come back to Verona's face. Sandy felt better about that.

And Verona was feeling better herself. If what Sandy said was true, this man, this Addie or whatever his name was, had lived on the island long enough that he couldn't have known her before, known her from wherever she was from. Maybe he was only trying to be friendly, but he shouldn't have said what he said. Couldn't he simply have said, "Hello?" She would gladly have talked to him then. He wasn't a bad looking man, after all.

She was glad, too, that she hadn't confided in Sandy. Not yet. Sandy had told her enough to put her mind at ease, almost.

No, there was no danger with this Addie, she could see that now. It was the way he'd approached her, however, the way he strode familiarly toward her that made her chest heave. She'd only seen him out of the corner of her eye, but her mind quickly flashed to someone putting a hand on her shoulder and saying, "Come with me. You don't belong here."

So she fled. Instinctively.

And she couldn't remember what happened to her ice cream cone, if she'd dropped it before she ran away, or if she'd continued licking it on her mad dash home.

Chapter Ten

A DDIE McDANIEL had a lot of stuff. It wasn't that he collected anything, it was simply what he had held onto over the
years. It wouldn't be important stuff to you or me, and it would
have been considered junk to the nouveau riche who elbowed
their way onto the island, but to Addie the detritus of his life had
meaning — it defined him.

He kept his possessions in boxes and milk crates, in large
manila envelopes, in folders, canvas bags, and shoeboxes. He
had books, record albums, compact discs, papers he had written through the years, letters, bank statements, telephone bills,
matchbooks, stationery, souvenirs — the bric-a-brac of a lifetime. He had carried it all with him, packing and unpacking his
books and records and, later, his CDs with every move. The rest
remained in their boxes, unopened for years.

It was what he had accumulated from the beginning, all the
little things he had picked up from grade school through high
school, into college and beyond, and over the years it had grown
from a collection to an obligation. He had managed to cram all
his stuff into one corner or another wherever he moved, at times

leaving a box or two behind in an attic or cellar, retrieving them months, or sometimes years later, when Digit or another of his landlords called for him to come and get rid of it. At one point, before he lucked into his year-round rental, his stuff was scattered in nooks and crannies all over the island, but gradually, box by box, milk crate by milk crate, it all came back to him.

And now was the time to deal with it. Addie was leaving, and his stuff — most of it, he hoped — wouldn't be going with him. "Simplify, simplify," he told himself, pulling a heavy box from beneath his bed. If only he could get it down to a box — or two. He could manage that.

What would he get rid of first? Which piece of his past could he jettison most easily? He opened the box. Books. His books would be the first to go.

Why did he still have his old college textbooks? Did he imagine he'd ever use them again? Was he saving them to hand down to some destitute college student? *Think about it, Addie.* These textbooks are all outdated now. He thought of closing the box and tossing the whole thing — but there might be something else inside. He riffled through a paperback book of poetry. This might be good to keep; you shouldn't throw poetry away. He set it aside. One book. What's one old text to remind him of the spring day when his class sat on the lawn discussing William Carlos Williams and Randall Jarrell, his professor taking them outside the classroom because that's what English professors could do, and how at that time he was enmeshed in the moment, as earnest in his attempt to understand why some words worked better than others as he was enchanted by the blonde sitting across from him that day, her hair radiant in the sunlight, her perfect features shining and unblemished?

Ahhh, but ... on to the next volume, a math book. He opened it and its spine snapped like new. Had he ever used it? He glanced at the pages, recalling none of it. Must have done great in that class. Out. Easy. Next, a history book, his notes scribbled in the margins; his penmanship, the work of an unsure student, was terrible, but still neater than his handwriting today. But what was this hiding between the pages? A note, from a girlfriend, inviting him to lunch that day. Out it goes, he thinks. But as long as that note survives the day lives on forever; the promise of a meeting yet to come, a luncheon date unconsummated. Surely, one little note wouldn't take up much space. He could keep it in his poetry book.

And on it goes, scraps from his past in every box: a birthday card from his mother ("On my son's twenty-first birthday" — a keeper); an old matchbook with a telephone number but no name — *that* he could throw away (but shouldn't he call the number first and see who answers? No, not this time); letters from his grandmother — these he had to save; as long as he had them she still was alive, still residing at her old return address. He should have written her more.

There were napkins with pieces of poetry scribbled on them. He read one:

People attract
as they appear
to be alike
they love
by twos
together
in groups
alone
in pairs
they are readied
for the ark.

(The poetry class wasn't a complete waste of time, he thought.) At the bottom of the box was a plaque he'd been given in high school for his part in an oratory competition. Should he chuck it? Later, maybe. He hadn't received too many awards in his life.

He'd had ambitions (to do what? Teach? He'd hated student teaching in college), but ever since he'd come to the island, it'd been too easy to float from one job to the next, from one season to the next, and, inevitably, from one year to the next.

And now where was he? He told himself he was preparing to leave, but leave to what? You couldn't just float along on the mainland like you could on the island. He needed a plan.

He thought of the girl/woman from Sandy's party. Conjuring her image made him forget the past, forget the present. He hadn't been with a woman in what, a year now, ever since Nora left? No, there'd been that one night with the girl he'd been dancing with at the Chicken Box. He should've married Nora. Although they'd never lived together, they'd dated steadily for three years.

And one day, as Addie and Digit sat at the Atlantic Café, Digit asked:

"Where's Nora, anyway?"

"She left."

"She left you?"

"She left the island."

Nora never pressured Addie, and they never talked marriage, but one night, as they snuggled, she told him she'd been offered a job as an account executive in New York, and she really couldn't turn it down.

"It's my field," she told him. "I'd worked in finance for years."

"I thought you were a chef," Addie said.

"I am, now, sort of. But that was just to do something different for a while. I'd burned out in New York, but now I'm ready to go back.

"You can't be Peter Pan forever," she said. "Sometimes you have to grow up."

It hadn't occurred to him at the time, but had Nora meant him?

———

Addie got up to stretch and his knees cracked. He'd gone through, what, three boxes? And how many more were there, under his bed, crammed in his closet? The task was too daunting. Each box held memories, some meaningful, some long forgotten, but inside every box were pieces of his life.

The bathroom beckoned: the burdens of memory weighed on him and he needed a break.

What Addie wanted at this point was to forget he even had all this stuff. Why bother going through it at all? Because each memento, each scrap of paper, brought him back to his life at that time, to what he was thinking then, to the people he cared about. These boxes held his dreams.

The phone rang. It was Digit. "Let's go fishing," he said. Good. Hallelujah. Any excuse to stop what he was doing, stop his mind from recollecting. Besides, he had put it off long enough — he really needed to tell his friend he was leaving, and at this point, after the screw-up he'd had with that girl/woman that afternoon, talking to Digit would be a relief.

But how easy would it be to tell his old friend he was leaving?

Of all the good things that had happened to him since moving to the island, getting to know Digit had been the best. Their friendship had grown, evolved, so that most of the time they didn't need to speak; they were comfortable simply being with each other.

When Digit had allowed Addie to stay after his girlfriend moved on that first summer it opened the door to their companionship. Unlike his relationships with the opposite sex that hinged, predictably, on just that, there was no other agenda with

Digit. No matter what happened, no matter how far away Addie moved, their friendship would endure.

"What the hell are you doing?" Digit said when he saw the boxes and piles of paraphernalia strewn around Addie's living room. Digit had entered without knocking, as always.

"Sorting through my life, old friend, sorting through my life."

"Talk about your waste of time," Digit said.

"What do you mean?" asked Addie. "This stuff is valuable."

"Show me one thing that's worth more than a dime."

"A dime?"

"All right, a dollar."

"You know what, Digit? That's your problem. Not everything has monetary value."

"In this life it does." While everything Addie had was personal, everything Digit squeezed into his garage was useful, or could be useful someday.

Digit surveyed the room, looking thoughtful. "Tell you what," he said. "I'll back up the truck tomorrow and help you take all this shit to the dump. No charge."

"Eat me," Addie said.

———————

They headed out in Digit's four-wheel-drive Ford pickup to the west end of the island, to Madaket. "The bass are back," Digit told him.

"Great," Addie said, although he really didn't care. He was happy to be doing something mindless, driving along saying nothing, listening to the Martha's Vineyard station, WMVY, on the radio. When they got to the beach, they let the air out of the tires to drive along the sand. The night was black, cloudless, and the stars, their luminosity undimmed by the artificial lights of the mainland, shone brightly.

Addie liked to fish, but he only fished with Digit. The trouble with fishing was that you might catch one. Addie went alone once, landed a bluefish and didn't know what to do with it — the fish's razor-sharp teeth kept snapping at him. Unable to get at the hook, Addie let the fish flop around on the beach until it died and then he got the hook out. It made him uneasy, seeing the fish flop around like that. Digit's method of killing a bluefish with a single blow on the noggin with his small, baseball bat-like club was a lot more dignified. With bass, which had no teeth to speak of, extricating the hook was a lot easier, although the fish was still jumpy, and slippery. If a caught bass wasn't big enough you threw it back. The way bluefish often took the whole lure meant they'd end up as supper, no matter their size.

As usual, Digit had brought the poles, the lures, and a six-pack. In spring and late fall, he would pack waders for him and his friend. Because they were going for bass, Digit affixed Bombers to the lines — light, fish-like lures that supposedly mimicked bait. He lit a small cigar and cast, the lure dancing and contorting in the wind before it hit the water.

The two fished about ten yards apart, casting into the cresting waves, reeling their lures back slowly, and casting again.

"We'll give it a few more casts, finish our beers, and drive down the beach a bit," Digit said. "You're pretty quiet tonight."

"Just enjoying the stars."

There was no one around, the night was perfect. Why mess it up by talking about leaving?

Not that Addie had a plan. It would take six months to sort through his things the way he had gone about it tonight, and he had less than two months to get his act together. He didn't even have a car that was mainland worthy. The old Chevy he drove had a ragtop that was ripped, a passenger door that only opened from the inside and tires that were nearly as bare as the beach they were standing on. Who was he kidding? If he was really going to leave he needed to get serious about it, get a new car at least.

He spoke, finally, but not about his intentions that seemed pretty half-baked now that he was thinking about it. He said, instead: "Been out to the lighthouse since they moved it?"

"Nope. You?"

"Today. Took a group out there, even though we're not supposed to; the people out there don't like seeing the buses."

"Screw them."

"That's what I thought. Anyway, I walked up to the old foundation, they don't let anybody near the new foundation yet, must be that they want to be sure that it's stable, or something. So I walked up to the old foundation, which is now a hole, and I felt something."

"What, a breeze?"

"Right. A breeze. No, I can't explain it; it was like something was pulling me."

"That's the wind, you asshole. You weren't being pulled, you were being pushed."

"Seriously. I felt this strange attraction. It freaked me out a little bit."

"So what did you do?"

"I left."

"Coward."

"You got that right. But, really, what do you think it is?"

Addie knew he could tell his friend about the experience without some kind of judgment attached. He didn't care if Digit believed him or not, Digit would listen to him.

Digit said nothing for a time, just puffed on his cigar, reeled in his line and cast again. "Originally," Digit said after a time, "the Indians lived out there at Sankaty, the Wampanoags. Thousands of Indians lived on this island before the English showed up — well, several hundred anyway — not many people know that. Wouldn't it be just like the white settlers to build a light-house on sacred ground? Maybe it was some kind of spiritual place."

"It had that kind of feeling to it," Addie responded. Digit was smart, there was no doubt about it. It was one of the things Addie liked about him. "It definitely had that feeling to it."

"Remember when they were building that housing pro-ject, and they found out it was an ancient Indian burial site? The tribe's chief and medicine man came over from the Cape to consecrate the ground and that put an end to that development. Think of all the places on the island the Indians lived before the English showed up; it wouldn't surprise me if Sankaty is hal-lowed ground." Digit reeled in his line. "Let's try further down the beach."

They drove a bit and Digit put his cigar in the ashtray. "Why don't you research it? Find out about it. You like history; it might make a good story for your tours."

"I don't think so."

"I don't think so," Digit repeated mockingly. "Why not? You're the one who said he felt something out there."

"I'm not going to be doing the tours anymore."

"You got fired?"

"No … "

"Hey, wait a minute. You don't believe that crap about them shutting down the buses, do you? You must know there's a lease that has at least two more years to run."

"Yeah, I know all that." It was now or never. "I think I'm leaving."

"Leaving the job? It's about time."

"No, the island."

Digit said nothing, drove a little more, pulled his truck to-ward the shoreline with his headlights hitting the ocean. The spot was less wavy than where they had been. "Right, you're leaving," he said, cutting the engine and opening his door. "You're not leaving."

But I am, Addie thought. At least I think I am.

Digit cracked a beer, looked out at the starlight reflected on the water. "So where are you going? You got a job somewhere?"

Addie grabbed a beer for himself. "I've got nothing, Digit, you know that."

"You've got the island."

"I don't even own a house here."

"So what does that mean? The Indians didn't own houses, either." He turned the radio off.

"You know," Digit continued, "the island's part of you now, you're part of the island. Think of all the people you've known over the years who've tried to live here but after six months, a year, two years, they were gone. It wasn't in their makeup; they weren't islanders, and you, my friend, are an islander."

Addie shrugged. Digit relit his cigar.

"All my life I've seen them come and go. They move here, thinking they're getting away from it all, thinking it's a fairy tale land, but in the end the isolation makes them look inward a bit more than they'd like. How many married people have come here, hoping the fantasy they'd shared during their honeymoons would save them, bring them closer together? Well, this is no fantasy land, you know that. Look at how many of them wind up getting divorced, a lot of them pretty soon after they move here." He paused for a second, leaned against the hood of his truck.

"When you're on the boat, and I don't care if you're coming or going, what do you see when you're rounding Brant Point?"

Addie thought for a minute, saw the gold dome of the Unitarian Church standing sentinel over the town; the wharves stretching like welcoming arms into the harbor; the tops of the trees cresting protectively over the shingled houses; heard the soothing sound of the foghorn. "I see home," he said.

"You know what some people see? They see clouds, they see grey skies, they see Alcatraz. Or, worse, they see dollar signs."

Gedoudamyway, Addie thought, smiling to himself.

"What's so funny?"

"Nothing. I'll tell you later."

"This is my home, Addie, our home, not a stopover until we get it together; not an address, not a fancy zip code, not some diversion from the real world. It's where I was raised, where my parents and grandparents were born. There's graffiti scribbled in the attic of the old Coffin School that was put there by my grandparents. How proud was I when I saw that? You can't buy your way into something like that." He was on a roll now; Addie shut up and listened.

"There are people getting married here who have never set foot on the island in their lives. Can you believe that? And why are they getting married here? Because it's the thing to do, that's why. Destination weddings, they call them. That's what this island is to them, a destination." He almost spit out the words. "I suppose that's all right, but these are our churches, where weddings have meaning because we've grown up in them, it's our home."

And Addie remembered Digit's own wedding, attended by people he'd seen around town for years but never knew they were part of Digit's family; people from both sides because Marsha, too, was from the island.

"No," Digit continued, "how many people have I met who said they sincerely cared about the island, and who knew all the history, a lot of them even better than I do, but it was all gloss in the end, they were only passing through. You can know all the history you want and never really know the island.

"No matter how many people come here, no matter how expensive it gets to live here, we'll still be here. You can count on that, we'll still be here."

The wind was picking up. Digit reached into the truck's cab, pulled his headlights on. The ocean was choppier now, the spray tossed upward by the wind. "Storm's coming up," Digit said. "That's why I wanted to come out tonight; there won't be any fishing for a couple of days."

He killed the lights and they both looked at the clouds racing through the stars. Addie turned his back to the wind, there on the western edge of the island, where, beyond the swelling waves, America reached out behind him.

He had never planned on moving to the island, never planned on staying, but then he had never planned much of anything in his life. What was he doing here? Spinning his wheels, that's what. The wheels on the bus go round and round, all right, but Addie couldn't get out of neutral.

Chapter Eleven

THE STORM of which Digit spoke was a tropical depression that kissed the Carolinas before veering out to sea. Although it was well over a hundred miles from the island when it passed, its residual force still had a lot of kick. High surf warnings were issued by the National Weather Service, and the surfers attacked the waves on the south shore as the storm approached.

Late that night and into the early morning, the wind howled outside Verona's window. Rain pounded the roof, lashed at the shingles. Verona pulled her blanket up to her chin as the weather raged. She usually liked the sound of rain on the roof, but tonight's storm was different, angry almost, seeming to threaten her shelter, as if it would tear the roof tiles apart. She lay awake, staring into the darkness as the leaf-laden trees slapped the sides of the house. Why, oh why was she here on this island?

She seemed to be meeting more people as time went on. She hadn't wanted to, not at all. People nodded with a kind of recognition now as she walked down the street, which she supposed was a good thing — it meant she was accepted, they weren't questioning why she was here — but she wanted, simply, to be allowed to remain in her own world, which was getting harder and harder to do. When she'd first arrived, it was so easy to live on the edges, alone, witnessing what was going on without being involved. She was able to exist on the fringe, interacting only when necessary, like the times she worked, but for the most part she was able to drift along unnoticed.

But one can only be a visitor so long; at some point you belong, merely by being there.

She was lucky, she supposed. She had no cell phone, no social security number, no driver's license, no savings or checking accounts. She received no mail. She needed a little more time, that was all. With a little time she'd be able to think more clearly. Until then, she'd do her best to continue to think as little as possible.

Chapter Twelve

THERE WERE no boats that day; there would be no boats the next day either.

The rain had ceased, but the winds on the backside of the storm continued to blow a near gale. The charter fishing boats tied up at the wharf bobbed in their slips like toy boats in a bathtub. Digit had been right — there'd be no fishing for a while.

The drivers showed up for work, nonetheless; there might be some tourists hanging around with nothing better to do. It was late August, and although they were pretty much sick of each other by now, the drivers who weren't sleeping or reading on their buses, like Frankie, were hanging around the office, not talking, just hanging. They were all pretty much talked out.

Passengers began straggling in. Ken sent out buses half full to give the drivers something to do, and to get them the hell out of the office. The passengers on the tour had been stuck on the island because of the storm and the wind and they took the tour out of boredom. They wanted to know what the plan was if there was a hurricane, what the evacuation plans were.

"Evacuation?" Addie said. "There are no plans. What are

they going to do, take fifty thousand people off the island in the summer? There's no way. The only thing we can do is head for higher ground and batten down the hatches."

He looked in the mirror; these people couldn't wait to get the hell off this island and never come back.

Addie met up with Digit at the end of the day at the Atlantic Café. He asked him if there really were any evacuation plans for the island because he'd just made up the answer on his tour.

"Damned if I know," Digit said. "I wouldn't leave anyway, but you'd probably be the first one out at the airport looking for a helicopter."

"Very funny."

The island had been lucky, Addie knew. The last hurricane to cause any real damage was Hurricane Bob in 1991, when the wind seemed to tunnel up Main Street, uprooting many of the old elms that had graced the town for a couple hundred years. Still, it was nothing compared to what happened on the Cape and the mainland, where trees were snapped like pencils by the wind.

No, the worst storms Addie had witnessed were the northeasters, the storms that no one on the mainland worried about because they were all "blowing out to sea."

"I suppose if a storm was bad enough you'd head to higher ground," Digit was saying. "You could head out to the middle of the island, to the moors, but there's no shelter out there. The Unitarian Church might be good, but it's old, and I don't know how safe the clock tower would be, but that's where I'd head. You can pretty much see the whole town from up there."

Addie had been up in the church tower and knew what Digit was talking about; it had been the island's fire lookout for generations.

"But then, you could head for highest ground and wished you hadn't," Digit went on. "Imagine if you'd been out at Great Point during that nor'easter and climbed to the top of the light-house for safety?" He shook his head. "You would have been screwed."

Addie had heard about that storm, too. He told people about it on his tours: how, during the night of March 29th, 1984, a northeaster wiped out the old lighthouse at Great Point, the fragile northernmost tip of the island where the lighthouse had resided since 1818. The erosion was so severe that the sands had shifted away from the light, exposing it to the Point's eastern shore where waves regularly battered its foundation. During that storm, when winds were so fierce that there were no boats, planes, or anything coming or going for three days, the lighthouse could take the pounding no more and fell like an old heavyweight, toppling onto itself like a planned demolition. The force hurled the light's metal top like a giant Frisbee yards down the beach, imbedding it in the sand to the tip of its lightning rod. It took a ton of digging and a backhoe to get it out.

"Wonder what that must have sounded like when it fell?" Digit asked.

"It must have been wicked," Addie guessed.

"I'd like to be wicked." It was Chuck. "Hey, Chuck," Addie said, "tell Digit what you told that guy from New York."

"That I'd make his apple big?"

"Forget it."

"So, are you going to ask that girl out?" Digit said out of no-where. Addie pointed to his chest, gave Digit a look that asked, *Me?*

"No, I'm talking to Chuck. Of course I'm talking to you. I think you should get together with that girl."

Addie knew who he was talking about, all right, but he didn't even know her name. Sandy had introduced her around the table, but Addie, as usual, wasn't paying attention. "Do you remember her name?" he asked Digit.

"No, I'm terrible with names. What are you asking me for? Ask her."

"Ask who?" Chuck wanted to know.

"That woman none of us knew at dinner the other night."

"Who? Verona?" Chuck said. Chuck was great with names. "She's cute — older, but cute."

"See? Even Chuck thinks she's cute."

Addie didn't feel like going through the whole thing about how he had seen her and scared her away. He'd just as soon forget about it. "I don't know," he said.

"Oh, right, I forgot, you're leaving," Digit said, raising his glass to his lips.

"You're leaving?" Chuck said.

"Not right away," Addie whispered, as if someone was listening to their conversation. "In a couple of months, after the tours are over. Don't tell Ken. I mean, I want him to hear it from me."

"My lips are sealed."

"Your lips are never sealed, Chuck."

"You know, you're not getting any younger," Digit said. "Looked in the mirror lately?"

"What's that supposed to mean?"

"It means that you're not going to find a cute woman who's close to your age anymore, that's what it means."

Addie thought of the mystery woman's face. She was cute, there was no doubting it. When he was younger, when he'd first moved to the island, he would have thought she was old. Funny how perceptions of people and their appearances aged along with you. In his mind he was still twenty-five, although he was far from twenty-five now.

Addie looked into his glass of Coke. He didn't have a beer

because he still had to get the bus off the wharf for the night. Thankfully, talk shifted from Verona *(was that really her name? What kind of name was Verona?)* to the Red Sox, to the end of summer, and how they were looking forward to fall. None of them noticed the news bulletin that displaced the rerun of *The Honeymooners* on the TV behind the bar, how police in Hyannis were looking for a woman who'd stolen credit card and social security numbers and was now on the run. They said they'd had her cornered but she'd eluded their grasp.

And when Addie saw Fred from the Steamship Authority coming through the door he beat a quick exit through the back. He saw Fred sidle up to Chuck and overheard him say: "So, what's up this weekend? Getting laid? Getting high?" And then he saw Fred whisper something in Chuck's ear.

Chapter Thirteen

VERONA. VER-O-NA. Addie repeated the name as he drove his bus back to the lot. "Ver-o-na," he said out loud, almost singing it. He'd heard the name before (or had he seen it?), but he didn't know where. Verona. Who was she? And why was he suddenly so interested? Ver-o-na.

Cut it out, Addie, he told himself. *She probably has a boyfriend. More likely, she's married.*

What was he thinking, that he was seriously considering getting involved? Forget about her, he told himself; he needed to get serious instead about going.

After she'd finished working that afternoon, Verona bicycled back to the lighthouse at Sankaty. She'd had a compulsion to go to the light all day, as if something was tugging her there.

When she awoke that morning, the rain had stopped but the skies were still dark; branches continued to claw at her window. At first, her mind was wonderfully blank, as if nothing had happened at all, as if the wind hadn't pushed and pulled all night at her windows, seeming to single her out, threatening to carry her away. Was it all a dream?

No.

The fierce wind and rain had frightened her. For the first time since she'd awakened on the wharf she felt alone. She was alone in the world with no one to confide in, no one to comfort her; the isolation she thought sheltered her from the world mocked by the banshee-like wail of the wind.

As she sat in bed kneading the blanket she held tight to her cheek, she wished for the first time she could go back, back to the wharf where she'd awakened, back to the day her new life began. If she could go back, maybe she could start all over again; or continue the life she'd had. It could have been a good life. She shuddered as she realized she might never know her real story.

There were inklings, however; pictures that played along the peripheries of her mind; unsettling shadows that ebbed and receded like waves at the water's edge. She treated these involuntary images as a thoughtless tide, allowing them to come and go without dwelling on them. Perhaps one day she'd try recalling them, invite them into her consciousness, see if they held the secret to her past.

As she thought this, however, something deep inside her poured through her body like a warm drink. She closed her eyes and spoke quietly to the swirling wind: "I'm never going back."

It was a hard ride to the lighthouse. The wind pushed against her as she pedaled. There were no other riders on the bike path. There it was, at last, in the distance, across the island plains that resembled the African Serengeti, although to Verona, who knew nothing of the Serengeti, they just looked like open fields. When she finally got to the old foundation it was as if something was asking her why, but what she didn't know. The feeling had nothing to do with her — it was as if the wind itself was trying to tell her something.

"Enough," she thought. "I'm not listening to the wind anymore."

———————

There was one hitch in Addie's plans to move away, and it was something he'd never told anyone about, not even Digit. He'd lived on the island so long he couldn't drive on the mainland anymore. He had no trouble driving the little bus around the island, but driving on the highway was white-knuckle, death-grip terror.

It hadn't always been this way, of course. He'd grown up on the mainland, loved cruising the highways. Then, after being on the island for about ten years, he drove up to Boston one weekend, a simple drive, one he'd done hundreds of times before.

But something came over him when he got up to speed and hit the passing lane, a time where he used to sit back, relax and crank up the radio. This time he felt as if he would lose control of the car. That he had to keep moving, that he couldn't stop, frightened him terribly. He felt he was going to black out, or worse, turn uncontrollably into another lane. He made it over to the breakdown lane, shaking the whole time, and drove with his flashers on to the next exit. It was a rental car and he drove it to the nearest office and took the bus back to the Cape.

Since then he'd driven around Hyannis from time to time, but never again on the highway. He'd see an on ramp and sweat would pour from his palms. It was as if he was trapped on the island, and he was ashamed of himself. He couldn't tell Ken about his malady, that was for sure, nor could he tell any of the other drivers — it would kill his confidence if they caught on to this failing, and if there was one thing a good tour bus driver needed it was confidence.

That he'd never told Digit gnawed at him. He didn't like hiding anything from his best friend.

But how was he going to leave if he couldn't drive? He supposed he could move to New York or something, and perhaps that's what he'd do, but then he'd be trapped there, stuck on another island, an island where he didn't know anybody, except Nora, and she had a new life now; he was just a guy in her rearview mirror. The freedom a car once represented stood for another thing entirely — it made him feel inadequate.

And as he looked around his rental house at all the boxes holding all his things the elation he'd had about trying something new — embarking on an adventure — turned to cold feelings of doubt. Should he stay or should he go?

That was the question.

Chapter Fourteen

FROM TIME to time Sandy entertained thoughts about leaving the island, about cashing in and moving into a double-wide in Florida. But these were fantasies born during times of frustration, like today, a real scorcher, when the humidity hung in the air like damp towels. Still, the trippers came, insistent on taking a tour, no matter how hot it was.

"Where's the air conditioning?"

"Open the windows," Sandy advised them.

"But it's hot outside."

"The air conditioning kicks in at forty miles an hour."

Nobody laughed.

No, Sandy wasn't going anywhere. The times and trials she'd had on the island were a part of her now; the memories, good and bad, adding up to define her life, or what her life had become.

What rooted her most was her home, her house. It represented more than property — it was her retreat, her haven. Her house was her own shingled island where she could shut out the world and dwell within the history its walls contained.

And, as she'd discovered, her house harbored stories of its own.

She'd begun by researching its prior owners after her divorce, something to do to keep her occupied, keep her mind off the rumors that swirled in those days. When she thought back on it now, she appreciated how much work she'd put into it, although it didn't seem like work at the time.

She started at the town's registry of deeds, where all the home's owners were neatly recorded in the hand of whoever was registrar at the time.

In the beginning, in 1875, Herman and Irene Paddock were given the land as a wedding present and lived in the house they built on the property, until 1902, when it was sold to Benjamin Coffin. There was no mention of a wife on the deed. Coffin owned the house until it somehow became the property of Mary and Fred Worth in the 1960s (it wasn't clear in the deed), who in turn ended up selling the house to Sandy and her husband.

Sandy understood from her conversations with Mary Worth that she and her husband had lived in the house at first, but soon moved away from town. They rented the house out summers for a decade or so before deciding to finally get rid of it. Sandy sensed the relief Mrs. Worth had at the closing, racking it up at the time to her having one less thing to think about, one less responsibility.

In time, and through conversations with neighbors, Sandy learned about the previous owner, Benjamin Coffin, one of the last lighthouse keepers at Sankaty, who had bought the house from his cousins, the Paddocks, so that his daughter would be closer to school. Apparently, Sandy's neighbors told her, the daughter was watched over by an aunt, but that she more or less raised herself and returned to the lighthouse on weekends to stay with her father.

While scanning old newspapers on microfilm at the library

one day, Sandy found out that Benjamin Coffin had died after falling from the lighthouse during a violent storm. As for his daughter, Sandy assumed she had inherited the house, but there was no record of it.

One neighbor, however, told her this story: that Benjamin Coffin was a horrible man who treated his daughter like a slave. "She was perfectly happy in town," the neighbor told her, "but her father forced her to walk the seven miles out to Sankaty after school on Friday, and walk back into town on Sunday afternoons, after she had cooked and cleaned for him all weekend. Can you imagine that? Making a young girl walk all that way? He refused to let her have any friends, and boys, well, you can forget it.

"Living on her own as she did," the neighbor continued, "she became quite headstrong, and one weekend she had a run-in with her father. He was at the top of the light cleaning the windows outside the lens — yes, there was a storm as the paper said, and the salt whipped up by the ocean had coated the glass. She followed him up to the top of the light and they continued arguing up there. No one's quite sure what happened next. The accepted story was that he lunged at her, she ducked, and he fell over the rail. Terrible thing. Imagine the guilt she must have felt if that was the case.

"The island was different then. There was no trial, no blame attached. Everyone knew he got what he deserved. The islanders all pitched in, set up a fund for her to live on so that she could finish school.

"Some people, of course, believed she had pushed him over."

It was a fantastic story, but Sandy had read the newspaper report of his fall.

"What happened to the girl?"

"Oh," the neighbor said, "when she graduated high school, she left the island and never returned."

Something in the way she said it implied otherwise, but Sandy had no reason to doubt the neighbor's story.

Until she found the letters, that is.

She discovered them after her divorce in the room that was now Verona's. She had taken out the furniture to put in a new rug, and as she rolled up the old one — a tattered, woolen thing that had been there since she'd first moved in — it caught on a nail, lifting up the floorboard beneath it. When she came back to hammer it in she saw under the raised floorboard a glimpse of fabric.

She pried up the board a bit and saw the fabric was tied around an old newspaper. Carefully, she untied the ribbon and unfolded the paper — there was the article she had seen on microfilm about Benjamin Coffin's fall. In the pages of the newspaper were two letters, still in their envelopes. She peered at the top one, addressed to Rebecca Coffin, and delivered to a town post office box. She took the letter out of the envelope, postmarked September 8, 1938.

"My darling Rebecca," the letter began, "my heart aches at being apart from you. Since our last correspondence, I have been agonizing over how I should confront your father when I return.

"Please come with me. I do not wish to speak ill of your father, but he has lived his life, and it is time for you to live yours. Come away with me. When my tour on this ship is done, we will return to the island if you wish, for I will live anywhere you choose.

"If you would only come with me to the mainland as my bride our future together will be sealed, but if you insist that you can only go if your father consents to our marriage I'm afraid you will be gone from me forever.

"We are due back in New Bedford in two weeks' time. Hopefully, we'll be able to lay over on Nantucket. I'll think of something to tell the captain. I must see you.

"Devotedly, Gerald."

Sandy opened the next letter in the packet, postmarked a month earlier.

"Dearest Rebecca,

"How wonderful this summer has been. I never imagined when our ship reached Nantucket that its beauty would pale in comparison to you. I had heard the tales about the glories of your island, but honestly couldn't have cared less before my arrival. The old days are over, I felt, and the island was only a shell of what it once was, when the oceans teemed with ships from the faraway isle. All of us at sea had heard the stories of Melville and *Moby-Dick*, but were also aware that since the last whaler left port so many years ago the island sustained itself on fishing and cranberries, and on the generosity of the summer visitors, of course.

"But to see you upon my tour of the light at Sankaty, and to receive your father's blessing to have you show me and my crew a bit of the island was the day my life forever changed. How fortunate that our stay had been planned to be an extended one, that we were bound to remain as long as it took for repairs. In any other port, at any other time, the days would have been interminable, but how quickly they have flown in your company.

"I intend to ask your father for your hand when I see him next. I will come by the light tomorrow. I write you now only because I cannot wait to speak with you, even if it is only through this letter.

"Until tomorrow, I remain, your trusted friend, Gerald."

What happened? Sandy wondered. Rebecca was, obviously, the lighthouse keeper's daughter. What had happened in a month?

The answer came when Sandy happened across a leatherbound book, a journal, while she was cleaning out the old cupboards in the pantry. The book was in one of the lower cabinets, standing flat against the cabinet divider, overlooked in all her years of living there.

And it was through the journal that Sandy learned Rebecca's story.

"How boring, how tedious my life has been, until this afternoon. A group of merchant seamen visited my father and me at the light. Usually, I would be in the house, and away from the light, and usually I would have nothing to do with sailors and their salty language. I have heard them on the docks and seen their coarseness, as they display animal-like behavior when they feel no one is watching. Not that they care if anyone is watching, or listening!

"But today, I was sitting outside the light with my father when the men arrived, escorted out to meet us by the Coast Guard. They exchanged pleasantries and my father took them for a tour to the top of the light. It was a glorious day, and the view from the top on such a day is breathtaking; where you not only see for miles to the horizon, but down to the little village of 'Sconset and out across the golf course to the moors beyond.

"One of the group came down from the top on his own, and introduced himself. He told me how he and his crew were to be in port for at least a month while they repaired their ship. He seemed pleasant, and his language was fine. He is also quite handsome.

"I said little to him, my shyness something I cannot help as I am around few people near my age except at school. And soon, I will lose that contact, as we graduate next year. I so want to go to college, to see what wonders the world holds beyond this island, but my father so far forbids it. He depends on me, as he has since mother's death, and I fear he will remain dependent on me forever! Although I have tried countless times to sway him, there is no talking to him!

"To continue, for reminiscences of this day remain sweet,

this sailor told me his name. Gerald. He said it once, but I remember it as though he whispered it to me this instant! He spoke with me about the sea, and inferred that I probably knew as much about being on the water as he did. I must have looked foolish to him, for I said nothing.

"And then, boldly, when the others descended the stairs, he had the nerve to ask my father if I could accompany his group into 'Sconset, as they were going to tour the village and would appreciate the knowledge of 'a native.' Perhaps my father was taken off guard, he is not used to being in the midst of large groups of men, or perhaps he felt confidence in the Coast Guard chaperones, for all he said was, 'She'll be back in an hour,' and they agreed.

"Oh, the roses adorning the little summer cottages never looked lovelier! The men — but I can't really call them men, for they are not much older than I — were all very charming, and they egged me on to tell them more about the island, what it was like living here. I made it seem all very pleasant, which, as for comfort and beautiful surroundings, is true. We went down to the beach at Codfish Park and they marveled at the wide expanse of sand, at how fine it was.

"We laughed all the way back to the light, it seemed. And as I prepared to say my good-byes, Gerald surprised me by asking my father and me to visit his boat the next day. My father said it wouldn't be possible, he had to tend to the light. 'Then your daughter will just have to come alone,' Gerald said. He said that he was sure at least one of the Coast Guardsmen could again come along as chaperone.

" 'But no,' said one of the Coasties (for that is what they call themselves, I know) 'it would not be right for Mr. Coffin not to be able to make the trip as well. We will man the light while you and your daughter tour the vessel.'

"How my heart skipped. Had he not said anything, I know

my father wouldn't have let me go. I could have hugged him then and there.

"I cannot wait until tomorrow."

Sandy turned the page.

"Oh, glorious day. Father and I have just returned from what I can only call the trip of a lifetime, even though I have yet to leave this island. Gerald and his crew gave such a masterful tour of their ship that even my father was impressed, I could tell. Gerald insisted we stay for lunch, and the galley was more than ship-shape, with linen tablecloths laid out for us and bouquets of hydrangeas on each table.

"After lunch, the crew showed my father the engine room and pointed out the various places where repairs would have to be made. Gerald said an engine room was no place for a young lady and so we took a walk along the docks. How my heart raced when we first stepped off the ship, but I dared not show my feelings.

"He told me he was twenty-two years old. Twenty-two, only five years older than I! He said he was fortunate to be first mate, but that he had been on boats since he was fifteen years old, and knew his way around a ship. Some may call that cockiness, but I think he was merely being confident.

"Soon, too soon, we were back at the ship. On the walk back he said he would visit us again at the light. I can only hope so."

Sandy read on. Gerald did indeed visit Rebecca again, ostensibly to ask her father's advice about some ship related item or other. By his next visit, it was clear that old man Coffin was getting a bit annoyed by the young man's questions. But Rebecca revealed this:

"On his way to his car, he slipped me a note, which I secreted away. But I am placing it here within these pages, so that I will have it always."

And there was the envelope, which Sandy opened and read:

"Dear Rebecca,

"I'm afraid I won't be able to fool your father much longer with the reasons for my visits. I would ask his permission to take you dancing at the Yacht Club, but I think I know what his answer will be.

"I know as well that you reside in town from time to time at the home of your aunt. If you'd like, I would be pleased to share a lime rickey at the drugstore soda fountain on your next visit to her. You may call at my boat. Please don't think me too bold.

"Your friend, Gerald."

And Rebecca did visit, and they did sit at the soda fountain, and Rebecca couldn't wait until she came to town again. She took her aunt into her confidence, who made up a story about needing Rebecca's help at the annual Grange meeting the next weekend so that Gerald could take her to the Yacht Club dance. The pages of Rebecca's journal became filled with matchbooks, paper napkins, and pressed flowers.

And then came the inevitable day before Gerald had to shove off when, as Sandy had first discovered in the letter hidden under her floorboards, Gerald asked for Rebecca's hand. Now she learned the outcome of Gerald's expectant words.

"It is two days later, and I force myself to write. Gerald came alone to the light yesterday afternoon. Although he has always worn a tie when we've gone out together, on this day he wore a suit, and he looked resplendent. I only hoped that to my father he would look mature, kind, and thoughtful.

"My father was in the living room of our small house here by the light, examining the tide charts, when Gerald arrived. My father did not acknowledge him at first, but when he did finally look up it was as if he had been expecting him to call. Every word is still etched in my mind. My father was blunt: 'State your business,' says he, but before Gerald can speak he rises from his chair. 'Do you think me a fool?' he roared so that the little house seemed to shake. 'This is a small island, my boy. You must think us some stupid to think we wouldn't know what's been going on. Did you have fun at the Grange, dear?' he said, turning to me, and then, to Gerald:

" 'You come to ask for her hand, you, who have done nothing but deceive me? You, with your trips out here seeking my advice, advice any cook or cabin boy would know. You, whose family we know nothing about. You have shamed us by slinking around with my daughter through town, while all who know me have seen it. You may leave now, and never return. If I could, I would ensure that you would never return to the island.'

"And Gerald tried to speak, but my father stormed past him and walked to the light and locked the door behind him.

" 'Come with me now,' Gerald whispered, but, no, I said, I could not leave, for I knew if I did I would never see my father again. And I could not bear that, no matter what he is like. I must leave tomorrow, Rebecca, he said, to which I replied that I knew all too well the day of his departure. He said that he would write, that he would somehow get a letter to me.

Father never left the lighthouse all night."

———————

"I cannot bring myself to write," the next entry began. "Father and I have not spoken although we continue to live and eat and breathe in the same house. At night I cannot sleep. I have cried, for days I have cried, but never in front of father.

"I have not heard from Gerald, and fear I never will again."

But, then, this entry:

"A letter at last, delivered to me by my aunt, my dear, sweet savior. He is coming back! He insists on seeing father, although I know it will make no difference. I will write and tell him so.

"And yet I must see him. My heart is torn. Gerald will have to think for both of us."

Sandy closed the journal, not wanting to read on. Even though this had all happened in the past, the ache, the yearning, was real. With her heart in her mouth, she turned to the next page.

It was blank.

As was the next, and the next. She flipped through the pages, but there was nothing. Would this be all? Oh, Rebecca, she thought, please say there's more.

There had to be more. Something happened between Gerald's arrival and Benjamin Coffin's terrible demise.

Chapter Fifteen

A SHORT walk from Sandy's house and the Lily Pond was the North Cemetery. The cemetery was cut in half — into Old North Cemetery and New North Cemetery — by New Lane, a former horse and buggy trail that over the centuries had turned into a paved thoroughfare. The tour buses drove past the cemetery as part of their route, and the drivers pointed out how the tombstones all faced in the same direction so that you could see the inscriptions on one side of the road but only the backs of the tombstones on the other.

Addie had driven by the old cemetery hundreds of times, but had come on his own maybe two or three times, no more. He was here now because he wanted to revisit different historic areas of the island before he left, affix some images in his memory.

A song went through his head, something he'd heard an island folk group singing in the Brotherhood: "Life in this tourist town is getting me down/ Oh, the breadlines keep getting longer every year." He grappled with how he was going to leave the island, if he was just going to say the heck with it, buy a car and get over his affliction, or if he would wait until he got to the mainland to do it. Probably be cheaper to buy a car over there.

But what would he do with his stuff?

He came to the cemetery to give his mind a break. The tombstones, he figured, were all placed the same way to face the setting sun. Nice touch. At least the early settlers could agree. He couldn't imagine getting islanders to agree on anything these days.

He wandered among the orderly graves in New North Cemetery, stopping every once in a while to read the inscriptions. The Chase family was well represented, including, he was surprised to find, Owen Chase, first mate of the ill-fated whaleship *Essex*, stove by a whale. Chase, one of the few survivors, wrote an account of the tragic shipwreck that caught the interest of another seafaring writer, Herman Melville. Nothing about the *Essex* on Chase's tombstone, though.

The gnarled trees at the edges of the cemetery gave the place a Halloween-type feel. Some years ago people came to rub the gravestones, to transfer the inscriptions onto waxy paper. The practice was discouraged after the engravings started to wear away. Time and weather were taking their own toll, slowly eroding the markers so that the names were fading on their own. Other stones teetered on the edges of their pedestals, while a few had succumbed to the wind and toppled.

Few people visited the old cemeteries now. That was fine with him; he welcomed the solitude as he meandered amidst the rows, among the people who lived what must have been a harsh, solitary existence on the island. Unless they left for a few years on a whaleship, many of them stayed on Nantucket their whole lives — far from the mainland and its progress and its problems. Did they ever want to leave? Did they feel trapped here?

Should he stay or should he go?

Staying would mean, what? Well, he'd have to find a new rental. He really didn't want to go through that hassle again. But, then, he'd have to find a rental on the mainland. If only he had someone to go with him, that would make it easier. He wondered what his old girlfriend was up to, the one with whom he'd moved to the island in the first place. Must be married, he thought. He was sure she'd never returned to the island, but perhaps she did, she and her husband and their kids, staying at one of the fancy summer homes on the beach, living the good life, as she pointed out to her husband the house she once lived in when she was "slumming it."

Addie didn't notice the other person two rows over, the one standing in front of a gravestone, intent on the inscription. When he finally sensed her out of the corner of his eye, she was only a row away. She said nothing, and gave no inclination that she saw him, but when he looked again, he saw it was Verona.

Verona. Ver-o-na. It couldn't be. But it was.

Great. Probably figures I'm stalking her, he thought. Why else would I be here? Why do we have to be the only two people in this cemetery?

Should he leave, pretend he didn't see her? But what if she did see him? If he turned and left now and she did see him she'd really think he was a jerk. It was too late now; he couldn't ignore her. Seeing her there made him flush — he did want to see her again. What could he say? What could he say so he wouldn't frighten her again? Think fast, you idiot, he told himself.

And don't bring up any old movies.

Verona came to the old cemetery often since she'd moved into Sandy's house. Walking by the old gravestones brought her serenity, calm. When invasive thoughts came to call, losing herself amid the grassy paths made them disappear. To her, the inscriptions were like stories, stories with a definite ending, ones with no surprises. The past was the past, unalterable, complete, finished.

She was standing before a grave she hadn't noticed before, even though she was positive she'd traveled this row previously. How did she miss this one? It was funny, too, how she'd at first been across the road but something made her come to this side, to this remote tombstone. "Benjamin Coffin," the inscription read. It had meaning, she could feel it, but what was it supposed to mean?

Although Verona did not want to know her own history, she was comfortable learning about Nantucket's history. It was safe — the old stories had happened years before, their consequences long over. Learning about the past had no bearing on the here and now.

There were other people named Coffin in this cemetery — why did this one seem so important to her?

And who is that? Is someone here? She turned and saw a man, a row away, looking down at a gravestone before casting a glance in her direction. Her instinct was to turn and walk in the other direction, but he looked familiar, as though she should know him. He looked back at her then, gave a little wave. He was smiling.

Obviously, this person felt he knew her because he started walking towards her. After he'd taken a few steps she recognized him — that bus driver, the one she'd overreacted to. He wasn't young, that was for sure, but he was cute.

"Verona?" He was talking to her. He knew her name.

"Hello," she said. She didn't know what else to say.

"Do you have family here?" he said. Good, she didn't flinch. He was going to say, "Do you come here often?" but was glad he'd thought that one over.

"Oh, no, I was just taking a walk."

"Me too. It's peaceful here, isn't it?" A pause. Spit it out, Addie. "Say, I'm sorry about the other day," he stammered. "I didn't mean to say anything wrong."

She looked at him caringly. How could she tell him he didn't say anything wrong at all, even though she ran?

Getting no reaction from her, Addie said this: "I can be a jerk sometimes."

"Oh, I don't think you're a jerk."

Great. A woman of few words. Still, the way she spoke, her soft voice, was pleasant. Keep it up, Addie, you've got nothing to lose. You're leaving the island anyway.

"Do you think any of these people would recognize the island today?" he said. "Would Main Street still look the same to them? I wonder if one of them was plopped downtown, could he still find his way home? Maybe a few of their houses are still around. Like Sandy's house, for instance. I wonder if anybody here lived in Sandy's house."

"How about this person?" Verona asked, glancing down at Benjamin Coffin.

Interaction. At last.

"Why not? What's the name? Benjamin Coffin? Maybe. Sandy would know; she knows a lot of Nantucket history."

"Have you heard about him?"

"Nope. I mean there are a lot of Coffins on Nantucket, no pun intended. Have you gone to the other graveyards? You know the guy who invented power steering is buried over in Prospect Hill. True story. But so is the nation's first woman astronomer, Maria Mitchell, and Robert Benchley, the humorist."

"You seem to know something about Nantucket history yourself."

"I guess I know more about Nantucket than I do anywhere else. I've lived here long enough. Besides, I have to — it's part of my job."

Yes, that's right, Verona thought. This man worked with Sandy. "I can't imagine driving one of those tour buses around; so many people to be responsible for."

"Oh, it's not so bad. It beats working," he laughed. "Have you ever taken a tour?"

"I don't think I'd like being on a bus full of strangers."

"You could bring a friend. My treat." He was getting somewhere, he could feel it. *Don't give up on this, Addie,* he told himself. *Come up with something.* "I could give you a private tour, in my car," he blurted out. Then, gaining composure, "That way we can go where the tour buses can't go. No big deal. We could go on my day off, or after work sometime."

They began to walk. Moving and talking seemed like the natural thing to do. "Would you like that?" he asked her, trying to sound casual.

The way he said it was so genuine, so non-threatening. For the first time since starting life as Verona, she felt like taking a chance with someone other than Irene or Sandy. "I'd like that," she said.

Great. "Great," he said. "How about tomorrow? I have to work, but we could go about five, five-thirty. Just a couple of hours. I'll have you home by dark. I can pick you up at your place."

And without knowing it, feeling much as she did when she unconsciously followed Irene home, Verona simply said, "Yes."

"Perfect. Are you heading home now? I'll walk you back. My car's in town."

And as they walked through the cemetery, Addie said to her: "Have you ever noticed how the gravestones all face the same way? They're all facing west, toward the setting sun."

Chapter Sixteen

S UMMER WAS winding down, and there were seats at the bar at the Atlantic Café. There were rumors that the Café was going to close after the season, either because of the downturn in the economy or because the owner of the building wanted something a little more upscale for the new brand of summer person. No one paid much attention to the rumors: after all, the Atlantic Café was an institution. Addie hoped Digit would be there, and he was, eating nachos and watching a soccer game.

"What's the score?"

"Who cares? I can't understand this game, anyway. I don't get how the rest of the world goes crazy over it." He turned from the TV to his friend. "What are you doing here? I thought you'd left the island."

"Very funny. Well, I did it."

"Did what?"

"Asked her out."

"Who out?"

"You know, that girl, Verona."

"No kidding?"

"No kidding."

"So, what are you going to do? Watch the submarine races?" There were no submarine races, of course. To watch the submarine races you parked at the ocean — at night and, hopefully, alone.

"Right. No, I'm taking her on a tour."

"Big spender. That should be exciting. And on your left ... "

"Not on a bus. I'm driving her around in my car."

"Oh, I get it. And then you'll watch the submarine races."

"For your information, my froggy friend, she happens to be very interested in Nantucket history."

"I've got some history right here she might be interested in."

"Aren't you married? I thought you'd be happy for me."

"I am, I am. Take it easy. Here, have a nacho."

"No, thanks." Addie noticed that Digit had a booger hanging out of his nose. "Hey, Digit," he said, and he pointed to his own nose.

"Hey, what? Your nose itch or something?"

"No," he whispered. "You've got a snot hanging out of your nose."

"Jesus." Digit took his napkin and wiped his nose. "Is it gone?"

"Yes. Good thing you weren't giving anyone any history lessons."

"Yeah. I just saw Marsha, too. I wonder why she didn't tell me? She usually does."

"She should have told you that your fly's down, too."

Digit nearly choked on a nacho as he leaned back on his barstool to check.

"Gotcha."

"You're an asshole, you know that?"

"Speaking of assholes ... "

"What?"

"Don't look now, but here comes Fred."

"We've got to find a different bar."

The seat on the other side of Digit was open, and Fred plopped into it as though he was welcome to it. "Hey, guys. Boy, what a day. Seventy-five cars on standby all day. Everybody's trying to leave the island."

"What number in line is your car, Fred?" Digit said.

"What?"

"Nothing." Digit stared at the television. Fred leaned over Digit's plate of nachos to talk to him and Addie.

"So, what are you guys up to this weekend?"

"Hey, Fred, I'm trying to watch this game."

"What's the score?"

"If you'd shut up maybe I'd know."

"You guys kill me, you know that?"

"I'd like to kill you," Digit said.

Fred either didn't hear him or pretended not to hear. He leaned in closer, so that Digit had to lean over in turn towards Addie. "Seriously, you guys know where I can score a little blow?"

"What?" Addie said.

"You know," Fred was whispering now. "Coke. My girlfriend's coming over, and I'd like to have some fun. You guys are pretty cool. You must know where I can score."

"Sorry, Fred," Addie said. "Why don't you just order a Coke here and let it go at that?"

"No, I'm serious," Fred said. "I've been dry since I got here."

"Why don't you ask your friends on the Vineyard?"

"I would, but I can't take a chance with the dogs. They're sniffing everything that comes over. I don't want to lose my job."

"That'd be a real shame, Fred," Digit said. "Look, can you move over? I'm trying to watch the game."

"You like soccer?" Fred asked.

"I'm trying to learn how to kick your ass," Digit said.

Fred wrote something down on a napkin and passed it to Digit. "Here's my number. I can understand how you maybe wouldn't want to talk in here. Give me a call. I'll pay top dollar; you could grab some fast cash."

Digit looked at the napkin lying on the bar and left it there. Turning to Fred he said, "You know what, Fred? You've got a kind face."

"Really?"

"Yeah, the kind I'd like to throw shit at."

Chapter Seventeen

VERONA WAS at work. Passing by her room, Sandy paused, noticed the rug. It had been years since she'd replaced the old one. She walked to the window and looked down on the shrubs and trees and wildflowers of the Lily Pond. She took a deep breath in affirmation of her love of living in this house. Rebecca, she thought, I hope there was some comfort for you here. She sat on the edge of Verona's bed and let her mind reach back …

———

… She had given the room a last-minute once-over before the new rug arrived. There was the floorboard that had hidden the letters. Were there more secrets stashed there? Perhaps she should have pried up all of the floorboards in the room, but that would have been crazy. There were only a couple of letters, after all, and the journal was found in the pantry, not here. She walked across the bare floorboards, thinking that if she stepped on a loose one she'd pry it up. Nothing, not even a creak.

So what led her to the attic, and up the stairs? What led

her to look beyond the unfinished canvases left by her husband, where, hidden since she'd moved into the house, was a chest, a small sea chest? Why had she never seen it before?

The chest wasn't heavy and she carried it back toward the stairs where the hallway light gave more illumination. There was a clasp, but no lock, and she slowly opened the lid, her fingers trembling a bit, as if something might fly out at her.

Nothing flew out at her, but still she drew back when she saw what was inside.

———

A lacy gauze and white fabric unpillowed and seemed to spring out at her. It was a wedding dress. She took it out carefully but did not unfold it, fearing she would damage the fragile lace. Beneath that was a navy blue peacoat and beneath that a cap, like a policeman's cap, but with a crest that said U. S. Life-Saving Service. Did Rebecca marry after all, and was this the uniform of Gerald? Did he enter some branch of the service after his time as a merchant mariner? Yes, she thought, he must have during World War II.

Beneath these items of clothing, wrapped in an old news-paper, was a picture, an old framed photograph of a married couple. The groom, though young in the picture, looked severe, while the bride had only the faintest hint of a smile. Sandy studied the picture closely, then the wedding dress, lifting it onto her lap where she could see it and the photograph at the same time. Could it be? She stood and unfolded the dress. The neckline, the sleeves, were the same. She would need a magnifying glass to study the lace in the picture, but she was sure it was the same dress the bride was wearing. She did not know what Rebecca looked like, but the picture seemed too old for it to be her.

Beneath that was what looked like a package wrapped in tissue paper. Inside was a plain, but pretty, dress, calf length she discovered when she unfolded it and held it up.

She looked back in the chest and saw an envelope. There was nothing written on the outside, and the back was tucked into the envelope and not sealed.

Inside was a handwritten note on plain stationery. It said: "Contents of chest

"Mother's wedding gown

"Father's uniform

"Photograph of Mother and Father on wedding day

"Dress I wore to Yacht Club dance"

Beneath the dress, however, was another journal, tied with string. Sandy recognized the handwriting at once.

"I put no date for there is no time left for me to measure, no calendar with meaning. I write this merely as my own testament to the truth.

"I begin a new journal. The one I wrote in years before was of another time, penned by a girl with hopes, a girl I do not recognize today (nor would she me). How stilted, how formal, my thoughts were then, written in what I thought was proper English. I write now only to clear my memory. I do not want to think of these things again. I do not want to think of being a girl, of Gerald. I do not want to think of my father.

"Gerald arrived that day amidst gathering clouds and small craft warnings. I had remained in town with my aunt, for my father did not seem to care where I went at that time. At least, he did not speak to me about it. We hadn't spoken since Gerald had left. Part of me thought that Father did not care what I did at all, and I hoped when I went to see Gerald that because of his seeming indifference Father would now allow me to marry him and leave the island.

"When I thought that, yes, I would go with Gerald, my mind grew sad at the prospect of leaving Nantucket, for I was sure I would never be able to return. Perhaps I should not marry

Gerald if the price was exile from the island I knew so well, the island that had contained my life to that point. It would be so much easier to stay.

"How foolish of me to think that way. Of course, I could have returned to the island. Had I known that this island would become my prison, I would have gone with Gerald without even seeing Father. In retrospect, that may have been the best course of action. But how were we to know?

"How were we to know?

"And how was I to know that it was a mistake, a mistake I have been forced to live with and endure?

"Gerald had made up some story to the captain about needing to see a relative on the island, and had persuaded him to lay over on their way back to New Bedford. As it turns out, he needn't have bothered because the wind had come up and they would have tied up at Nantucket regardless. Neither the captain nor anyone on Nantucket knew what kind of storm was brewing. And neither did we know of the personal storm that would forever alter our lives.

"Gerald had arranged to borrow a car from one of the Coast Guardsmen. When I saw him, it was as if I hadn't seen him in years, although it had only been several weeks. Our embrace could have lasted forever, and how I wish it had.

"He was prepared to face father alone, but I insisted on accompanying him to the light. On the drive out, he said to me: 'Rebecca, we are meant to be together. Please come with me. I know you love your father, but what will become of us if he won't consent? Are you willing to come with me, no matter what?'

"And I looked out the window at the moors and their subtle red/grey hue, and I thought of the Rosa rugosa in bloom along the shore in summer, and of the Queen Anne's lace in the fields and meadows. And I had no answer. And as we drove, the wind picked up.

" 'I should be back at the boat,' Gerald said. 'This is an unusual wind. They'll need all hands.'

"I did not know what Gerald was prepared to say to my father, nor could I imagine my father's reaction, nor did I want to. I felt as if I was in a dream, not necessarily a bad dream, but not a good dream either. I wanted to reach the light, to get it over with, but I also feared going there.

"When at last we arrived, the door to the light was open. Gerald said nothing as we left the car, and he walked ahead of me, but Father was not there.

" 'He must be at the top,' I said. We ascended the staircase, Gerald before me, and as we got halfway up, I could hear Father coming down. When he met Gerald on the stairs, he said nothing, yet I could see the anger in his eyes. He turned and walked the winding stair back to the top. Gerald and I followed.

"I could feel the wind blowing outside the light, hear it beating against the glass. Father was back at the top now, and soon Gerald and I were inside the light as well. Although it was afternoon, the darkening sky and the closely turning light accentuated their features so that Father appeared to be as tormented as Ahab, and Gerald much older than his years. 'I have nothing to say to you,' Father said at last. 'Take your leave.'

"But Gerald was steadfast. 'Please, can we go down and talk? I love your daughter.'

" 'Love.' I had never heard the word from his lips before, yet because of the gale that was blowing, and because of the strange light cast by the turning beacon, it was as if the word had a different meaning, as if Gerald was shouting it in defiance.

" 'You know nothing of love,' my father shouted back. 'You mean to take my daughter from me? I will not allow it, not to you.'

" 'But why, sir?' " he asked. "It is her wish as well." And they both looked at me then. Their glances stung, as if I was the cause of some great misery, as if I was the cause of the gathering storm itself.

I turned my face from the light as Father roared: "You will not have her," and he pushed past Gerald to open the metal door to the outside rail.

"The wind was raging. Father braced himself against the rail. Gerald followed him outside. I could hear their shouts, could see their agonized expressions through the glass, but could not understand what they were saying. 'Please,' I thought. 'Please come inside.' I did not want this. Without me, none of this would be happening.

"They continued to argue as they moved along the rail. The wind obscured their words, and seemed to snatch them from their mouths and hurl them into the void. The sky grew dark and ominous. I watched my father and Gerald as they moved around the top of the light, and while each grasped the rail, neither seemed cognizant of the wind.

"Then Gerald began moving away from Father, and back toward a panel that opened to the inside. My father came behind him, and Gerald tugged at the panel, which was held fast by the wind. My father then put his arms around Gerald's shoulders as Gerald was putting all his weight into opening the panel. Suddenly, Gerald fell backwards.

"I saw him fall against the rail, but the wind knocked him back onto the platform. He literally crawled through the open window.

" 'Where's Father?' I asked him. We looked through the glass, and my eyes searched along the outer rail. 'Where's Father?' I asked again desperately.

"Gerald struggled against the panel to the outside, forced it open and rushed to the rail. I saw him looking over the side …

"Whether the wind had suddenly let up, or if Gerald had newfound strength, he flung the panel open, entered the light and made his way to the stairs. 'Where's Father?' I shouted this time, and I dared not think. I followed Gerald as he ran down the winding stair. When we got to the bottom, he turned to me and said, 'Don't. Stay where you are.' But I could not help looking beyond him, where I saw Father lying on the ground.

"I was too numb to wail, too shocked to cry. I saw Gerald go up to Father and kneel by him. Then, he turned and came back to me. He put his hand to his mouth and looked at me with sad eyes. 'I'm sorry,' he whispered. 'Rebecca, I'm so sorry.

"I wanted to get to my father, but Gerald held my shoulders. 'No, Rebecca, you mustn't. You cannot see him.' And he tried to hold me in his arms, but I turned away. I walked in circles inside the bottom of the light, lost in grief, inconsolable.

" 'Because of me,' is all I could think. 'Because of me.' I wished I had never met Gerald, never been so selfish to think only of my own happiness. I sank to the floor, then, and sobbed.

"Gerald stood off to the side in that little room, leaving me to myself. After I don't know how long he came up to me and whispered, 'We must go to the house. I need to make a telephone call. There's nothing you can do out here, Rebecca. Please come with me.' And he put his arms gently on my shoulders and urged me up, and he shielded me with his arms as we walked to the lighthouse keeper's house.

"I remember feeling as we walked what seemed like a mile, yet was only several steps, how calm everything had become, as though time had stood still. Where all I had noticed at the top of the light was how the wind roared and rattled, now it seemed as if there was no wind at all.

"And then I thought of my father. What had I done? I wanted to run to him, shake him awake, hold him. But the reality of what had happened descended on me and a numbness took over my being.

"We entered the house, I sat at the table, and Gerald went

to the phone. I remember him clicking the receiver. 'There's no operator,' he said. 'The lines must be down.'

"He paced the room for a while before sitting down next to me. 'Rebecca,' he said. 'He was trying to help me open the panel. The wind must have carried him backwards. I'm so sorry.

" 'But we can't stay here,' he continued. 'We must get help. The phones aren't working and we can't take a chance that the phones in 'Sconset are working. We have to get to town.'

"I must have stared at him, but, truly, I do not know what I did other than saying nothing at first. Then I said, 'I'm not leaving Father.'

" 'Rebecca, you must. There's nothing either of us can do for him. We need to get help. The storm is going to get worse, I can tell. This wind is different than any I've ever encountered, on land or sea. If this storm gets worse, the roads may be impassable. We must get to town, or we may be here all night, or longer. We have to leave now, or else we'll be forced to stay here, and staying here won't help anyone.'

" 'I cannot leave him, Gerald,' I said through tears. 'I cannot leave him out there on the ground like an animal.

" 'I'll take him into the light,' Gerald said. 'He'll be out of the rain and the elements until help arrives.'

" 'Maybe we can help him.' I stood, thinking I'd rush out to help Father. Gerald stood by the door. 'He's beyond our help, Rebecca.'

" 'I can't leave him,' I said again. 'I can't leave him.'

" 'We have to. I've got to get back to the boat. We can both go there and they can help us. Rebecca, we must go now.'

"He left the house then and I did not watch as he dragged Father into the light. Against everything I felt, I left with Gerald, and he had to push me towards the car with his arms around me in order to get to the car, the wind was so strong. As we started down the drive, I looked back at the light to make sure the beacon was working. It was.

"On the way to town, the wind railed and shook and twisted the lines that hadn't already fallen from the telephone poles. Even the car struggled against the wind, and the bushes and small trees were in constant motion. There was no one else on the road and no birds were flying.

"Gerald told me his version of events. 'He was trying to help me open the panel. We were getting nowhere, and I said I had to get back to my boat, for that was my responsibility. He said that was the problem: that the boat would always be my first responsibility, as the lighthouse was his. He said he didn't want you having the same life as your mother.'

"I heard these words and sobbed. My father had never told me. I never knew the pain he must have felt. Why had I been so selfish, thinking of myself, and not of my father who was, I knew then, only trying to protect me. Grief washed through me as I realized how much I loved him.

"Gerald continued: 'At first I thought he was trying to grab me, to stop me from getting back in the light. But he said, "It'll take two of us," and he was reaching for the panel when I heaved and we both fell backward into the rail. The force of it must have carried him over.'

"Gerald then said nothing for a while. The driving was treacherous, with fallen limbs all over the road. At one point, the water had come up onto the roadway and Gerald splashed through, seeming to will the car to make it without stalling. It was worse trying to get back to town; we should have stayed at the light. What was I doing with Gerald? My place was with my father.

" 'I do love you,' he said. 'We'll get through this together.'

"And the joy I should have felt hearing those words was replaced with a feeling of emptiness. His words only made my grief more real.

"In town, the streets were filled with water. Gerald got as close as he could to the docks but could get no further than the gas plant and we left the car there. Boats knocked against the piers; those that weren't tied down properly were thrashing about. There was no one in sight.

"Gerald and I made it to his boat at last. There was no one above deck, and he motioned for me to come with him below.

" 'Where have you been?' the captain wanted to know. 'There's a hurricane raging. And who's she?'

" 'This is my fiancée,' Gerald replied. 'Sir, there's been an accident.'

"And he recounted the whole, horrible story. And the captain listened intently as the boat heaved and was knocked about. The wind seemed to be screaming, a sound like I'd never heard before. It was as if the elements themselves were trying to tell the story. Gerald slumped when he was finished, clearly exhausted. The captain said to me, 'I'm very sorry, miss, but there's nothing we can do now. Winds in New Bedford are up to one hundred miles per hour. We can't be sure it won't hit here harder. You can try and find a policeman if you'd like, but we have to stay with the boat. Is there somewhere you can stay?'

"I was in a trance but managed to say, 'With my aunt.'

" 'Then I suggest you go there now,' the captain said. 'We can get this straightened out tomorrow. We won't be leaving now for a couple of days.'

"Gerald stayed with the boat, and I said my good-bye to him as if I was saying good-bye to someone else. I hadn't thought of my aunt during the tragedy and I yearned to see her.

"People always thought it was my aunt's house, but it was indeed my father's house. My mother's sister, who never married, agreed to stay with me after Mother died. I was always thankful for her company, and when I thought about it afterwards, grateful to my father for making the arrangement, rather than having me live alone with him at the light.

"The water was rising up Main Street as I made my way to our house. The wind at times seemed to lift me and at others to push against me as I walked. The elms in town bent and swayed, but did not break, although there were fallen branches everywhere. The back of our house, which faced the old Lily Pond, was flooded, but I was able to enter through the front door.

"Seeing my aunt, I broke down and sobbed. 'Father's dead,' I told her, 'and it's my fault.'

"And now it was my turn to tell the story, and with the retelling, relive once more the terrible ordeal. My aunt sobbed also, and held me and said, over and over again, 'You poor, poor dear.

" 'He loved you so,' she said to me. 'He was overprotective, but he didn't know any other way. Don't blame yourself. He would never blame you.'

"She, too, said there was nothing to be done at the moment. And I, exhausted and spent, fell asleep in her arms.

"The next day, I woke thinking it had all been a nightmare, but it was all too true. My aunt accompanied me to the boat, where the men were scampering over the deck and on the dock, inspecting her from stem to stern and making necessary repairs. Although shutters were ripped from houses, and many streets were still flooded, the island seemed to have weathered the storm. My aunt spoke below with Gerald and with the captain while I stayed on the dock.

"Finally, my aunt came up top, shook hands with the captain and told me to come with her. I hesitated, hoping that Gerald would come up, embrace me, and tell me everything was going to be all right. But my aunt put her arms on my shoulders and told me to come along. Her tone with me was short, and I had never heard her address me in that way before.

" 'Gerald won't be coming out, dear,' she said sternly. 'We must go. And you must put him out of your mind.' I looked at her then, and she must have read the despair in my expression. 'It's best if you never saw Gerald again,' is all she said."

Chapter Eighteen

THERE WERE more pages to read but Sandy had to put the journal down for a moment. Her hands shook. Oh, Rebecca, she thought, I wish I could have been there to comfort you. But she couldn't embrace words written on a page, and she couldn't travel back in time and change what had happened. All she could do was read on.

"We walked in silence back to my aunt's house, my house. I knew I was walking through town but my vision was hazy, as if I was in a dream. I did not feel as though I was in my body anymore but somewhere someplace else and the person who was walking had nothing to do with me.

"I heard what my aunt had said, but my mind would not let me believe that was the end, that I had lost my father and I would not hear Gerald's voice, or smell the aroma of his presence ever again. It was as if I had been plucked from my life and assigned a new one.

"But when we reached my house, and sat in the kitchen, my aunt told me what she had agreed upon with the captain.

" 'It is best, dear, that you forget all about him. You are still young, and you will find someone else who will not be tainted by this terrible tragedy. I will go to the police now, and tell them that you were with your father during the storm, that he had to attend to the light, and that by accident he fell, which is the truth. It is best not to involve Gerald in this. What if he is not believed? Is it worth taking the chance that he might go to jail? That he might go to jail for years?'

"I could not believe what I was hearing. Jail? Why would Gerald go to jail? I was there. I knew Father's fall was an accident.

And my aunt knew what I was thinking.

" 'Can you be certain a jury would believe your story, a girl taken in, under the spell of a seaman? Anyone sitting on that jury would know your father, and know he did not approve of your seeing him. What would they be more apt to believe? Gerald himself told me, and he told the captain that he could not say for sure how your father fell. It is best that we not mention him at all, and that you get on with your life. I know you can't believe me now, but you will get over it in time.'

"I said nothing, but thought desperately of a way to change things. This could not be happening. And I remembered that Gerald had moved Father's body into the light. My aunt once again perceived my thoughts.

" 'We will say he fell down the stairs, and that in your grief you walked back into town through the storm, not knowing what you were doing. If it is the only story they have to go on, it will be believed.

"I could not believe what I was hearing.

" 'It is best to put it all behind you and get on with your life,' is all she said."

———————

Sandy could not believe that anyone would buy the story, but, again, the island was more isolated in those days. The police, knowing the family well, would not want a teenaged girl to suffer. They would accept the aunt's story, or make themselves accept it. It would be easier that way.

———————

"When my aunt went to bed that night I stole down to the docks, but Gerald's boat was gone. I understood then that my aunt wasn't worried about my seeing him; she knew he wouldn't be there, that they most likely shoved off as soon as we left the boat.

"The police believed her story. They did not even question me, thinking they were sparing me.

"And I put it out of my mind, and in so doing I became a shell."

The next few pages were blank, but then the journal resumed.

"I waited to hear from Gerald, by letter, or through the words of a fisherman or fellow seaman, for years. I never heard from him. The war years came, and those were hard times for the island. The war seemed to be the final barrier to any thoughts I had of ever seeing Gerald again. After the war, I cared for my aunt until she passed away, and by then other girls my age had been long married and were occupied with their families.

"Once, and only once during those hopeful times right after the war did I envision Gerald returning, taking the boat to the island, seeking me out at my house. Those thoughts only made me sadder, and I could never let my mind have them again. I became a recluse, and stayed in this house alone. At times, I would retrace my walk out to the light, the same walk I took countless times in my youth, but as soon as I spied the light in the distance, I would turn around and walk home.

"At times I wondered what I would say if I saw Gerald again, if I could tell him that the Coast Guard decided to automate the light shortly after Father's accident, that he was the last keeper of the light. In some strange way it made me proud. I suppose I had to have something to hang onto."

More blank pages, and then:

"My neighbors ignore me. To them, I may as well have moved away. But I am here, imprisoned on this island, never to leave."

After that, nothing more was written, nothing more included within the pages of the journal. Sandy retied the string, put the book back in the sea chest and closed the lid, as if by so doing she was putting the story to rest.

But it was not a work of fiction and she could not wave aside what had happened, even if it had happened years before. But she realized as well there was nothing, after all, she could do. It was history.

———

Engrossed in her recollections, Sandy had forgotten she was sitting on Verona's bed. She rose slowly and left the room. She wondered why she was thinking of the journal, and of Rebecca, now, after so many years. By her own account, the journal ended sometime in the 1950s. Poor Rebecca, she thought. No matter what my life's been like, it's been nothing like yours.

The neighbor had been wrong, or had lied. Rebecca never left the island. Did she die in this house? Did anyone attend her funeral?

But Sandy knew that the answers to these questions would never bring her comfort. It was best to let it go.

Chapter Nineteen

A DATE, a date. He was going on a date. Well, not really a date, but, yes, it was a date.

Like his fellow driver Margaret on one of her good days, Addie was up, he was perky. He even got into work early and beat Sandy to be first in line. He wanted to make sure he'd finish his day before five o'clock.

He was washing his bus windows, for the first time all summer, when Sandy pulled in.

"Well, what have we here?" she said as she stepped down off her bus. "Is there a special tour group I don't know about, or is there some kind of lunar alignment where everything is now the opposite?"

"And what's that supposed to mean?"

"You're usually last in line. Hungry for money?"

"Can't a guy get into work early without getting harassed? The rest of the island seems to pride itself on being at work before everybody else."

"That's so nobody can talk about them behind their backs."

"I didn't know that. Is that why you're always here first?"

Sandy gave him a stare, walked around to the driver's window where she reached in and pulled the lever to close her bus doors. She headed to the office.

"Hey, Sandy, wait. I was just cracking a joke." Sandy ignored him.

Addie ran up to intercept her. "Seriously, Sandy. You know I didn't mean that." Sandy said nothing, kept walking toward the office.

"Look, Sandy. If I tell you something will you promise not to tell anyone? I'm here first because I need to get out early today. I'm taking your tenant out after work."

"What?"

"Verona."

"What?"

"Verona. I'm taking her out for a drive."

"You can't use the bus."

"I know that," although he also knew Sandy used the bus all the time for personal errands, but he wasn't going to mention that now. "I'm taking her in my car."

"That piece of shit?"

"Hey, it's all I've got. So, whaddaya think? Tell me about her. Tell me everything you know."

"There's not much to tell. She's nice, she's cute."

Inside, however, Sandy was pleased. It was about time Verona got out of her routine of working, biking to who knows where, and hanging out in her room or at the Lily Pond. Funny that Addie had made the arrangement on his own. She had lightly considered involving Irene in a scheme to get the two of them together. She knew Irene helped out a caterer on the side, a caterer who was doing a big clambake for some billionaire who'd just built a mega-mansion in the dunes. Sandy would be transporting the catering crew and some of the equipment to the clambake because they didn't want the help clogging up the driveway with their cars. Sandy toyed with the notion of asking Irene to have Verona help her out that night, while she'd make up some excuse to get Addie to do the final pickup at the end of the party. Irene would make sure everybody else got off the bus first, and Addie would have to take Verona home.

But this was better. She only hoped Verona wouldn't stand Addie up.

Addie put in his requisite three tours, sticking to the proper route each time, adhering to the standard tour driver script. "And on your left ... " He was done by 4:15. Unfortunately, he began the day first in line and ended the day first in line.

"I need you to do a five o'clock," Ken told him. Damn. He should have dumped his passengers at the end of the wharf after his last tour and headed back to the lot without checking in at the office, ending his day by calling in on the radio when he was safely away from base. It was a trick Sandy used all the time, and Ken never called her on it.

"Oh, come on, Ken. I've done my three tours."

"You're first in line."

"So I'm being punished for being responsible?"

"If that's how you want to look at it."

"I'll do it," Sandy said.

"No, it's his turn for a five o'clock. You can go home."

"Really, Ken, I could use the money."

"Suit yourself."

Addie could have kissed her. "Thanks," he mouthed to her as he made a quick exit. The look Sandy gave him in return meant, "You owe me one."

His car was a piece of junk, but Addie liked to think it had character. It was an old Chevy convertible, the top was ripped and duct-taped, but with the weather still nice he put the top down. Like the rest of his life he had never upgraded. He popped in a cassette, music from his teenage past, Bob Dylan's *New Morning*: "Can't you hear that/motor turnin'?"

"Yes, I can," Addie said out loud.

And as he turned the corner near the Lily Pond, there sat Verona on Sandy's front steps.

Perhaps it was the sunbeams kissing her hair, or the glow radiating from her skin, but Addie thrilled at seeing her.

"Hop in," he said, and as he opened the door for her and she sat next to him on the front seat, Addie felt an excitement he hadn't felt in years. He was older, true, but not that old, and he was driving around — alone — with a girl/woman.

"What's this?" she asked when she got into the car.

"It's a convertible."

"No, the music."

"*New Morning*. You've heard it before. By Bob Dylan."

"No. I don't think so."

He wanted to say: "Where've you been living? In a convent?" But he checked himself. Instead he said: "Oh, then you'll really like it, I think. You don't hear it too much these days, but it's one of his best."

"Is it new?"

"God, no. It's almost 40 years old." Just who Bob Dylan or *New Morning* was Verona had no idea, but she liked that it was old. She liked that a lot.

They drove up to the Oldest House, built in 1686, and Addie explained that it was considered the Coffin family homestead, and wasn't that weird that they were just looking at Benjamin Coffin's tombstone yesterday?

"Three hundred and one years later, on October 1st, 1987, it was struck by lightning. You could hear the crack all over the island. I remember the silence after the crack and then, like the pain hitting your brain after you stub your toe, the sudden wail of police and fire sirens. The lightning strike blew half the roof right off." Verona listened to his monologue in silence.

"From here," he continued, "we can either head out to 'Sconset and stop by the lighthouse, or go in the other direction and visit Madaket. Your choice."

Verona didn't want to go to the lighthouse with Addie, not yet; it was too personal. And she'd been to Madaket only a few times to clean houses.

"I'd like to go to Madaket," she said.

Which was what Addie hoped she'd say: if he timed it right, they'd be there for the sunset.

———

There was something homely about Madaket that Addie liked: it wasn't overrun with the fancy feel that consumed much of the island. Madaket retained a laid-back ambience, where it was still expected that of course you'd track in sand at one of the unpretentious summer cottages. It was the way people once summered all over the island and the way most did still on the west end.

Along the way, Addie pointed out various points of interest. "And on your left," he couldn't believe he was saying that, as if they were on a real tour, "is the old dump, which became the sanitary landfill and which is now the landfill-slash-recycling center. Have you been there? It's fun just to go to the take it or leave it, or, as most people call it, the Madaket Mall. It's where people drop off old furniture or clothes, things like that. And you wouldn't believe what these rich people throw away. I know a woman who furnished her whole house from things left behind at the take it or leave it. There's another woman on the island who weaves rugs out of the old towels they leave behind."

Beyond that was Long Pond, and the bridge where people fished for crabs. Bob Dylan continued: "If dogs run free, why not me … "

To Verona, driving along in an open car, feeling the soft summer breeze caress her face, was a sweet sensation. It was better than she'd expected, although, in truth, she'd had no expectations at all. This was good, she was glad she had taken a chance. She liked being in the company of this man who spoke so soothingly, but sitting across from him in the front seat was as close as she wanted to get.

As Addie entered the little village of Madaket, he looked over at Verona and smiled. He hadn't been out here since he'd been fishing with Digit.

He was convinced that night he'd had enough of Nantucket, that he'd seen all there was to see, experienced all he was going to experience on this island, this floating mish-mosh of cultures and attitudes and classes; of rich and poor, and the dwindling in-between.

Now, driving to the sunset with a woman who interested him terribly, he wasn't so sure.

He drove on the bridge past Madaket Millie's house — Millie who was long gone now, but who once counted the scallopers as they went out in the winter and would assure the families who called when the weather turned ugly that, yes, their husbands were fine, she could see them tying up their boats that minute; Millie, who speared a rogue shark with a pitchfork in the creek near her house, and who lived with a pack of dogs, preferring their company, she said, to people, although there were few people more human than Millie.

At the end of the road, he stopped near the public landing and asked Verona if she'd like to walk along the beach. The sun was dropping behind Tuckernuck, the small island to the west that was populated by long-time summer residents who valued their privacy. He pointed it out to her, noting that it was the Coffin family who had originally purchased the tiny island from the

Indians.

They were sitting on the beach when a crane flew overhead, gently soared over the low treetops and landed gracefully on the water. The color of the sky was turning soft purple. The water casually lapped the shoreline and the sand made a soft sucking noise when the water receded. Everything was serene.

"Why do people celebrate beauty in nature, but not in each other?" Verona asked after a while. "Why don't we see the beauty in ordinary human movements every day?"

"Beats me," Addie said, as he watched a seagull pluck a crab from the water, drag it up onto the beach and deliberately peck it to death. But he liked what she said, this absorbing, poetic girl/ woman.

He had brought a blanket with him and they sat on it and watched the sunset. Stars appeared in the darkening sky and a shooting star crossed over the horizon.

"Make a wish," Addie said to Verona.

I wish I never find out who I am, she thought.

On the drive home Addie contemplated asking her out for a drink, but he didn't want to push it. Take it slow, Addie, he thought, take it slow.

Chapter Twenty

L ABOR DAY had yet to arrive, but the selectmen, led by one Mr. Jason Bonere, a Round-the-Pointer if ever there was one, were stirring up a storm.

"He wants to put up that traffic light," Digit told Addie while he mended his scallop nets, getting ready for the season; the dire forecast predicted in April replaced by one of anticipated abundance. "It's all over that website. He's going to propose a test light at the first meeting after Labor Day. People are already talking about protesting."

If there was one thing the island prided itself on it was that it had no traffic lights — a last statement against the excesses and glare of the mainland. Addie wasn't surprised that this vestige of the faraway island's character would evaporate like everything else.

"I'm not surprised," he said.

"There'll never be a traffic light here," Digit said. "He just wants to make people feel he's doing something. He's nuts. He listens to these town planners who try using mainland solutions to island problems. You know the reasoning: everything's better if it's done on the mainland. The only problem is we've got too many off-islanders trying to tell us what to do."

"So, are you going to join the protest?"

"What, are you crazy? I've got better things to do. Believe me, that traffic light's not going in."

Addie noticed something on Digit's teeth as he spoke, a green blot. "What did you have for lunch, Digit?"

"A tuna fish sandwich. Why?"

"You've got lettuce on your teeth."

Digit licked his teeth, picked between them with his thumbnail. "Damn," he said. "Why did Marsha let me leave the house like that?"

Marsha had a cousin the same age whose name also was Marsha. They were both named after their paternal grandmother, so they had the same last name as well. It drove her crazy, especially in grade school when they were in the same class.

"Marsha Stetson," the teacher would call, and both of them would say, "Here."

The teacher tried to rectify it by looking toward their middle names and calling one Marsha L. and the other Marsha S., for instance, but they had the same middle names as well, a family name, Coffin. So, she did what seemed reasonable at the time, and called one "Big Marsha," and the other one "Little Marsha." Marsha was "Big Marsha," and she hated it.

Like Digit, the name stuck, and she was known as "Big Marsha" throughout middle school and high school. That may have been why she and Digit hit it off, because of their misnomers, and why they clung to each other. She couldn't wait to get married and change her last name. Although they lived together after high school, Digit took his time getting around to asking her, and she had to broach the subject.

"Don't you think it's time we got married?" she asked him when they were fishing one night.

"Oh, Marsha, don't hassle me now. Ask me tomorrow."

And she did. And that's how they got married.

Only now she didn't feel like being married anymore, not to Digit, anyway.

That's why she hadn't told him about the shaving cream behind his ear, or the boogers in his nose, or the food stuck between his teeth. It was her way of saying, "I don't love you anymore."

The other way was by sleeping with Thom McArthur, a summer person whose family had plenty of money. Thom McArthur had already been married and divorced twice, so ending a marriage didn't seem like much of an impediment to him. Marsha, evidently, felt the same way.

Digit trusted her, that was the problem. He never questioned her when she left the house for hours, purportedly satisfying a sudden interest in "birdwatching." He wasn't the suspicious type. It made telling him difficult. Marsha wasn't cold-hearted.

She'd wait until scallop season began. Maybe he'd accidentally drown himself before she had to say anything.

Chapter Twenty-One

VERONA WHISTLED as she worked. She didn't know she could whistle, but it seemed to come to her naturally. She had enjoyed herself with this man, this Addie, the night before. He didn't ask questions, which was good.

Besides, he was leaving the island. He told her that. She was safe with him.

Since her awakening, she focused on staying in the present. Oh, she'd had a life before — she was not stupid, she knew she had — but she was happy now, and she did not want any encumbrance — or friendship — to spoil that happiness.

Life could be burdensome, she knew. She saw it in the people she worked with who worried about making ends meet, who were anxious about their children's schooling, or if their husbands were faithful. The more attachments people had, whether it be to a house, a car, or the number of people they had to answer to, the more they worried, the more concerns they had.

And that is why Verona vowed to keep it simple. If she lost her job, she'd find another; if Sandy sold her house, she'd find another room; if her bike broke down, it wouldn't cost much to fix it.

She had no debts, she had no plans. What could be better?

And if this man, this Addie, wanted to offer her a little companionship, what could be bad about that?

Besides, he seemed to know a lot about the island's history. She liked that.

Perhaps he knew about the history of the lighthouse. Perhaps he could shed light on what it was she felt out there.

———————

Besides the talk about the traffic light floating around the web, another rumor was circulating: that Dr. Molly Malone had returned to the island.

Which would be a small miracle in itself because Dr. Malone had been declared officially dead over twenty years before.

The saga of Dr. Malone was well known to islanders: how she, a research scientist, had apparently made a breakthrough discovery that would have made her famous, a candidate for some prestigious honor. People had seen her in town that winter's day, shopping for a celebratory dinner.

But Dr. Malone never had the dinner that night. Before she could celebrate she mysteriously disappeared, never to be seen again.

What was found as search parties combed the island in the frigid January days following her disappearance were her clothes, a pair of sandals, her wallet and her passport, all in a neat pile in the moors halfway between her house and Sankaty Head light. It was assumed she had decided to do herself in by going for a swim in the icy waters off 'Sconset when she realized her findings weren't as earthshaking as she'd assumed. Digit had told Addie about it one time.

"They say she committed suicide," Digit had said, "but if she walked into the ocean she would have washed up somewhere, wouldn't she? The thing is, it was a bitter cold night, so cold that if she'd started out walking to dive into the ocean, she'd have to be real determined to do so. And why would her clothes be found hundreds of yards away from the ocean? And there's no way she would have been wearing sandals. It just doesn't make sense."

Her body was never found. There was no sign of foul play and no warrants were issued. In time, all searches were called off. Several years later, her family petitioned the court to settle her estate and she was declared legally dead.

The police chief at the time said privately that he believed her to be alive, that she faked her death in order to start a new life. On the record, however, he said her disappearance remained a mystery.

In the years since, there had been several Dr. Malone sightings, all of which turned out to be false. For all intents she had vanished, and her story faded as the decades passed.

The new rumor circulating over the Internet said she had been seen bicycling near the lighthouse, and that she was living clandestinely on the island under a new identity. Someone added that she had even undergone plastic surgery to change her appearance, and that she looked younger than her years.

———

Addie hadn't yet moved to the island when Dr. Malone disappeared, so her alleged reappearance didn't faze him one way or the other. People could talk all they wanted to. So what if she came back? She hadn't committed any crime, had she?

All he was interested in was Verona. Verona, who, as he thought of her at that moment, was sitting in her bedroom, making a list of the pleasant things she'd discovered since her awakening. "Things I like," she wrote, noticing that her handwriting flowed effortlessly. "I wonder how I learned to write like this?" she thought, but, like all her other thoughts, she wouldn't let her mind dwell on it. Too risky. And so she continued:

"the lighthouse
"my room
"sailboats on the water
"walks through town
"A — — "

She stopped herself. She had almost written "Addie."

"That's the end of that," she said to herself as she put her pen down and hopped on her bike to clear her head.

———

The hollyhocks were in full bloom as Addie walked with Verona along Easy Street. He had noticed the flowers before — heck, he drove past all kinds of flowers on his route, from the daffodils in spring, to Scotch broom in June, to forsythia, to lilacs, to Rosa rugosa, rose of Sharon, lilies and hydrangeas — but he hadn't really seen their beauty until now. Before this, before Verona, they were mere decoration, backdrops, but now the hollyhocks, in all their varied colors, trumpeted the glories of the day.

They had been seeing each other with frequency as August slipped away; Verona appearing at the wharf at the end of the day, happening to be there as Addie rolled in. After a week or so their meetings became routine, so that neither made plans with the other — it was simply expected that they would see each other.

Verona had gone to the wharf the day after she'd almost included Addie on her list of favorite things. As it had since she'd been on the island, the wharf gave her comfort, grounded her somehow.

And when Addie pulled in in his bus her heart lightened.

She took that as a sign.

For Addie, Verona's innocence and simple ways had him seeing the island as he did when he first arrived, when every trip to town held its own surprises, when every narrow street was a new treasure. Summer was no longer a pain in the ass — everything was bright and beautiful.

Including Verona's eyes, which saw everything in the best possible light.

He didn't know her last name but he didn't need to know everything about her, did he?

Well, did he?

One early evening she surprised him with a picnic basket. They walked through town and over to the Lily Pond where she led him to her favorite spot. There, in a secluded area of reeds and trees, she laid out a blanket and they ate chicken, tomatoes and mozzarella drizzled with olive oil, and a pasta salad that made her stop for a second when she was making it because she put it together unconsciously, as though she had made it a thousand times before. She had simply started reaching for the ingredients instinctively. To her knowledge, she had never had pasta salad in her life.

But in her mind she had seen herself cooking, with someone, a shadowy presence now lost in the vapors of her memory.

"This is delicious," Addie said to her. "Are you a chef or something?"

"No," she said sheepishly.

"Well, where did you learn to cook like this?"

"Stop it," she wanted to say. "Stop asking me questions." His queries, though innocent enough, were unsettling. Questions could only lead to more questions. She needed a diversion.

It came to her quickly.

Chapter Twenty-Two

"Do you have a bicycle?" Verona asked Addie.

A bicycle? Sure, he had a bicycle, an old, rust-threatened hulk of a ten-speed that he left outside year-round. It was rideable, he thought; that is, if the chain hadn't rotted off.

Verona wanted to ride right then and there to the lighthouse with Addie. "I'd have to go home and get it," he told her.

But wait. Sandy had a bicycle. She wouldn't mind if Addie borrowed it.

"Let's go to the lighthouse," she said.

"Now?"

"Why not?"

If Verona had told him to climb a tree or a telephone pole he would have done it. He would have done anything she asked him.

Since Nora, he really hadn't had the companionship of a woman. Sure, he'd been on a couple of dates in the past year (not including that tryst with the girl from the Chicken Box) but he had little, if anything, in common with either of them. On his last date he went to the movies, where the woman constantly checked her phone, the glow from its tiny screen distracting him, while her incessant tapping on its miniature keypad annoyed him. They hadn't left the theater before she had the damn thing up to her ear.

In the short time he'd known Verona, he'd never once seen her with a cell phone. She didn't have the need for constant contact that seemed to infect the rest of the population.

Verona was different, there was no doubt about that. If she seemed a little standoffish at times that was all right with him. He didn't need the complications of an involvement. Not now.

Still, he had to admit, the more he saw her, the more he liked her.

And when he wasn't with her, he couldn't stop thinking about her.

———

They rode through town and out to the bike path. As they passed the Shipwreck and Life-Saving Museum, which featured as one of its exhibits the salvaged top of the former Great Point Light, Addie wasn't so sure this was a good idea after all. Although he had taken sporadic bike rides over the years, most recently back to the lot after his bus had broken down, he had never pedaled all the way to 'Sconset. He wasn't convinced he'd be able to make it, but watching Verona as she glided effortlessly in front of him took his mind off his strained leg muscles.

Fog descended suddenly. It rolled across the moors as it formed, a grey blanket that seemed to simultaneously fall from the sky and unfold from below, an ethereal cloud that enveloped the land, obscuring all that it touched. At low points, it hovered over the street and bike path like a misty bower. Addie pedaled to keep up with Verona as she disappeared in and out of the fog.

As they neared the light at last all that was visible was the murky glow of the beacon as it swept the sky. Verona liked the mantle of fog; it made the world seem more private, as if she and Addie were the only two people in the world.

But after they biked the slow climb up Baxter Road to the lighthouse, Verona saw they were not alone. At first she thought her eyes were playing tricks on her, but it was no mirage. There, revealed by the light made faint by the fog, was a silhouette. As they got closer they saw it was a woman.

And as they got closer still, they saw that she was an old woman.

Curious, thought Verona.

———

Rebecca knew how quickly the fog could come up at Sankaty, but still she hadn't expected it. She had set out from town wondering if she could make it to the light at all, and now here she was at the old foundation. But the fog was a damp curtain and she could never make the walk back to town, not with her eyesight, not on her old legs.

Oh, they'd be angry with her at the Homestead, they probably had the police out looking for her by now, but she had to come, she needed to make one last walk to the lighthouse.

She hadn't been out to the light for all these years. When she saw the scars of the old foundation it was as if her heart was being ripped from her again. She remembered it all: the storm, the words, the fall. And now the light itself had moved, as if it couldn't remain where the awful event had occurred.

That the light had been moved didn't make it any easier. It was still there, the light that had been so much a part of her life, the light that had changed her fate so unalterably.

She had been out there alone for nearly an hour when two people showed up on their bicycles. Was that a girl or someone older? She couldn't tell. Through the fog, the way this person moved reminded her a bit of herself when she was younger.

"Are you all right?" a man, a younger man she could tell, was speaking to her. She didn't feel the need to answer.

Verona sensed the woman was distressed. The pull she'd always felt at the lighthouse now drew her nearer to her.

The two women looked at each other through the fog, the mist obscuring their features so that each appeared ghostlike.

"Do I know you?" the older woman said.

"No, but I feel that you belong here," Verona said to her quietly.

Now that was an understatement, Rebecca thought. Who was this, some old hippie trying to spiritually connect with the elements? But, no, she seemed kind. If only Rebecca could see her face better.

"Something happened here," Verona said to her.

"Yes, that's right," Rebecca answered. "Something happened here. Long ago."

Rebecca welcomed the distraction of talking to this girl. If only it wasn't so cold. The fog was wet and chilling. She was tired.

"Do you live near here?" Addie asked her.

"I used to live right here," she said. "My father was the lighthouse keeper."

"Oh? What was his name?" Addie wanted to know.

"Coffin," Rebecca replied. "Benjamin Coffin."

The name didn't click with Addie, but Verona took a step backward. Benjamin Coffin was the name she and Addie had seen on the tombstone.

"Do you live on the island?" Verona asked her.

"I've been here a few more years than you have, if that's what you're asking," Rebecca said.

The fog was getting thicker now, and Verona guessed the woman was tired. "How are you getting home?" she asked her.

Good question. "I don't know," is all she could say. Getting out to the light had taken every ounce of her energy, one foot in front of the other, not thinking of how far she'd traveled or how far she had to go. When the fog came up she'd wished it would surround her completely, envelop her, carry her, finally, away.

But now she was weary, just weary.

Verona turned to Addie. "Ride back to town and get your car," she said to him. "We'll wait here."

Addie looked at her as if to say, "Are you joking?" but Verona couldn't see his face in the fog. "We'd have to ride back no matter what," she said to him. "We need to give this woman a ride home."

Addie had a better plan. "I'll ride into 'Sconset and call a cab. We can leave our bikes here and pick them up tomorrow."

Off he went. Verona led Rebecca over to some large rocks that had been unearthed during the lighthouse move and sat down with her. She put an arm around the old woman's shoulders. She could feel the sadness in her body. Finally, Rebecca said, "My father died here."

The two of them sat in the fog, the lighthouse's beacon tracing a shadowy arc around them.

Chapter Twenty-Three

SANDY HAD been meaning to talk to Verona for days, ask her a little about herself, but Verona was seldom around anymore, ever since she'd taken up with Addie McDaniel. Well, Sandy told herself, it was what I'd wanted, and they seem to have hit it off. Be careful what you wish for, she thought.

The back door opened then, and it was Verona with Addie McDaniel in tow.

"You'll never guess what just happened," Verona said, walking quickly into the kitchen. This was a new Verona, Sandy thought, a woman more sure of herself.

"Don't keep me in suspense."

"We were at the lighthouse … I hope you don't mind that Addie borrowed your bike … we were at the light and this woman was there."

"And … ?"

"And she was older, and her father used to be the keeper of the light." Verona was talking quickly now. Sandy had never seen her so animated.

"Here, sit down," Sandy said. "Should I make some tea?

Hello, Addie."

"I'd love some tea," Addie said. "You got decaf?"

"What are you, trying to get healthy all of a sudden?" Sandy said. "I've got some herb tea. Is that okay?"

"Her name is Rebecca," Verona said.

Sandy stopped. Rebecca? Must be a coincidence. The Rebecca she knew was dead.

"Rebecca Coffin. Her father was Benjamin Coffin. The strange thing is that I was just looking at his grave over in the cemetery the other day."

Sandy dropped the teacup she was holding and it shattered on the floor. It couldn't be. Sandy sat down, stared at some place beyond the kitchen. No, this wasn't right, she thought. It couldn't be right. "Tell me more," she said quietly.

"It was pretty foggy out there, and we really couldn't see much," Addie piped in. "I had to go find a cab in 'Sconset to take us all back to town. ... Are you okay?"

"I'm fine. Can't a person drop a teacup in her own house? Verona, you tell me what happened."

"She lives at the Homestead. I didn't know what that was, but she told me all about it."

If Sandy wasn't sitting, she was sure she would have fallen over. This had to be a joke, a bad joke. She knew Rebecca, or felt that she did. She couldn't be alive. "Verona," she said as calmly as she could. "Go back. Tell me the whole story."

And Verona told Sandy about biking out to the light and finding the old woman there, and how the woman had walked all the way from town, and how they sat on the rock, and it was while they were waiting for Addie that the whole story came out about her fiancé, and the storm, and the horrible fall.

"I felt so badly for her," Verona said. "But it all happened years ago."

Sandy sat, stunned. Someone knew the story and was playing a little game with Verona. What kind of sick mind would do such a thing?

This person was senile, that was it, demented.

"Verona, you can't believe everything you hear," Sandy said. "There are a lot of crazies out there."

Verona said nothing. Rebecca's story was true; the old woman wasn't crazy. It all added up: Verona's attraction to the lighthouse, finding the grave, seeing Rebecca in the fog.

"Verona," Sandy said. "We've got to talk." And the way she said it let Addie know that it was time to go. "Look at the time," he said. "I better get going if I want to be first in line in the morning."

Verona gave Addie a look that said, 'Don't go,' but she knew that Sandy wanted to talk to her alone.

"I'll see you tomorrow," Addie said, "after my tours. Sandy, I'll see you bright and early."

"Tomorrow's my day off," she said.

"Even better for me," he said. "First in line, it is."

Chapter Twenty-Four

CHUCK HADN'T been around the office in a while, and Addie asked Ken where he was.

"None of your business."

"All right, okay. Just wondering."

"He said he had something important to attend to. He'll be back next week."

Not that Addie really cared where Chuck was. He just missed his whacked out sense of humor, his cowboy grin. Sometimes he and Chuck would have contests to see who could do the tour the fastest. If they were both in line together, they'd load up, start out at the same time, and take off in different directions. The first one back to base won.

One time, Chuck was counting his tips as Addie pulled in.

"You couldn't be back so soon."

"Went to Surfside," Chuck said. "Went through town and out to the beach. They never knew the difference."

"Didn't they ask about the lighthouse?"

"I told them it fell over in the last storm."

The next time they had the contest, Addie drove up Main

Street, took a left onto Pleasant, straight out to 'Sconset, around the flagpole, and right back to town. He was back in 45 minutes. Gotcha, Chuck.

But Addie had a bigger problem to deal with than racing with Chuck. He hadn't told Ken yet that he was thinking of leaving.

And he still had to pack. September was coming, which meant that he had just over a month to go.

But he didn't want to think of that now. He had a plan, a plan he couldn't wait to tell Verona about.

"Let's you and me go away for a day or two," he said to her when she met him after work.

"Away?" Verona didn't understand what he was saying at first — she was still thinking about finding Rebecca in the fog.

"Earth to Verona," Addie was saying. "Can you hear me?"

"I'm sorry," she said. "I was thinking of something else."

"I've got a couple of days off coming. Let's go to the Cape or, better yet, the boat's still going over to the Vineyard once a day, let's go over to Martha's Vineyard for a night, see something different."

"I don't think so," Verona said.

"Why not? It'd be fun. The Vineyard's twice the size of Nantucket."

"I can't get the days off work."

"Sure you can. You never take a day off."

"Not now. I can't do it right now."

Or ever, she wanted to say. The island was her shell. She had never considered leaving, not even for a day. If she left, something might jar her memory, trigger something inside her that would bring back the life she'd had.

And whatever that life was, she didn't want it back.

———

There had been a death. The image had pushed its way into her mind and persisted. She couldn't ignore it as she had so many others, not this one.

She could see it, the body, looking down on it, the terrible gnawing in her gut.

The image kept coming back, getting clearer each time, until, after her talk with Sandy, it sharpened, and the truth became clear, the reality manifest.

She was responsible. It had been her fault.

———

Although she'd spoken with Verona, Sandy was anything but comforted by their conversation. Verona insisted that she and Addie had come across this woman named Rebecca who claimed to be Benjamin Coffin's daughter. But when Sandy asked her what she looked like all Verona could say was: "She's old."

Who was this Verona? True, she was just a tenant, and a good one, but there was a mystery about her that Sandy needed to unlock. There were things Verona wasn't telling her.

But she wasn't being entirely honest with Verona, either. She hadn't told her what she knew — about the letters, about Rebecca's diary. She still couldn't make herself believe that the Rebecca Verona told her about was the same Rebecca whose journals she'd discovered under the floorboards and in the attic.

Ever since she'd read the letters and journals she had assumed Rebecca was dead, that she had lived her lonely life in this house and pined away. Rebecca couldn't still be alive.

Sandy walked upstairs to Verona's room. She leaned on the windowsill, puzzling over the prior night's developments. But wait a minute. Verona claimed this woman lived at the Homestead. Why not just go over and see if she was for real? It was simple.

Sandy ran down the stairs, not wanting to allow herself the thought that Rebecca was alive. If she was, it would be like finding a long-lost friend. She had so many things to ask her. If it truly was Rebecca, what had her life been like after her journals ended? Sandy needed to know.

She also needed to know a little more about her housemate. There was more to Verona than the demure wallflower she presented herself to be.

Chapter Twenty-Five

Jason Bonere had high aspirations. As chairman of the Board of Selectmen, he was determined to lead Nantucket into the new century. The island wasn't changing, it had already changed, as surely as the private jets that clogged the tarmac in the summer were the sleek signs of the ultra-wealth and the new attitude that ruled. It was true, the millionaires were now mowing the billionaires' lawns, and the billionaires when they came wanted comfort, they wanted convenience.

And if that meant that traffic lights had to be installed to facilitate the flow of their hybrids and SUVs then so be it.

The studies had all been done, every planner the town hired had recommended traffic lights. True, none of these planners had taken into account the island's history, the long-standing reverence for the past islanders had always held dear. Well, history be damned. If Jason Bonere could, he'd pave over every cobblestone on Main Street. Didn't somebody write that history was dead anyway? He was sure he'd seen something to that effect on his Blackberry.

No matter what the feelings were against it, a traffic light was going in. And then Jason Bonere could take his accomplishment, his solution to the island's traffic problem, and ride it to a seat in the state senate. He leaned back in his chair at the selectmen's office and could see it now: Jason Bonere, state senator, and then, why not?, United States Congressman.

Oh, he'd been teased about his name as a kid, but every taunt he received made him more determined to flaunt it. "Yeah, you bastards," he'd think. "People are going to remember my name more than they will yours." He was not going to hide from his name ("It's pronounced 'Bone-*Air*,'" he'd say through gritted teeth), and people would know when they heard the word Bonere that Jason Bonere meant business. He took glee in the nameplate he sat behind at selectmen's meetings, the nameplate the island's cable television station never shied from zooming in on: "Mr. Bonere." Yes, he was Mr. Bonere, and he wanted to ensure no one ever forgot it.

Others on the island had a different name for him.

"You see what Mr. Asshole is up to?" Digit said to Addie.

"And which Mr. Asshole are you referring to?"

"You know, Bonere, that prick."

"The one whose bumper sticker you had on your car?"

"Look, at the time I thought it was funny; it was a collector's item. People only voted for him because of his name. But now he's gone too far. He's really going to put in that traffic light."

"That's what I hear."

"Well, it ain't going to happen. There's posts all over the web. People are getting organized."

"Won't that just alert the cops?"

"They're going to go underground with this. Something's going to happen, you'll see."

Addie didn't care. He was thinking about why Verona didn't want to go away with him. He'd thought they'd been getting close these past couple of weeks. He'd only suggested a trip to the Vineyard, it wasn't as though he was asking her to run away with him.

Her excuse was pretty lame, too, now that he thought about it. She had to work. Why didn't she just say she wanted to be friends? Then at least he'd know where he stood. It was only a couple of days away. He figured she'd like to take a little trip with him.

But maybe that was it: a couple of days. What was he thinking? Asking her to go away for a couple of days meant he wanted her to sleep with him. True, he did want her to sleep with him, but he was moving way too fast. What an idiot.

"Just call me Mr. Prick," he said under his breath.

"What's that?" Digit said.

Addie had forgotten Digit was there. "Oh, nothing," he said. "I said maybe I'm being too quick."

"Not with me, you're not. You've been acting pretty sluggish lately. Oh, I forgot, you're in love."

"Am I, Mr. Smarty Pants?"

"Mr. Smarty Pants? What are we, in fifth grade? You're losing it, Addie."

"I probably am. If you must know, it's that I asked Verona to go away with me for a couple of days and she turned me down."

"She's smarter than I thought. Where did you want to go?"

"The Vineyard. You know, take the inter-island boat while it's still running for the summer."

"The Vineyard? Well, there's your answer right there. Who'd want to go to the Vineyard?"

"I thought we'd see something different for a change. Ride bikes. Go out to Gay Head."

"Man, you've been living here too long. They don't call it Gay Head anymore, it's Aquinnah."

Addie looked at him questioningly. "Aquinnah," Digit repeated. "It's the Indian name. Come to think of it, Marsha's going over to the Vineyard for a couple of days herself."

"By herself?"

"She's meeting a girlfriend. Someone she hasn't seen in years. From the Cape. They thought it would be fun to meet in neutral territory."

"You're not going?"

"Like I told you, who'd want to go to the Vineyard?"

Chapter Twenty-Six

I T WAS a short walk from Sandy's house to the Homestead, the stately, white-clapboard old people's home established by Nantucketers in the early twentieth century to take care of their own. The Homestead wasn't a nursing home, but a rooming house for the elderly, with a staff and meals served three times a day. Sandy had been there only once before, at Christmastime, when they held an annual open house for islanders to greet the residents.

Sandy stood on the brick sidewalk fronting the home, wondering just what in hell she was doing. What was she going to say to this woman? "Look, I've read all your private journals and I really cared about you, but it was so much easier to care knowing there was nothing I could do?" She did not want to be confrontational. After the initial shock of hearing Rebecca might really be alive, and her instant reaction of denial, Sandy recognized it was her own version of events she was clinging to. She had filled in the blanks of Rebecca's life story, coming up with her own melodramatic ending to suit her needs. Somehow it made her feel better knowing that someone's life was worse — much worse — than her own.

On her walk to the Homestead she realized how childish, how selfish, that interpretation had been. She thought of how years before she had wanted to hug Rebecca. Now she may get that chance.

She approached the front door tentatively. This visit should be easy, but it wasn't, even though she was filled with questions.

———————

"When did my life get so complicated?" Verona thought as she plopped onto her bed. Her aim all along had been to keep things simple, but now she was being forced to think.

She didn't want to think — about going away, about being afraid of finding her identity. It made her mind hurt. She just wanted to exist — which she had been doing in the beginning when she kept to herself.

But it felt good to open up to Addie, share things just a little; it seemed right. She didn't know that it meant she'd have to make decisions about coming or going.

Or that her opening up would allow her past to so forcefully intrude.

Was it real? Were the images something her mind conjured?

She lay on her bed, hoping all her thoughts would evaporate. To distract herself she focused on last night's talk with Sandy. She wondered why Sandy seemed so upset about the old woman she'd met at the lighthouse.

And what was the connection of all these things: the woman, the light, the graveyard?

And why should it matter to her?

She walked over to her mirror, looked into it as though it could speak to her. "Who are you?" she asked herself out loud. In the beginning, when she first woke on the island and Irene had taken her in, it was enough to let events wash over her, not wonder how she'd gotten to this place, or what kind of life she'd led before. It was just as easy to let it all go, start fresh, be some-one new: Verona.

Verona. It was her name now. She couldn't imagine what her name had been before.

She peered at her reflection. The face that looked back seemed like someone else's, different even from the face she'd seen when she'd first moved into this house. She must have seen this face thousands of times before. Was it a face she was com-fortable with? Was it a face that represented success, failure, loneliness?

It was her face, there was no doubt about that, but what kind of life had it led? *Who are you?* she asked herself again.

As if the mirror was speaking to her, the thought crossed her mind that when you ask questions, sometimes you get answers.

She turned from the mirror, left her room, closed the door. Her intention was to go downstairs, but as she approached the top step her attention was drawn to the door at the end of the hallway, the attic door. Even though she had no reason to go up there, and despite her instincts not to pry, the urge to explore was stronger. She could use something to occupy her mind right now, she reasoned.

"And," she thought as she walked down the hallway, "I'll sleep better at night knowing there's nothing to worry about up there."

Besides, Sandy wasn't home.

Chapter Twenty-Seven

Sandy got up her courage and knocked on the Homestead's front door. As soon as she did she felt like turning and running away, like a schoolgirl, but the door opened and a woman close to her age stood behind it. "Can I help you?"

Sandy was stuck, she couldn't leave now. The first thing that popped into her head was to say she was lost, but she had seen this woman around town. She didn't want her thinking she was nuts, so she said the only thing she could say.

"I'm wondering if I could talk to one of your residents. Rebecca?"

"Oh, yes, Rebecca. She seems to be making a lot of friends lately. I'm not sure if she's still napping — she took a long walk yesterday — but let me see if she's up. Can I tell her who's calling?"

"Well, she doesn't really know me."

The woman at the door cocked an eyebrow, as if to say, "And why do you want to see her?"

"I think we may have a mutual friend. I found some pictures in my house that may interest her."

"Well, all right, then. Have a seat in here."

And as she pointed Sandy to a chair, she said: "I've seen you around the island. How do I know you?"

"I drive a bus," Sandy said.

"Yes, of course. The little blue ones."

"That's right."

"That must be interesting. I'll bet the tourists have a lot of questions."

Not as many as I have, Sandy thought.

———————

Verona climbed the wooden staircase. A solitary light hung from a cord above her head and she pulled on the string. There was nothing much to see: a few boxes, some clothes hanging on a rafter.

As she turned to leave, however, she noticed a couple of stretched canvases off in the corner. As Verona approached, one of the canvases fell over, revealing an old, weathered chest.

Verona knelt by the chest and opened it. On top was a wedding dress that fluffed like rising dough. Verona took it out gingerly, careful not to unfold it. Underneath was a package of some sort with an old newspaper wrapped around it. Verona put the newspaper aside, studied the framed photograph it enclosed, a stern looking couple, probably on their wedding day.

She thought she heard something downstairs. Sandy might be home. She reached for the newspaper to rewrap the photograph, but paused when a headline caught her eye.

It was the front page of the New Bedford *Standard-Times.* "Allies March Against Axis," one headline read, while another stated: "FDR urges sacrifice in radio address." Neither held any meaning to Verona. She put the paper down, reached for the photograph, and as she turned her head back to the newspaper, she noticed different headlines.

"Boy Scouts pitch in for local war effort," she read, and then, below the fold, this headline: "Nazis sink Merchant Marine vessel off Canada; New Bedford man among those aboard."

And Verona read the story: "A German U-boat sank a Merchant Marine vessel in the Canadian Maritimes last week that was carrying supplies to United States warships in the North Atlantic. A New Bedford man, Gerald Hopkins, is among those listed as serving on the vessel which is believed to have lost all hands in the disaster."

Verona looked up, listened. She couldn't hear anything; nobody was home. Still, best not to take a chance; she really wasn't comfortable snooping around like this.

She wrapped the newspaper around the photograph, and as she moved to put it back where she'd found it, she noticed something else, a notebook with a string tied around it. She picked up the journal, sighed, and slowly untied the string. She felt like she was doing something wrong, but she wanted to do it anyway.

And she opened the journal and began to read.

Chapter Twenty-Eight

WHEN SANDY saw Rebecca for the first time she felt as if she had known her for years. There was something in her plain features that seemed familiar, even though she had no photograph to go by, no other point of reference. When she looked into the old woman's eyes she detected no overriding sadness, just weariness.

Sandy offered her hand, but Rebecca just stood there and said: "Who are you?"

"Sandy Bronson. I live in your old house by the Lily Pond. I wish I had known you were here; I would have visited sooner."

Rebecca sat in the chair opposite Sandy and motioned for her to sit as well. "And because you live in my house you've come to see me." She sat back, said nothing for a while. "Is there something you need from me?"

"No, not at all. It's just that I found some of your old things and was wondering if you wanted them."

"There's nothing in that house I want. You can have whatever you've found."

Sandy didn't know what to make of the response. Wasn't

this woman curious as to what she'd found? She tried a different approach.

"The girl — woman — who saw you at the lighthouse the other night told me about you. There was an old chest left behind in the attic."

"And you went through it."

"I didn't know what it was. Yes, I did go through it, years ago. There's a wedding dress in it, that I assumed was your mother's … "

"Please," Rebecca said, and she held up her hand. "I've done my best to put the past behind me."

But my heart ached for you, Sandy wanted to say. I can't believe I'm talking to you now. But she said, instead: "I understand. It's just that I was so surprised when I heard you were … "

"Still alive?"

"No," Sandy interjected hurriedly. "No. I just wondered why you left those things in the attic. Surely, they hold meaning to you."

"If I left them there, I don't want them anymore. I don't even know what 'things' you're referring to."

"Well, the wedding dress, for one. And there's a dress that I believed belonged to you." As she said this, she looked at Rebecca's face, but her expression revealed nothing. "And I found your journals as well."

"And you read them, I suppose."

"Yes, I did," Sandy said softly. "I did."

Rebecca didn't respond. The two sat in silence for what, to Sandy, seemed an interminable length of time. She wanted to blurt out: "So, what happened to you? Did you ever find happiness?" But she said nothing.

"Well, if you've said everything you have to say," Rebecca said, putting her hands on the arms of the chair as if to rise, "I'll be getting back to my room."

No, Sandy thought, it couldn't end like this. "Wait," she said. "I'm very interested in your life. Verona said you told her about your father … "

"I said too much. And I don't feel like saying any more to you."

This couldn't be happening. This wasn't how this meeting was supposed to go. "Please," Sandy said. "I'd really like to get to know you better. I've lived in your house for over twenty years, I've taken good care of it."

"It's not my house any more," Rebecca said. "I never really felt it was my house at all, if you want the honest truth. And I don't appreciate your dredging up the past. I just want to be left alone."

"But why?"

"I don't even know you," Rebecca said. "I don't owe you any kind of explanation."

"No, you don't, you absolutely don't. I just thought I could give you some company from time to time. I feel as if I know you. And it's not just because I read your journals, either. I feel as though a part of you is still in that house. I was going to ask if you'd like to come back with me some time, have some tea … "

"I never want to set foot in that house again. Now, if you don't mind … "

This wasn't going well at all. Sandy figured she had nothing to lose. "Did you ever see Gerald again?"

Rebecca seemed to have no interest in the question. If she felt anything at all, she didn't show it. Was this the right Rebecca? But then the old woman sank back in her chair.

"I'm sorry," Sandy said. "I should never … "

"You should never have what?" Rebecca said softly but sternly, her eyes now closed.

Why did I say that? Sandy thought. She opened her mouth to speak, but Rebecca said suddenly, "What's done is done. That was so many years ago."

The old woman's eyes remained closed. Sandy thought she had fallen asleep. But Rebecca spoke again. "You say you still have my journals?"

"Yes, I ... "

"Throw them away. Burn them."

Sandy felt terrible. Why couldn't she have kept her big mouth shut? "I'm so sorry," she whispered.

Rebecca opened her eyes then, leaned toward her. "It's not as if you've told me something I didn't know. I assumed those journals would be long gone by now." She paused. "But I guess they're not. I had forgotten about them, to be honest with you. I never intended for anyone else to read them."

"I didn't know," Sandy said. "They were in the house. If I had known ... "

"That I was still alive?"

"No," Sandy said sincerely. "If I had known you, I never would have read them."

"Well, you know me now."

The way she said it lessened Sandy's guilt somewhat. Still, she was upset with herself for being so thoughtless. "I should never have come here and bothered you," she said.

"Perhaps you're right," Rebecca said, which stung Sandy like a dagger, but Rebecca continued, "I know you don't mean to hurt me. You seem like a nice girl *(a little heavy,* Rebecca thought, *but a nice girl all the same).* It's good to know there's someone in the house who cares about it.

"And don't worry, I came to terms with my past long ago."

"Look, you're tired, I can tell," Sandy said, figuring her best strategy was to shut up and leave. "I'll let you go, but can I come back and see you some time?"

And what Rebecca said made Sandy draw a breath: "I'm not going anywhere."

———

As Sandy walked the brick sidewalk back to her house she wondered if this was indeed the Rebecca of the journals. She hadn't denied living in the house, but she revealed so little about herself. No wonder, Sandy thought, I never gave her a chance. "Did you ever see Gerald again?" How insensitive, how thoughtless. She'd have thought her years as a bartender would have sharpened her intuition a bit more. It wasn't the warm meeting she'd hoped for, but that was her fault, and if it wasn't the Rebecca she'd expected, what did she expect? Rebecca, if that's who it was, had every right to try and forget her past.

No, Sandy thought as she approached the house Rebecca didn't want to set foot in, that first meeting wasn't great, but something could still be salvaged. Here I come, unannounced, and tell her I've read her private thoughts, make her think about things she's tried to put behind her. And after all that she said she'd see me again.

And as Sandy walked up her front walk she thought this: She really was just acting like an old Nantucketer.

And her spirits lifted.

But when Sandy walked inside, she was not prepared for the surprise Verona had for her.

———

Verona, of course, had no idea Sandy had read Rebecca's journal. So when she blurted out: "Rebecca used to live here," the look on Sandy's face made her stop short. "Are you all right?" Verona asked her.

Sandy's face drained of color. "How could you know that?" she said hoarsely.

"I read her journal."

"How?"

"How?"

"How did you find it? Where did you find it?"

"In the attic."

"And what were you doing in the attic?"

"Something led me there."

"Something led you there?" Sandy was getting upset now.

"I was just curious. I didn't mean to do anything wrong."

Was it wrong, Verona thought? It surely seemed so now.

"Oh, Verona," Sandy said, brushing past her. And then she turned.

"Tell me what you know."

————

They sat in the living room as Verona told Sandy what she had found, how she'd looked through the old sea chest.

Sandy interrupted her story. "That attic is none of your business." As soon as the words left her mouth she knew her tone was more severe than she intended. Well, too bad. Verona needed to be reined in, taken down a peg. Was she going through her bedroom, too?

Verona, head bowed, tried holding back her tears. "I didn't mean … I didn't think I was doing anything wrong."

Sandy relented. "Forget it." She looked at Verona, at this boarder she knew so little about. She was being hard on her, transferring her own frustrations with Rebecca onto this little exchange. Softening her attitude she told Verona what she hadn't mentioned before — how she'd found the letters and the journals years ago and how she'd been so sure Rebecca had passed away.

But now, she admitted, she wasn't sure what to think.

She was sure of one thing, however. She was going to get a lock for her bedroom door.

Chapter Twenty-Nine

BACK IN her room, Rebecca thought of the years that had gone by since her father's fall, and her aunt's death, and the time she had moved out of her house at last.

Why this woman had visited her, had resurrected her past, had made her contemplate once more what she had resolved to forget … but there was nothing she could do about that now. The woman had come, she had talked, and Rebecca allowed her mind to revisit the newly dredged memories.

Her father had no will but it was understood that he had bought the house for her. Although it was brought up that she should transfer title to her name, the tragedy of his fall overshadowed any legal proceedings, by her or anyone else. That Rebecca stayed on in the house, and paid the taxes every year, and cared for her aunt, was enough — everything to do with legal ownership was eventually forgotten. She sold the house for cash to one of her cousins and her husband and simply gave them the deed. It was one of the happiest days of Rebecca's life.

Rebecca remained on the island for a time, and rented a room from her friend Flossie on Pearl Street. Together they worked at the cottage hospital — an apt description since the hospital was quartered in three old houses downtown — and Rebecca took some comfort in caring for the island people she knew. The hospital was small enough then that Rebecca was placed in a variety of jobs, wherever she was needed. That she wasn't technically a nurse didn't matter.

One night Flossie asked her: "What are you doing with your life, Rebecca? You should see a bit of the world while you're still young enough to do it. Have you ever been off-island at all?"

It was a question Rebecca hadn't considered since she'd been asked by Gerald to go away with him. Like everything else about that time, she had buried the proposition deep within her memory. The island was all that she knew, and she was convinced it was all she'd ever know.

"This island holds too many memories for you," Flossie told her. "You never go anywhere. You may as well be in prison.

"What's keeping you here?" Flossie continued. "Don't you have cousins off-island? Why don't you go visit them?"

And after a few letters were written, and a telephone call or two, Rebecca prepared to take the boat off-island for the first time. The year was 1957.

It was the last boat trip she took until her return to the island fifty years later.

───────

Rebecca didn't stand on the deck of the boat that day as it made its way out of the harbor, didn't look back at the town and the church steeples and the summer houses along the beachfront. She sat as deep within the boat as she could, putting Nantucket farther behind her with every slow mile of ocean.

The crossing was rough. Rebecca was embarrassed that she felt seasick, which made her determined never to go back.

Her cousin met her at Woods Hole. Rebecca stayed with

her for a time at her home in Brockton, Massachusetts, until she found a suitable enough apartment in one of the city's three deckers. She found work in the hospital there, and told no one of her past.

The city brought its own distractions, but no romances.

Until she met him.

She sighed when she thought of him now, the one she had shut from her mind, as if he had never existed.

But he had, oh, yes he had. And the imprint he made was greater than anything that had happened in her life.

Gerald remained deep in her heart. But her job, her new location, occupied her mind and allowed her to slog through her day. The nights were hard.

Her cousin invited her to dinner from time to time. One night a man sat at the table, a friend, her cousin told her. Rebecca wasn't pleased about a stranger being there, but he was pleasant, and reserved throughout dinner and any minor irritation she felt at his presence dissolved as the evening progressed.

Two weeks later she was again invited to her cousin's, and again he was there. He spoke neither too little nor too much during dinner and his easy way relaxed Rebecca. She enjoyed the conversation and, she had to admit, his company.

The three of them went to the movies occasionally, he taking the innermost seat so that Rebecca and her cousin could sit together on the aisle. His presence at dinner, while frequent, was not constant, and Rebecca felt a slight twinge of regret when he wasn't there.

Her cousin had little to say about him, but she told Rebecca this: he had lived in the neighborhood while she was growing up and had recently moved back to the city. She had never known him well, and she was surprised when he called her. He said it would be nice to reconnect with someone from his childhood. It wasn't clear where he'd been all these years, he said only that he'd been "on the road," and Rebecca and her cousin assumed he was a salesman of some kind.

On a planned movie night, Rebecca's cousin begged off at the last minute, said she wasn't feeling well. He offered to leave, "take a rain check," but Rebecca's cousin waved his suggestion aside.

"No, you two go," she said. "You were looking forward to it."

He and Rebecca walked to the movie theater, talked about the weather, and for the first time he sat next to her at the movies.

At the end of the night, he asked if he could see her again.

———

They went out to eat a couple of times, and he was a gentleman on both occasions. Rebecca asked her cousin if she minded the two of them going out alone, and her cousin simply said: "I thought you two might hit if off."

His name was Jack. Jack Stanley. He said little about himself and didn't pry into Rebecca's past. She felt guilty about looking forward to seeing him; the memory of Gerald remained ever present. She could never give her heart to anyone else, but she did enjoy the companionship Jack Stanley offered. It would never go any further than that.

———

They began having weekly dinners together, sometimes before a movie, sometimes not. They discussed little beyond current events. Although he knew Rebecca worked at the hospital, she never inquired about his occupation, what prompted his return to the city, or what his plans for the future might be. She was content having someone to talk to, someone to help fend off her loneliness.

One night he reached for her hand as he walked her back to her apartment. Rebecca was taken aback but did not withdraw from this little intimacy. Hand-holding after that became part of their routine, and Rebecca considered it to be nothing more than that — casual contact.

He kissed her a few weeks later when he said good night, a friendly kiss, a peck, really. It happened so suddenly, so smoothly, that Rebecca didn't have the chance to recoil, although she knew as she readied for bed that night that she wouldn't have resisted. A kiss is just a kiss, she reminded herself.

When it happened, it occurred as the natural culmination of two people who were tired of being alone. That's what Rebecca told herself anyway; she needed to justify it somehow.

It was his first time in her apartment. Rebecca had wanted to cook him a meal, give a little of herself to Jack Stanley. She had never intended to give all of herself, but the frustrations she had suppressed for all those years needed release. It felt so right at the time.

He was gentle, he was kind. She didn't know what to expect, and was thinking too much as he kissed her on the couch and her body craved more.

She had wanted it to be Gerald, wanted with all her soul for it to be Gerald, but that was never going to happen. She was 38-years-old and had never been with a man, never felt a caress of her naked body. She gave in to his advances, let her mind go blank, and hugged him, hugged him desperately as she shuddered at his touch.

When it was over, she turned away, wanting to be alone, wanting him to leave and, as if he could read her mind, he gradually stirred, slowly got dressed, and left without a word.

In the darkness of her apartment she thought of Gerald, how she'd never had the chance to have her love for him grow into a craving, didn't have the opportunity to anticipate the joys of their eventual coupling.

And now she had been with a man and felt neither sadness

nor joy, only hollowness, and the unwanted yet undeniable realization that her youth had been stolen from her.

————

She never saw, nor heard from, Jack Stanley again.

She was untroubled at first by his silence, relieved, in fact, that he didn't assume their pairing was the advent of a more committed relationship. When he called on her, as he undoubtedly would, she would tell him she needed time to sort out her feelings, but that she would, if he insisted, continue to have dinner with him, or go to the movies, nothing more.

But nothing was all she got.

After three weeks had elapsed, it occurred to her that something may have happened to Jack Stanley, and she was suddenly concerned. She went to her cousin and asked if she had heard from him.

No, she said, she hadn't heard from him.

Had he contacted her at all in the past three weeks?

No. Why? Was something wrong?

No. Nothing was wrong.

"You look worried, Rebecca. You don't seem yourself."

"I'm fine."

"Why don't you come by for dinner tomorrow night. You look as though you haven't eaten in weeks."

And Rebecca came, but there was no Jack Stanley joining them. Her cousin set the table without saying a word about him, as if Jack Stanley had never existed. Rebecca sensed a conspiratorial silence in her cousin's glances and movements; her actions and attitude seemed somehow contrived.

"Are you all right?" her cousin asked her over dinner.

And Rebecca realized she was simply being paranoid. Jack Stanley was an old acquaintance of her cousin's, and if he hadn't been in touch with her it simply meant that he hadn't been in touch with her. He evidently meant little to her, and Rebecca felt her blood drain because she had allowed him to mean something to her.

She cried herself to sleep that night and night after night after that, the long days turning into weeks. After another month had passed with no word from Jack Stanley, Rebecca could cry no more. He got what he had wanted and had moved on to other conquests. She had been a fool, but she had not given her heart to him, and she resolved to drive him from her memory, as she had the other painful episodes of her past.

The nausea was not surprising; she worked in a hospital after all and must have picked up a bug. Its daily occurrence, however, was a concern, especially since she had no other symptoms during the day. She was hungry all the time, and found herself stopping by the drugstore on her way home from work for a pre-supper sundae.

When her loose-fitting dress felt suddenly tight one morning, she fell back on her bed and thought the unthinkable: she was 38-years-old — too old, too old for this to have happened.

She went on a diet, passed by the drugstore even though she yearned the taste of ice cream, but still her hips expanded. No, she thought, no, but she knew it was true; she could feel it in every pore.

She confided in her cousin, who at first was determined to find that bastard Jack Stanley and make him confront his responsibility, but Rebecca was steadfast — she would bear this circumstance alone. Even if he reappeared, which she knew would thankfully never happen, she would do this on her own. For once, she would have control over her destiny.

That she was not on Nantucket was good. She didn't need the whispers, the suppositions, the unasked questions. If nothing else, there was slight comfort in that.

The doctor she chose was understanding, and when the baby arrived, it was adopted by someone the doctor knew, a couple who could not have children of their own. Rebecca met the couple and was satisfied they'd give her baby a loving home. On her insistence, she affirmed that she would have no future contact with the child. There was only one caveat: that on the child's twenty-first birthday it would be given a letter she had drawn up months before. After they were assured that the letter contained nothing that would affect their relationship with the child, the adoptive parents agreed, and signed a legal document in confirmation. The letter was placed in the care of the doctor, who would make the necessary arrangements for the letter's safe delivery twenty-one years later.

Chapter Thirty

AUGUST CEDED to September and the bus drivers couldn't have been happier. The mood lightened, spirits lifted as the crowds dispersed and the summer people returned to their lives on the mainland.

It was always a relief when Labor Day arrived. By mid-August, driving was more of an adventure than anyone wanted. It wasn't just the traffic: pedestrians and bicyclists crossed the street at will, in droves, no matter what size or type vehicle was coming at them.

"It's like their brains are on vacation, too," Chuck pointed out.

Yes, Chuck was back with his grin, adding to the lighthearted-ness of the office. Even Ken broke a smile at the thought of another season drawing to a blessed close.

"So where have you been, what have you been up to?" Addie asked Chuck, who sat on the bench outside the office, staring at who knows what through his sunglasses.

"Oh, you know," Chuck said, as he lowered his glasses down the rim of his nose and peered up at Addie impishly. "A little of this, a little of that."

"And a lot of you know what," Addie said.

"I haven't the faintest idea what you're talking about," Chuck laughed.

For his part, Addie had apologized to Verona about the little off-island trip he had suggested. "I don't know what I was thinking," he'd said.

"Don't think," she said.

Wouldn't that be great, he thought, don't think.

But he had only a month to go to get his life in order, and he told Verona about it.

"I've got to move out of my place," he said to her. "I was thinking I'd be all set by now, ready to go."

"Go where?" she'd said.

Where, indeed. But her question troubled him. Hadn't she been listening? Hadn't he told her of his plans?

Well, hadn't he?

Perhaps he hadn't. And the reason that he hadn't told her about his plans is that he didn't have a plan. All he'd been thinking about the past month was her: her smile, her laugh, her living in the moment.

———

Nantucket. Addie took out his map and looked at it. He had lived on the island for twenty years, but he had never visualized his place on it, never thought of himself as a dot on the map in a kind of 'you are here' way. He looked up, saw a gull floating high in the sky, a sky painted with thin strokes of clouds, wondered where the gull was. From here, Addie thought, he's probably over by the high school. But, from this perspective, what is beyond that?

He studied his map, a freebie handed out by the bike rental people. This little place contained his life. He knew more about it than anywhere else and yet he didn't know where he stood.

"If I'm here," he thought, and he put his finger where he was, in town by the wharves, "then beyond that is Surfside." It seemed reasonable enough.

But where was he really? He thought of how most of the time he wasn't aware he was living on an island almost thirty miles at sea. It was like being anywhere else: get up, go to work, go home. The only time he truly felt he was on an island was when he was out on Digit's boat, looking back at the storybook skyline, on the ocean, away from the cares and concerns and the boxes of stuff waiting for him back on the island.

The summer people had it right; Nantucket was a true getaway for them. They came around Memorial Day when the weather was getting perfect, stayed through the halcyon days of summer, and, before the winds picked up again — the winds that blew and howled for most of the winter — they were back on the boat and gone.

What was it Digit had said to him, that he was an islander? He supposed he meant that if you accumulated enough winters, if you loved the island enough to accept the northeast winds, grey skies, and occasional loneliness you had earned the designation. He supposed he was an islander, and he wondered if he'd ever be ready to move back to the mainland.

Why couldn't I be a summer person, he thought? Why couldn't I have been born rich?

But if he'd been a summer person, he never would have found Verona. The thought brought a wide smile as he stood outside his bus doors and waited for the latest gaggle of tourists to arrive.

Chapter Thirty-One

IN RECENT days there was more talk on the website about the mysterious reappearance of Dr. Malone. Digit scrolled through the back and forth comments as he drank his third cup of coffee that morning.

"What a load of crap," he said out loud, as he read the different hypotheses about the doctor's return.

"I saw her the other night," tuckerjim48 wrote in. "She was riding her bike by the lighthouse again. Isn't that where she supposedly went into the drink? She must have some attraction to the lighthouse."

"I'm pretty sure I saw her, too," ciscosue added. "But she was near the Oldest House. Does anyone have any idea what she looks like?"

"Contrary to what anyone believes," coatueman wrote, "the good doctor is not middle aged, nor did she have surgery to make herself look younger. She's in her eighties. No matter how good a plastic surgeon, no one could make her look 30 years younger. She looks her age, believe me. I thought I saw her walking last week near the lighthouse along the Polpis Road but when I turned my car around she was gone. Maybe she's a ghost."

"Now that's a good one," Digit said to himself as he clicked off the website and turned to his e-mail. "Now there's ghosts walking among us."

He couldn't wait to tell Addie about this one. He and Marsha shared the same e-mail address, 'stompthegrapes' and he scrolled through the usual garbage, deleting all the junk mail, and he was ready to delete a message from 'studpuppy21' when something caught his eye. He thought he saw the word 'Marsha' and he stopped to make sure the message wasn't for her.

Even though they shared an e-mail address, Digit respected Marsha's privacy and he never read her messages unless they concerned him as well. But this one was not addressed to Marsha, but to someone named Dude.

"Yo, Dude," the message began. "Just got back from the Vineyard. Thought you were going to meet us there. Great weather, great food, and great sex, as always."

"Man, this guy's full of himself," Digit thought, and he read on.

"At any rate, Marsha's ready to give her old man the boot. This has been going on way too long. Once she divorces him, she's moving in with me. I've been trying to talk her into moving in now but she says she's been with him too long and she wants to let him down easy.

"Get this, his name is Clarence. What a name! But he's a fisherman and I'd just as soon steer clear of him."

A jolt like lightning went through Digit. He felt his body instantly telescope far away, as though he was watching himself sitting at the computer. This couldn't be. He stopped and looked at the address the e-mail was sent to: 'stompthegrapes.' That was his e-mail all right. Obviously, it was sent to his computer by mistake. "Be careful what you e-mail, pal," he thought, marveling at how he still could think clearly.

He thought of sending a reply message, but thought better of it. Before he did anything, he needed to talk to Marsha.

———————

Chuck and Addie raced each other around the island on the last trip of the day. With the summer pretty much over, there were fewer cars on the road and Addie was able to get back to base in thirty minutes.

"Damn," Chuck said after he rolled in. "You couldn't have gone to 'Sconset."

"Yes, I did. Straight up Main, left on Orange, straight out to 'Sconset and straight back in."

"You owe me a drink for that one," Chuck said.

"Fair enough," Addie said.

There were seats at the bar at the Atlantic Café. "I hear they're going to close this place down," Chuck said as he settled onto the stool.

"They close this place down they'll be ripping out part of the soul of downtown," Addie said to him. "Where do you get your information anyhow?"

"On that website, Island Breezes. The same place everybody gets their information."

"You need to get out more, Chuck."

"Oh, I'm already out. Haven't you heard? So how's your love life?" Chuck asked after the beers arrived.

"All right. Fine. Fantastic," Addie said. "How's yours?"

"Oh, you know, I could always use a little on the side. I hear you and Verona have become quite an item."

"How do you know? Is that on that website too?"

"On this island? What doesn't anyone know? So what about the mystery woman? Where's she from?"

"Man, when you're not full of misinformation you're full of questions. I don't know where she's from, and I don't care. Does it make a difference?"

"No, no difference at all. It's just that now that you're serious, you'd think you'd know a little more about her."

"I know enough."

"I'll bet you don't. I'll bet you don't even know her last name."

"Let's change the subject."

"You don't know her last name, do you? Do you know if she even has a last name?"

"I'm sure she does. Look, what does it matter? Are you interested in her or something?"

"Wrong gender, my friend. But keep an eye on your credit cards; she might try to steal your identity when you're not looking."

"I don't have any credit cards. They got me into trouble once."

"Speaking of trouble," Chuck said … and in walked Digit.

Chapter Thirty-Two

ADDIE HAD never seen his friend so distressed, even when his scallop boat sank to the bottom of the harbor one winter. "We'll raise her and repair her," is what he'd said at the time.

But he saw in Digit's face that whatever troubled him now was worse than the threat of losing his boat.

"She's left me," he said.

Addie didn't understand.

"Marsha. She's leaving me for someone else."

Addie didn't know what to say. Chuck got up, motioned for Digit to take his seat, and walked over to where Steamship Authority Fred was sitting at the end of the bar.

Addie ordered a beer for Digit. "I don't want anything," Digit told him. "I don't know what I'm going to do."

"What happened? Not that you need to tell me … "

"I want to tell you. That's why I'm here. I need to talk to someone, or I'll go crazy. You think you know someone, spend most of your life with them, and then this." He put his head in his hands. "Look, let's get out of here."

The two old friends walked towards the wharf. "I found out

in an e-mail, isn't that great?" Digit said at last.

"She e-mailed you?"

"No, her boyfriend."

"He e-mailed you?"

"Not intentionally. He was e-mailing a friend and sent it to me by mistake. So that's it. I showed Marsha the e-mail, and she denied it, said it must be a different Marsha and Clarence ... "

"He called you Clarence?"

"The e-mail said Clarence, yes. I don't want to go into that now, okay?"

Addie's bus was still parked on the wharf. "Let's go in here and talk. At least it'll be private."

They sat on the bus and talked.

"I feel so stupid to have trusted her," Digit said. "I shared everything with Marsha. Here I was, thinking we were in this life together, for better or for worse, and she's banging this dickweed homewrecker. I don't know where to turn; I feel like my brain is going to explode."

"I don't think anything's going to make you feel any better for a while," Addie said. "This sucks. Are you sure this wasn't just a fling?"

"A fling? What the hell's a fling? Breaking someone's heart? I was so comfortable with Marsha, everything was easy. I didn't ignore her, did I?"

"No, you guys did a lot together. I remember how worried she was the times you were late coming in from scalloping. She'd call me and I'd remind her how well you knew the waters, and no matter how bad the fog was you could make it back blind-folded ... "

"I could, too. Aww, who gives a shit about scalloping now? I don't give a shit about anything. I don't know what I'm going to do, Addie. She was my life."

"I guess you can't know what's going on inside someone's

mind," Addie said.

"I guess you can't," Digit said so quietly Addie barely heard him. All Digit had now was time, and time was not on his side. If Marsha really had left him he'd be doing time for a while, but he couldn't tell his friend this; Digit would have to find it out for himself.

Addie knew all about it. He'd screwed up his own relationship years ago, before he'd moved to the island.

He had been married, too. Fortunately, they didn't have any kids. Unfortunately, he didn't have Sarah anymore either.

Perhaps they married too young, and Addie being Addie, he wasn't too attentive to Sarah after a couple of years. He just assumed they'd always be together, didn't think he had to do the little things, like maybe mention the word, "love" every once in a while, or plan a special weekend like the one he'd envisioned with Verona.

Stupid, stupid, stupid.

Oh, he did love Sarah, with all his heart, but he took her for granted and, eventually, a co-worker of his didn't. End of story.

He knew the hurt Digit was going through, but he knew as well that nothing he could say could change either the situation or how his friend was feeling. Addie would be there for him, but Digit had to go through this alone.

And it wouldn't be easy.

They sat on the bus in silence. The sun set and the sky was glorious in the gloaming, but Addie knew that Digit, even though he was staring at it, didn't see it.

"Come on," Addie said, "I'll drive you to my place. You can stay with me tonight."

———————

Digit woke on Addie's couch the next morning, hoping he was waking from a dream. He thought of how stupid he'd been, of the phone calls from an unknown number that ended in dial tones when he answered. He thought of the phony girlfriend Marsha was going to see on the Vineyard who turned out to be Mr. Dickweed. He didn't want to think about how long it had been going on.

He lay there, looking at the ceiling, noticed a spider moving along upside down. He wondered how insects were able to do that.

And then he thought of Marsha and wondered how he was going to be able to live without her.

Chapter Thirty-Three

ADDIE SAT on the bench outside the bus office thinking about Verona.

Why did she seem so familiar to him, as if he had known her before? No, that was crazy; he had just met her.

But what was her story? And did he want to know?

The way Marsha had blindsided Digit — that was a marriage that seemed as rock-solid as anything on earth. So what was the lesson? Was it better to keep your distance, not get too involved with anyone?

But then where would you be? Alone. Addie wasn't lonely, but he was tired of being alone.

He didn't notice Chuck sidle up to him.

"I heard what happened to Digit," Chuck said, startling Addie. "Whoa, big fella. Take it easy. A bit jumpy, are we?"

"I was just thinking," Addie said, thinking that being alone on the bench right now wouldn't be so bad.

"I like Digit," Chuck went on. "Besides his obvious physical attributes he's a nice man."

"Are you telling me you find Digit attractive?"

"Me?" Chuck said, moving closer to Addie so that their shoulders touched. "Oh, honey, what would ever give you such an idea?"

"Cut the crap, Chuck. Yes, Digit is a nice guy; he's my best friend."

"I could have that guy taken care of if Digit wants me to."

"What guy?"

"The guy who stole his wife."

"Taken care of?"

Chuck pulled his sunglass down the rim of his nose and looked Addie in the eye. "You know, a little message from a stranger."

Addie had always figured that Chuck moved in circles on the fringe, but he had never thought what kind of circles. "Are you talking about a hit or something?"

"Such language. Let's just say it wouldn't be in his best interests to see Digit's wife again."

"You're creeping me out now, Chuck. You really know people like that?"

Chuck smiled a devious smile, his teeth gleaming. "Had you going there, didn't I?" he said.

"What are you talking about now?"

"I was just kidding. Man, you're gullible. You think I'm a gangsta or something?"

"I don't know what you are, Chuck."

"But I bet you wish you did."

"Haven't you got a tour to do?"

"I'm at your service. Let's neck."

Addie got up shaking his head and walked back into the bus office.

"Aw, don't pout, Addie. It's not becoming," Chuck called to him. And then he laughed, "Hey, have you found out Verona's last name yet?"

Addie didn't know why the question bothered him so much.

———————

It was a question that circled through Sandy's mind as well. Who was this Verona?

It annoyed her when Verona told her she'd gone into the attic and read Rebecca's journal. True, her explorations were probably innocent enough; after all, Sandy had encouraged her to use the kitchen, to get more comfortable around the house, but Rebecca had been her special secret, her little intimacy. And now Verona had glommed onto it, as if Rebecca's story was hers to share. Why couldn't it have been me who met Rebecca out at the light, Sandy thought, me who Rebecca first confided in?

She's mine, Verona. Rebecca's story is mine to share. Or keep.

She found herself perturbed, too, by Verona's cloying innocence, her everything is beautiful demeanor. Where at first she found Verona's attitude refreshing, she now found it irritating. No one could be as uncomplicated as Verona let on.

She would talk to Irene, get to the bottom of things. She needed to unravel the secrets of this mystery girl.

"Girl? She's practically my age," Sandy said out loud. "Who does she think she's kidding?"

Sandy poured herself a glass of wine, pondered the Rebecca saga a bit more. Was this old woman truly Rebecca? If so, where had she been all these years?

Rebecca, if that's who this woman really was, had secrets of her own.

Chapter Thirty-Four

THAT EVENING, Addie and Verona walked silently along the beach at Surfside, the sky before sunset a deep cerulean. Addie was concerned about Digit, wondered if he should confront Marsha and find out just what was going on. Would that be a help, or would it merely cement her convictions to leave him?

Verona thought of Sandy, knew she had upset her, but wasn't sure why.

Why wasn't Sandy happy that Rebecca had been found?

"Can I talk to you?" Verona asked Addie.

"Sure," Addie said offhandedly, still focused on Digit.

Verona told Addie then of Rebecca's journals, how she'd found them in Sandy's attic. "She had a fiancé at one time — Gerald. Her father didn't approve."

"That's too bad," Addie said. "What happened to him?"

"He died," Verona said.

Addie looked hard at Verona, into her soft eyes. What was going on in there? She was being so matter of fact, she must be kidding.

"You're joking, right?"

"About what?"

"About this Gerald."

"No, it's true," she said. "I've seen it; I mean, I saw the newspaper that said he had died. I meant to tell Sandy about it, but she didn't seem too happy that I'd been in her attic."

"You were in her attic?"

"Uh, huh. I found an old chest, where I read Rebecca's diary and saw a newspaper article about his death."

"That's too bad."

"Yes, I suppose so. I probably shouldn't have gone up there, but I found out that Rebecca lived in Sandy's house."

"And Sandy knows about this?"

"Yes."

Addie could tell by her earnest expression, that she needed to continue. "Tell me more," he said.

———

They sat on the sand as Verona told Addie about the relief she felt after she and Sandy had shared their stories. "I think she understands," Verona told him uncertainly.

"Understands what?"

"That I wasn't trying to pry; that I'm not that kind of person. I just want Rebecca to be happy."

"She's old. How happy can she be?"

"Based on how she sounded at the light that night I don't think she's happy at all. I don't think Sandy's too happy with me either. Oh, Addie, it's all so confusing."

"Sandy will get over it," Addie said. "Believe me. This isn't that big a deal."

"What isn't?"

"That you went into her attic."

"I suppose not." Verona looked off across the ocean and towards the darkening horizon. Sunset had come and gone, and small stars twinkled faintly as they appeared. If only each sunset could wipe away the cares of every day, like a blackboard brushed clean.

She would talk to Sandy again, assure her that she'd keep to herself from now on. She'd learned her lesson: getting involved in other people's happiness only led to misunderstandings, convolutions, sadness.

Chapter Thirty-Five

SANDY MET Irene the next afternoon. The two of them hadn't seen each other since Sandy's dinner party, and Sandy used that as a pretense to get together for a cup of coffee.

They'd known each other almost as long as Irene had been on the island. In one of those serendipitous ways that people meet, Sandy, attracted to her accent at first, had been charmed by Irene's observations at an artist's reception on the wharf.

"He thinks he's God's gift," Irene had said through a mouthful of Brie and crackers. "Honestly, if it wasn't for the wine I don't think anyone would give a flying you know what for these paintings."

From that sentence on, Irene and Sandy became close friends.

Sandy wasn't sure how she was going to broach the subject of Verona, but Irene gave her the opening as soon as the coffee arrived.

"So, how are things going with you and Verona?" Irene said in her pleasant lilt. "I work with her, but Verona never was much of a conversationalist."

"Oh, fine," Sandy said hesitantly. "Tell me, Irene, what do you know about her?"

"Not much," Irene laughed. "I don't think anyone knows a whole lot about Verona. She keeps to herself."

Sandy got to the point. "Well, she hasn't been keeping to herself lately, not around my house at least."

"Oh?"

"She's been snooping around my attic, not that there's anything worth finding up there, but it's occurred to me that I should know a little something about her. She never talks about her family, or where she came from, or what she's doing here for that matter. It's not normal. To be honest, Irene, I'm wondering what her motives are."

"Motives?"

"She's up to something."

Irene sipped her coffee, looked around at the empty tables in the coffee shop. The waitress was up by the front, doodling on her guest-check pad, snapping gum. Good. Irene didn't want anyone overhearing their conversation.

"And what do you think she's up to?"

Sandy saw the questioning concern on her friend's face, pursed her lips, exhaled. "Oh, I don't know, Irene. Maybe I'm looking for things. Maybe I'm just frustrated. Maybe if she was a little more forthcoming … It just seems as if she's trying to hide something."

"And what would she be trying to hide?" Irene's questions weren't confrontational, but calm, friendly.

Sandy paused, leaned forward. "Have you seen the news lately?"

"I try to stay as far away from the news as possible."

"There's a woman who's been stealing people's identities, you know, credit card information, social security numbers. The police tracked her to the Cape and lost her. You never know … "

Irene leaned back and laughed. "Oh, Sandy. Whoever Verona is, she's not stealing credit cards. Would I have her working for me if I felt in the least suspicious? Don't you know I keep a close watch on my girls until I can trust them implicitly?"

"They say she's a master of disguise."

"And how many disguises have you seen Verona wearing? Has she ever not slept in your house, even for a night? Is she ever out at night, for that matter?"

"She goes out sometimes … "

"To the lighthouse. I don't think there's anyone who knows her who doesn't know that. Seems to me that she isn't hiding anything."

Sandy fell back into her chair, looked up at the ceiling. Irene was right, of course. Verona wasn't hiding anything; she didn't seem to have a duplicitous bone in her body. Now that she thought of it, Verona was forthcoming about going into the attic, came right out and told her about it. She wasn't sneaking around the house. Sandy's assumptions, quite simply, weren't fair.

It was all because of Rebecca. The neat string she had tied around Rebecca's story had become undone with Rebecca's return. She felt it was her duty, her right, to have the missing gaps filled in. Rebecca's reluctance to open up bothered Sandy more than she'd been able to admit, and Verona was a convenient target for Sandy's frustrations.

Sandy leaned forward, reached for Irene's hand. "I'm so glad I've talked with you. Forgive me for being so suspicious; I know you care for her." She paused. "I can't help but wonder who she is, however. She acts sometimes as if she's in her twenties, and we both know she's a lot older than that."

Irene pulled her chair next to Sandy, leaned close. "I probably should have said this before," she said quietly. "I did send her your way without any explanation. Let me tell you a story."

And Irene told Sandy how she'd found Verona on the docks

and taken her home. She admitted that she, too, was wary at first.

"Truth be told, I thought she might have some sort of medical condition," Irene confessed. "It seemed as if she was in a perpetual state of recovering from anesthesia. I had to constantly repeat myself to her, but I soon understood that she simply needed time to get used to her new surroundings.

"Here's my theory: someone sent her here to work, or offered her a job as a nanny or some such thing, and when she arrived she was told it was all a mistake, there was no job for her.

"Now, who knows, she may have been desperate for a job, chucked it all wherever she came from so she couldn't go back — there was nothing for her to go back to. She's broke, alone, and with nowhere to go. Seems to me I'd be acting a bit desperate myself under those conditions. Let me put it this way, she didn't hesitate one bit when I offered her a job, and she's been a wonderful worker. If you're looking for a secret, I think you'll find that's it."

Irene, bless her, Sandy thought, forever seeking the best in people. And she had the Irish knack for perception. Irene's explanation seemed to be as plausible as any.

"The poor thing," Sandy said. "And here I was thinking the worst of her." She looked down, folded her paper napkin in half, into quarters, looked into Irene's trusting eyes. Did she really want to do this?

"Now I have something I want to tell you," Sandy said to her. "Do you have a little more time?"

And Sandy relayed the whole saga of Rebecca: finding the journals, taking the story to her heart, assuming Rebecca had died, and then, years later, being told by Verona that she'd found her at the lighthouse.

Irene's eyes widened as Sandy told her tale. "What a fantastic story. And you say you met her yourself?"

"I'm afraid the meeting didn't go very well."

"Of course it wouldn't," Irene said to her. "Think of what you've told me. You've got to give her some time. She must have built up some pretty powerful defenses over the years. Wouldn't you have?"

"Maybe I should just leave her alone," Sandy said.

"Not on your life," Irene insisted. "She's been alone her whole life. She could use a friend like you."

Sandy wasn't sure what kind of a friend she was.

"Maybe," Sandy began.

"Yes, maybe," said Irene.

"Oh, forget it."

"No, you've got a plan, I can tell."

"I was just thinking ... No, forget it."

"I can't forget it now, Sandy. What are you thinking?"

"What if we somehow got her to the house. Would that be good? Maybe if she came home ... "

"That'd be grand," Irene said. "We'll get her back to her house and she'll realize that the past is past. It'll open her mind to new beginnings, new friendships. I'd love to be her friend."

Great, Sandy thought. Another person who wants to be Rebecca's friend. Can't I just have her for myself?

But before Sandy could ruminate any further, Irene was quickly talking.

"Right," she said. "Here's what we'll do ... "

Chapter Thirty-Six

As an outward sign of her conviction to eliminate unnecessary trappings from her life, Verona cut her hair.

She was careful with the scissors, watched herself in her mirror as she cut the strands that hung over her ears and the bangs that had gotten too long in the past months. She didn't cut away too much, just enough to be rejuvenated.

"There," she said to her reflection. "A new me."

And now, who am I? she thought.

The girls were cleaning a new place Irene had lined up, an old guest house in the center of town. Verona didn't watch television, but one of the girls had the TV on in the room she was cleaning. When she heard a woman sobbing, Verona stopped and looked at the screen.

"And you don't know who you are?" a man with a microphone was asking. The woman didn't speak but shook her head. "And how did you get here?"

Again the woman could barely speak. "I — don't — know,"

she said haltingly, crying again.

"Police are hoping that someone watching will identify this woman who for now remains in their custody. From Providence, I'm … "

Verona had left the room before he could finish. Her palms were sweating. Thoughts rushed through her mind, thoughts that screamed at her. *Who do you think you are?* the thoughts demanded. *How long do you think you can play this game?*

She grabbed a dust rag and feverishly attacked the furniture. This wasn't a game. She'd been given a gift, she reminded herself, several gifts.

The first was that she wasn't like that woman she'd just seen on the television; the situation she'd found herself in didn't make her sad.

The second was that she'd been found by Irene, dear Irene who didn't ask questions.

The third was that she'd met Addie.

But she couldn't keep her past at bay forever, she knew that now. Little by little, fragments had returned: that she had been loved, for instance; she was sure the cloudy figure at the margins of her memory had loved her.

But someone had died, and the question persisted: was she responsible? Had it been her fault?

She wanted to wipe it all from her mind, go back to that day Irene had first found her.

But it was too late to go back.

It might be good to unburden herself, tell Addie her story, but then again, it might not. Telling him might only lead to more questions, more unrelenting thoughts.

And yet she didn't want to keep her secret any longer. It was tiring, keeping a secret.

As she mopped the kitchen floor, she decided to put it out of her mind. That was easiest. Yes, that was the easiest thing to do.

And if she ever saw or heard a television again, she'd turn it off.

———————

As they were packing up the vacuum and the other cleaning gear, the guest house owner returned, passed Verona as she was lugging a mop and bucket down the front stairs. The guest house owner did a double take, saw the back of Verona's newly-shorn head as she made for the work truck. There was something about Verona that seemed familiar to her, and she craned for a better look, but ... there, the phone was ringing, and she quickly climbed the stairs to answer it. As she went behind the front desk, she accidentally kicked the suitcase that had been there for months now, left behind by a guest, a suitcase she'd been too busy to deal with. "I should have the police pick this up if the owner doesn't want it," she thought as she answered the phone.

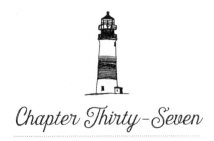

Chapter Thirty-Seven

GIVING UP the baby — although she had determined from the outset that it was the right, the only, thing to do — was harder than she'd imagined. She'd had several discussions with the doctor during the course of her pregnancy and it was agreed that the baby would be taken from her at birth to better bond with its new parents.

After the delivery, however, the doctor insisted she hold the baby, that the connection, however slight, had to be made; it would be best for both mother and child.

Rebecca wasn't prepared for the outpouring of love as she looked upon her baby. Peering into her newborn's eyes, she had never felt such happiness, nor, despite the terrible circumstances of her past, known such sadness. "I love you," she whispered into her baby's ear. "My love will always be with you."

————

As best she could, Rebecca got on with her life. The baby had been healthy, she had prayed for that, and would be given a much better home than she ever could have provided. She was not comforted by this knowledge, but took solace in it, and solace was all she could expect.

The new family soon moved away from the city, their departure easing the pain of proximity, and Rebecca, drawing on reserves of strength she never knew she had, put it all behind her. She had done the right thing, and there was no sense dwelling on what-might-have-beens.

That was something she had learned long ago.

———

Rebecca buried herself in her work, joined women's clubs in the city, and determinedly kept herself occupied. As time went on, as the years went by, she nurtured her self-sufficiency, clung to it as if her life depended on it.

She allowed herself the painful pleasure of thinking of her baby once a year, on the anniversary of its birth. She consoled herself by thinking of its happiness and by willing her love into the cosmos.

———

Rebecca remained in the city and seldom thought of Nantucket. It was as if Nantucket was a place that existed in a fairy tale, a story that ceased to hold meaning.

She worked at the hospital until retirement age, and then filled her days with volunteer work, her most pleasant assignment reading to the influx of immigrant children at several of the city's elementary schools. If happiness had eluded her, contentment had taken root, a satisfied sense of self that she had done the best she could given the circumstances.

———

On her eighty-fifth birthday, Rebecca decided it was time to go home. She hadn't been back to the island in fifty years, but her cousin had died, she had no remaining ties to the city, and before she, too, faded away, she decided it would be best to fade away on Nantucket.

She wrote the Homestead, told the people there of her situation, and was invited back to the island.

Things had changed in the years since she'd been away. The boat, a high-speed catamaran, left from Hyannis now and the crossing took only an hour. This time, Rebecca did not hide away on the passenger deck. As the boat slowed to enter the harbor, Rebecca stood at the outside rail, her heart unexpectedly lifting as the church steeples materialized on the horizon, and the dome of the Unitarian Church glinted in the sunshine. It was as if all the years she was away had been erased. She was home.

———

There had been another reason for her return: she needed to see the lighthouse again.

Although she had banished thoughts of the island from her waking consciousness, the image of the light continued to haunt her dreams. In order to ease her nights she needed to confront this part of her past, come to terms with it, put it to rest.

On her slow walk to the light that afternoon, her memories were surprisingly nostalgic. She thought back to when she was a girl, before Gerald, before her father's horrible fall. The island seemed as beautiful to her now as it did to her then, and she found joy in her innocent remembrances.

Despite her age, her steps seemed to lighten as she recalled the many times she'd taken this same route, when her thoughts were blissfully free from concern, when her future was still a distant horizon.

The rapidly descending fog, however, seeped into her bones, obscured her pleasant memories. When she reached the light, she was painfully mired in the present, the awful reality of what had happened had returned, but she was too spent to mourn the past.

And then that girl materialized, as if she had been created by the fog.

Rebecca was upset with herself for confiding in her that night. But she seemed so honestly concerned that Rebecca let her defenses down. She was glad she hadn't told her she'd had a child, however. A child. The child was well into adulthood by now. Still, she was oddly comforted when the girl put her arm on her shoulder, and she allowed herself the fantasy that her own child would have done the same.

The thought chilled her now. She could never let herself think that way again. Thinking like that could only lead to sorrow.

And she didn't need that other woman coming along to remind her of the life she'd left behind on Nantucket. Yes, she remembered the sea chest and the things she'd put inside it. When she'd closed the lid that last time, she'd thought she was shutting everything away forever.

But there was no lid to close, no sea chest to shut, on what had happened after that.

It seemed her return to Nantucket had been a mistake, but it was too late to reconsider. There was no going back. To think she'd thought the island was a prison when she was a young girl.

The girl she'd been had no idea what a prison truly was.

Chapter Thirty-Eight

WITH KEN's permission, Sandy called the Homestead and offered a free tour to the residents.

"That would be wonderful," the woman said. "But why?"

"We're community minded," Sandy told her. "We thought that since things were slowing down a bit we'd do something nice for Nantucket's older residents as a way of giving back."

"Wonderful," the woman said again. "When will this take place?"

"Anytime you can get all the residents together. Tomorrow afternoon?"

"Tomorrow afternoon would be fine."

"Perfect. We'll have a bus outside the Homestead at say, around 2:30? And please come along if you'd like."

"Thanks, I may do just that if I can get away."

"Please do. It wouldn't be the same without you."

Sandy hung up and smiled at Irene. "It's all set."

———

The plan was this: if they could get Rebecca home, back

to her old house, she might open up a bit, bring Sandy into her confidence, tell her what had happened between the end of the journals and now.

Sandy simply had to know.

Addie would pick up the Homestead's residents and give them a tour. If they were all going it was a good bet that Rebecca would have to go as well, especially if the house manager went along for the ride. Addie would not drive near the lighthouse; they didn't want to chance any bad vibrations for Rebecca. At the end of the tour he'd surprise them by pulling into the Lily Pond, where Sandy and Irene would have tables set up and tea and cupcakes waiting for them.

Of course they'd all have to use the bathroom, and wasn't it convenient that Sandy's house was right there?

"No bathroom stops along the way," Sandy reminded Addie.

"Got it. Why am I doing this again?"

"You owe me one, remember?"

Addie pulled up in front of the Homestead with explicit instructions that Rebecca must get on the bus. The residents were already on the sidewalk and sitting on the bench when he arrived. He was glad to be given this mission. He didn't know what Sandy and Irene were up to, but with all that was going on with Digit the distraction was welcome. As the people slowly piled on, he looked for Rebecca but couldn't see her. Maybe she was wearing a hat.

Everyone was smiling as they took their seats. The Homestead manager came on and counted heads. "Thirteen. You're all set," she said. "Have a good time everybody."

"But aren't you coming?" Addie asked her. He turned to look at the people on the bus. There were supposed to be fourteen. Where was Rebecca?

"I'd love to go," the woman said, "but one of our residents went for a walk and I have to be here for her when she returns."

209

"We could wait here for her."

"Oh, no, go ahead. Rebecca won't be back for at least an hour. Have a good time," she said to the eager passengers before exiting the bus and walking back into the Homestead.

Great. Now what was he supposed to do? He couldn't kick everyone off the bus. There was nothing to do but give the tour. "Hello everybody," he said as he closed the door and put the bus into gear. "My name is Roger … "

"Hello, Roger," everybody said.

Why did he say his name was Roger? He had been hearing "Chestnut Mare" by the Byrds in his head and was thinking of how the group's singer, Jim McGuinn, had changed his first name to Roger. It just popped out of his mouth.

So he'd be Roger for this trip. Didn't matter, he supposed. This tour was a failure before it even began. Sandy wasn't going to like it, but what could he do?

At least he didn't have to avoid the lighthouse anymore.

He drove up Main Street to Caton Circle, the small traffic island that the Caton family had been decorating with lights at Christmastime for generations. He turned left past the old Quaker cemetery. "Robert Lowell wrote a poem about this cemetery," he told the passengers, a couple of whom had already nodded off.

"Who's that, Roger?" somebody asked. Addie thought she was talking to another passenger. He'd forgotten his name was Roger.

"I think he may be hard of hearing," the woman said to the person sitting next to her.

"Either that, or he's forgotten his name," an elderly man said loudly. "I hope he hasn't forgotten how to drive."

Everybody laughed.

Addie continued on past the Old Mill, and the high school and out to 'Sconset, and tried to keep in mind that his name was Roger.

The passengers brightened up when they reached the small village of 'Sconset. Some of them, evidently, hadn't been out to this end of the island in years. "Look, the post office is still there," one of them said. "This place hasn't really changed at all. It still looks like it did when I was a kid."

"Remember walking all the way back out here from town?" one woman said to another. "When the last movie was over we'd have to walk home. What did it take us, an hour and a half?"

"Walking quickly," the other woman said. "I can't imagine how long it would take us to walk it today."

"Rebecca did it a few days ago," someone across the aisle said.

"She didn't!"

"I heard she walked to the lighthouse."

"Well, she used to make that walk all the time, remember? When her father was the keeper of the light? Nothing unusual. We all walked in those days."

"That was a tragedy."

"What? Walking? What's so tragic about that?"

"No, what happened. You remember how her father died. Some people say Rebecca pushed him."

"Oh, I heard all that talk. It was an accident, a terrible accident. I remember feeling so sorry for Rebecca. Everybody did. She became a virtual shut-in after that. She never left her house."

"I'm surprised she came back to the island at all."

"Well, it's good having her back.

"But I wonder what she did for all those years she was away?"

Listening to the conversation, which wasn't difficult because they all spoke so loudly, Addie was glad Rebecca wasn't on this trip. She may have recognized him as the person who helped get her home from the lighthouse that night and figure out that something funny was going on.

But if she was on the bus, he wouldn't have gone to 'Sconset.

Still, what he'd overheard was troubling. Were they exaggerating past events? What did they mean when they said Rebecca pushed her father?

Addie didn't want to know. They could talk all they wanted. He'd do his best to ignore them.

Addie drove by the lighthouse on the way back to town. While some of them remarked about its recent move, no one said any more about Rebecca's father's fall. Addie tried figuring out the height of the light: it was a long, long way to the ground.

"Hey, Roger," someone said from the back. "Are we going to make a bathroom stop at all?"

"At the end," Addie said.

"Well hurry up and get it over with." And everybody laughed again.

Back in town, Addie drove by the Oldest House and finally, mercifully, he pulled in to the small parking area at the Lily Pond. "We have a little surprise for you," he said as he opened the door.

And there at a table set up on the lawn were Sandy, Irene, and … Rebecca.

The passengers shuffled towards the picnic tables. "Roger, you said there'd be a bathroom," one of them asked,

"Yes, right in that house. Take a right before the kitchen."

"Roger?" Sandy said to him.

"Don't ask. But what's going on here?"

"Isn't it wonderful?" she said, looking over to where Irene sat drinking tea with Rebecca. "She came here on her own as we were setting up. I saw her on the sidewalk. She started to walk away when she saw me, but Irene convinced her to come around back to the Lily Pond where we already had the tables set up. She hasn't gone inside yet, but I think she will when she's ready."

"So what's the deal?" Addie asked, wondering if he should

bring up what he'd just heard about Rebecca. He decided to let it drop. The whole thing with the tour seemed kind of crazy to him anyway.

"It's complicated," Sandy said to him. "I'll tell you all about it later.

"Where's Verona, by the way?" she asked him over her shoulder.

"Working, I guess. Why? Is she supposed to be here?"

Sandy didn't answer, but walked into the house to bring out the tea and cupcakes. Rebecca was here, everything had turned out just fine. When she saw Verona she'd assure her that everything was all right between them. After all, if it wasn't for Verona, she may have never found Rebecca. What if she'd never discovered that Rebecca was living right up the street at the Homestead? Now that would have been a tragedy.

Addie walked over to where Irene was sitting with Rebecca. The old woman was smiling. Irene had charm, there was no doubt about that.

Rebecca hadn't intended to walk to her old house that afternoon, but when she'd heard about the tour she decided she'd rather be alone. She didn't want to be told things she already knew about the island. All those drivers made everything up anyway. As she left the Homestead she found herself walking towards her old home, as if she was being led there. "It wouldn't hurt to have a look," she told herself.

She was prepared for the worst as she approached, fearing that the bad memories that flooded over her at the light might hit her again. But as the corner of her house came into view, the sight of it was oddly comforting. Contrary to what she'd expected, she was glad to be standing outside her front door again.

She didn't expect Sandy, for now she knew her name, and that other woman to come up to her like that. Nor did she expect them both to gush over her as they did. But when they offered her a seat outside, she was glad for the chance to sit.

The house looked the same. Sandy pointed out the windows on the second floor. "My bedroom's to the far left, the one to the right is my tenant's." Rebecca looked up, recognized the windows to the right as her old room, the place where she'd poured out her heart in her journals. She saw the room in her mind and felt that she was seventeen again.

Sandy saw Rebecca's expression change as she gazed up at the window, and while she wanted to ask if she'd like to go take a look, she had to tread very carefully. She and Irene had talked about it: they didn't want to overwhelm Rebecca too quickly. Things had to develop at her pace.

And then the bus showed up, which was fine. Everything had to be revealed one step at a time.

"Would you like some tea, Addie?" Irene asked him.

"No, thanks. I've got to get back to base. Ken's expecting me for the next tour; there's another bus waiting for me there. I guess Sandy can drive everyone back when they're done here."

The man looking for the bathroom came up to the table. "Thanks for the tour, Roger," he said. "You got most of it right," and he gave Addie a friendly pat on the shoulder.

"Roger?" Irene asked when the man moved toward the cupcakes.

"It's complicated," Addie said, smiling. "I'll tell you later."

———

Rebecca seemed content. She didn't talk, but Sandy could see her taking it all in, turning occasionally to look around the Lily Pond.

Again, Sandy was going to ask Rebecca if she wanted to take a step inside, but a doubtful glance from Irene reminded her that she shouldn't push it. When it was time to go, Rebecca boarded the bus with the rest of the residents, who all greeted her as a long-lost friend.

"Give her time," Sandy thought as she closed the bus door and put it into drive. She knew from Rebecca's expression as she surveyed her old home that this *was* the Rebecca who'd written the journals all those years ago. She could put any further need to know on the back burner for the moment: all she wanted now was for Rebecca to find some semblance of happiness.

Chapter Thirty-Nine

HIS HEART leapt when he saw her standing there as he walked onto the wharf. It seemed as if he hadn't seen Verona in weeks.

There was something different about her, however.

"Nice haircut," he said.

Verona had forgotten she'd cut her hair — she'd stopped looking in mirrors. "Oh," she said, lowering her eyes, patting the back of her head with her hand. "Do you like it?"

"It makes you look younger," he said honestly.

Verona had biked home after work, eager to talk to Sandy, tell her she had no interest in Rebecca anymore. But when she saw the crowd of people out back by the Lily Pond, she headed to the docks, hoping she'd find Addie there. Being in his company kept her mind off things.

"I just saw Rebecca," Addie told her.

Verona didn't know why the statement bothered her. "Where?" she asked him.

"At your place, at Sandy's. I gave everybody at the Homestead a tour."

Good, Verona thought. Sandy had Rebecca all to herself. It was best that she hadn't gone home; better to give them time alone.

"What are you doing tonight?" she asked him.

"I was going to try and finish packing, but I can skip that."

"No," she said, "let's go to your house. I can help you."

"My place is a mess," he said. "I've got stuff everywhere."

"It can't be that bad," she said.

When they later arrived at Addie's house, however, Verona couldn't believe that one person could have so many things. Boxes and paper bags were everywhere. "What is all this?" she asked him.

"My life. I've been carrying it with me everywhere. It's quite a load."

Is that all it took to have a life, she thought, boxes of things? "Do you know what everything is?"

"Some of it. But I'm not sure where some things are, like my birth certificate. It's kind of taken on a life of its own."

Unlike the neatly tucked away treasure she'd uncovered in Sandy's attic, Addie's accumulation was chaotic. It made Verona uneasy just looking at it — the piles emitted an aura of heaviness that was nearly suffocating. She had nothing but her clothes, a toothbrush, and a hairbrush. And her bicycle, of course.

"I was going to go through all this and consolidate," Addie said to her, "but I just don't have time before I have to get out of here."

He didn't tell her how wrenching it had become just looking at it all, to consider what was important and what wasn't. He opened a box that had loose papers on top. He picked one up. "These are some poems I wrote in high school. Man, what was I thinking?"

"So you can throw those away?"

"No way. It'd be like throwing out a piece of myself. Of

course the younger me would probably say, 'Heave them!' "

———————

As Addie sorted through his possessions, Verona wondered if there was a secret stash of hers somewhere. What would it contain? Would she, like Rebecca, have saved a dress? Did she, too, have poems describing her teenaged feelings stuffed into a cardboard box?

What was she like as a child, what things made her happy? And what were her parents like? Was she an only child; did she have brothers and sisters?

Was she married? Did she have children? She'd had no hint of who she was when she'd first wakened on Nantucket, not even a flicker. Lately, however, she'd been stung by glimpses of what had been.

Her mind returned reluctantly to what she'd seen on the television, the sobbing woman she'd tried expunging from her mind. It had stunned her, to the core, but it hadn't shocked her into remembering.

Thank God for that.

Still, it was too close. Why hadn't she reacted like the girl on the television? Why hadn't she cried out for help?

She couldn't say. These past months it had been enough to focus on getting by, on taking care of her immediate needs, on living day by day, on being alone.

But people wouldn't let you be alone, that's what she'd learned. No matter how hard you tried, no matter how much you kept to yourself, there'd be someone wondering what your place was, where you were from, how you fit in.

"What are you thinking about?" Addie asked as he sniffed two old bottles of shaving lotion he'd packed away.

"What are those?" Verona asked him, happy to change the subject.

"These? Oh, nothing. A present from an old girlfriend." He didn't want to tell her they came from Sarah, his wife. It seemed like such a long time ago now — another lifetime ago.

Could he tell Verona that she was helping him forget he'd even had that life?

The box the shaving lotion was in also contained cards Sarah had sent him when they were dating, letters expressing her love for him, photos of the two of them together. He closed the box quickly and turned to another.

In this he found old baseball cards, a copy of Woody Guthrie's biography *Bound for Glory,* old cassette tapes, a melted homemade candle, a paperback edition of *Howl,* a ticket to the Empire State Building.

Verona watched his expression as he sorted through these things. He seemed flustered, almost sad.

"It's okay to let go of your past," she said to him softly.

Addie looked at her, looked into her caring eyes as he fingered an old tie-tac he'd had since high school. "You're right," he said. "This stuff is weighing me down; it's controlling me. Look at this," and he held up a beer mug with the words 'I Drink to Remember' written on it. "I've had this mug for over thirty years. I don't even use it anymore; I just carry it around with me because I can't throw it away." He glanced behind him and his mood lifted. "I've got a couple of boxes and bags over there I've already gone through, old newspapers and T-shirts that don't fit me anymore, and a manual from my first job scooping ice cream when I was sixteen. Let's burn them."

"Burn them?"

"A ceremonial so long. We can have a bonfire on the beach. Time to jettison some of this crap."

"When?"

"Tomorrow night. Let's have a cookout."

219

Chapter Forty

SANDY WAS still up when Addie dropped off Verona.

"So, tomorrow, late afternoon," he said to her. He wanted to kiss her goodnight, but there was nothing in her demeanor that suggested he should, so he let the moment pass. "It'll be fun," he continued. "I haven't had a beach cookout in years."

To her knowledge, Verona had never been to a beach cookout. Whatever it was, Addie seemed excited about it.

"You can ask Sandy to come," he said. "We'll have a party."

Verona had assumed it was going to be just the two of them. Whatever she did these days, it seemed, there was always a bunch of people around.

Although she had intended to speak to Sandy that afternoon, Verona wanted now to slip unseen up to her bedroom. When she reached the bottom stair, however, Sandy called out to her.

"Verona?"

"Yes," she said quietly, hoping Sandy would simply say, "goodnight."

"Come in here, please. I want to talk to you."

Sandy was watching television. A chill shot through Verona; she didn't want to see or hear that woman she'd seen that afternoon. Sandy mercifully clicked the television off. "Rebecca was here today," Sandy said to her.

"I know. Addie told me."

"Of course," Sandy said. "Verona, I owe you an apology for the way I last spoke to you."

Verona wasn't sure why Sandy needed to apologize to her, but before she could say anything, Sandy blurted out, "What did you do to your hair?"

"I cut it."

"I can see that."

"It was time for a change."

"Can you sit for a minute?"

Verona sat on the chair opposite Sandy. "You could probably tell I was upset with you the other day," Sandy began. "It wasn't fair of me." Sandy shifted her position on the couch, drew her legs under her. "Maybe I've been alone too long," she continued. "My thoughts ran away with me. It's just that I had taken Rebecca's journals as my own private retreat from the world; it was as if this house," and she gazed about the room, "this house was offering up a secret to comfort me. I was sure nobody had seen those journals since Rebecca had written them; it was like discovering a long-lost treasure, a piece of history. In my mind Rebecca was dead. Her writings seemed to be of another time. I never did the math, never let myself think that they were only about fifty years old. It all seemed so safe, so long ago. Had I thought for a minute that Rebecca was still alive, even though I'd never met her ... ," her voice trailed. "I'd never invade someone's privacy that way."

She paused. "You do believe me, don't you?"

Verona nodded. Why wouldn't she believe her?

"I'm hoping you can imagine my shock, then, when you

told me Rebecca was alive," Sandy went on. "I'd never told you about her — it was a real bolt out of the blue." Sandy shook her head. "It was … surreal. Imagine someone you think's been dead suddenly coming back to life. I just couldn't believe you."

Sandy looked at Verona, waited for her to say something. Verona had nothing to say. What could she say?

"And then I was mad at you," Sandy went on, "mad because you were the one who found her — and I apologize for thinking that way. If it wasn't for you … " and her voice trailed off, became choked, "if it wasn't for you I may never have known Rebecca was still alive." She wiped a tear away with the back of her hand. "And today Rebecca was here. Isn't it wonderful?"

Verona nodded yes. She was gladdened more that Sandy seemed happy again. "It's too bad about Gerald," Verona said absent-mindedly.

"Yes, I know," Sandy said. "I wonder if they ever got together. Her journals ended so abruptly … "

"But he died," Verona said quietly. Surely, Sandy knew that. She had seen the old newspaper.

The blank look Sandy gave her told her otherwise. "He died?" she said in a whisper. And then her voice rose. "How do you know this?" she said, her eyes now locked on Verona.

Verona wished she hadn't said anything, wished she had stolen off to bed. She couldn't escape Sandy's stare, however. "It was in that old newspaper," she said haltingly. "The one in the old chest."

"Show me."

And they took the stairs in silence to the attic, and Verona opened the sea chest and handed the wrapped photograph to Sandy. "It's in here."

Sandy unwrapped the newspaper and shined her flashlight on the headlines. "It's on the other side," Verona said.

Sandy read the story and let the newspaper fall to the side.

She hung her head and said nothing. After a long minute of silence, she looked up at Verona. "Do you think Rebecca knows?" she said hoarsely.

"She must," Verona said. "She wrapped the picture in it."

Another terrible revelation, Sandy thought. Why hadn't she noticed this before? She felt angry with Verona yet again but quickly put her anger in check. This, too, wasn't Verona's fault, but Verona sure seemed to have a knack for finding bad news.

"Verona," she said, "we must never mention this. I'd hate to think what this would do to Rebecca if she didn't know."

I hate to think, period, Verona thought.

Chapter Forty-One

Anticipating the cookout helped take Verona's mind off things. People sure were complicated. After her talk with Sandy and her inadvertent slip about Gerald, she was more determined than ever to mind her own business. She wished she had never gone into Sandy's attic, wished in a way that she had never found Rebecca in the first place.

At work that day, Addie asked Sandy and Chuck and Ken to come along. "It's an end of the summer blowout," Addie told them.

"I'm into anything that blows," Chuck said. "Count me in."

And so, after the day's last tour, and with Ken's permission, they loaded up Sandy's bus at the A&P. Addie rounded up Digit who had moved back into his house and who he knew would have plenty of wood hanging around for the fire. "Come on, Digit," Addie said. "I know you've got nothing better to do. Get that truck of yours in gear."

They got to the beach a couple of hours before sunset. Addie parked his car next to Sandy's bus in the dirt parking lot. Digit's pickup was already there. Digit, who had grown up having clambakes with his family, had finished digging a pit in the sand. Into this he'd thrown in bits of scrap wood he had lying around his yard and then a bag of charcoal.

He scattered some littleneck clams onto a grate he'd laid over the coals. The clams opened quickly and he passed them around. He tossed on whole ears of corn that he had partially shucked, removing the silk, and leaving the husks intact. He soaked these in a tub of fresh water he'd brought along before chucking them onto the grill.

"It didn't take you long to get all this together," Addie said to him.

"Be prepared," Digit said.

"So how's it going?" Addie asked him, devouring another clam.

"Better," Digit said. "I've been thinking: I've got that whole house to myself again; why don't you move back in? You could even have your old room back."

"Are you kidding?"

"Do I look like I'm kidding?"

"But I'm supposed to be leaving … "

"You haven't done dick to leave, and you know it. Come on, stay with me until you figure out what you're going to do. First six months are free."

"I couldn't do that."

"Marsha's giving me the house outright. She says it ought to stay in the family."

"That's nice of her."

"Nice, my ass. Her boyfriend's loaded, remember? She just wants me to evaporate. She never liked the house anyway. But I'm not taking any chances: I'm having the papers drawn up now before she changes her mind.

"So," he continued, "are you in?"

"What the heck. Why not? Thanks, Digit."

"And you may as well have Verona move in with you."

"Verona?" he said.

"Yes, Verona." The look Digit saw on Addie's face seemed to transform his friend into a sixteen year old. "Don't tell me," Digit said.

"Don't tell you what?"

"Don't tell me you haven't done it yet."

"What's that supposed to mean?"

"You haven't, have you?"

"Life's not all about sex, you know."

"Oh, don't I know it; don't I know that all too well. But you guys aren't teenagers anymore."

"It hasn't been that kind of relationship."

"And what kind of relationship are we talking about?"

"I'm not exactly sure. Besides, I'm taking it slow, real slow. I just like her company. She's different."

She's different, all right, Digit thought.

"When are we going to get those weenies going?" asked Chuck abruptly, who along with everyone else had ambled close to the fire.

"Yes, let's get cooking," Digit said as he cracked a beer.

After everyone ate, and Digit threw more wood onto the fire, they sat around and soaked in the twilight, looked out over the beach, saw the waves build and crash on the shoreline. It was nice, Addie thought, to simply be here with his friends and not have to think about leaving, or what he was going to do with his life, or anything.

But then he remembered why he was here.

"Hold on, everybody. I've got some things to add to the fire."

"A little spice," Chuck said. "Bring it on, Addie."

"Hey, Chuck, maybe your mind could crawl *into* the gutter," Addie said. "But since you're wondering, I could use your help."

Addie and Chuck returned from Addie's car, each carrying

two boxes. "This is it," Addie proclaimed, as he opened one box and took out his old work manual. "Goodbye to my past." And as he chucked it onto the fire, Chuck let out a whoop and everyone joined in, even Verona, as the contents of the boxes were thrown onto the fire and the flames leapt into the darkening sky.

"How does it feel?" Sandy asked Addie, glad to be away from her house and all its secrets. She breathed the salt air deeply, let it rinse her mind.

"Liberating," he said, putting his arm around Verona and pulling her close.

They all sat around the fire then, enjoying the warmth; everyone contentedly silent. "Anyone seen Digit?" Sandy asked after a while.

"He's had a few beers. He must be seeing a man about a horse," Chuck said.

But then, rumbling down the road, came Digit's pickup.

No one had seen him slip off. Returning now, Digit drove beyond where the other cars were parked and up onto the beach. "Let's go," he said loudly. "I've got my own past to get rid of."

And he let down the tailgate and began tossing his stuff onto the fire. "See you later, Marsha; have a nice life," he said, as he pitched their wedding picture into the inferno.

When he was finished, Digit danced around the flames. Everyone joined in, holding hands as they circled and skipped and laughed around the fire.

A tossed T-shirt made the flames leap, followed by a pair of jeans that the fire also gladly consumed. "Where'd those come from?" Digit asked, as everyone turned to see Chuck dancing around the fire, bollicky bare ass in the flickering light.

No one noticed the headlights approaching from down the beach, the headlights that snaked around the dunes before stopping next to the bonfire.

"You got a permit for this fire?" a young policeman asked

as he hopped off the all-terrain vehicle the cops used to patrol the beach.

"Yes, sir, right here," Digit lied. "Got it from the fire department this afternoon."

"That's fine," another voice said as he shined a flashlight in their faces. It was a man whose suit looked incongruous on the beach. "Is there a Charles Finley here?"

"Right here," Chuck said, waddling closer, crossing his legs as best he could.

And the man in the suit walked over to him. "I've got a warrant for your arrest," he said, as he slapped handcuffs on him. He apparently didn't notice, or care about, Chuck's lack of clothing.

"Hey, wait a minute," Digit said. "What's the charge?"

"Distributing a controlled substance." And as he led the naked Chuck away, they could hear him say, "You have the right to remain silent … "

The cop on the ATV, meanwhile, said: "Time to put this fire out and go home. Party's over."

Chapter Forty-Two

A S THOUGH she was caught in a vortex, Verona woke with a start that jerked her into a sitting position. She went from sleeping to waking so quickly that it took her a second to realize she was in bed. She didn't recall dreaming; there was nothing she could imagine that would shake her from sleeping so suddenly.

She was in bed, that much she knew, but as her brain adapted to consciousness she wasn't sure of her surroundings. In a second she realized she wasn't in her bed at all, and the room she was in wasn't hers.

She gazed at the unfamiliar bed frame and looked around at the walls that were covered with a white and red striped wallpaper. She put her elbows on her knees and sat with her head in her hands. "Think, Verona, think," she told herself. "How did you get here?"

She remembered the bonfire the night before, how they had thrown some of Addie's things onto the fire and how Digit had backed up his truck onto the beach. But things got confusing after the police arrested Chuck and the party broke up. She was tired. All the excitement had made her weary. The last thing she could recall was falling blissfully asleep in Addie's car.

That was it — she must be at Addie's house. Was this his bed? Did he sleep alongside her? She felt the space next to her on the bed. It was warm. But that could be her own body heat.

Light peeked through the closed curtains. It was morning. What time was it? Where was she?

And then, outside the door, she heard the murmur of voices, or was it a voice? Footsteps approached, and a man's voice called her name: "Verona. Verona? Are you awake?"

Was that Addie? It didn't sound like him, although through the closed door she couldn't be sure. She looked at the door, it opened, and a man she had never seen before walked into the bedroom.

"Good morning, baby," he said to her, holding out a cup. "Coffee, fresh and black, just the way you like it."

All she could do was look at this man who held the cup in his hand, this man with a neatly trimmed salt and pepper beard and glasses, this man she had never seen before, this stranger. "Are you all right?" he said to her. "You look like you've seen a ghost."

"Where's Addie?" she asked softly.

"Addie?" he said, sitting now on the side of the bed. "I don't know any Addie. That must have been some dream." Again, he held out the cup to her. "Here, have some coffee and tell me all about it."

Coffee? She didn't drink coffee, and if she did she wouldn't drink black coffee. She didn't know what else to say, so she said, "No, thanks."

"Hey," he said. "Is everything okay? Are you feeling all right? You look weird." He put the coffee down on the chest of drawers near the bed, held out his hand to touch her forehead.

Verona recoiled. "Whoa," he said, standing up. "Calm down. Why don't I let you wake up a bit? I know how nightmares can make you feel. Take your time. I'll be out in the kitchen making breakfast." And as he turned to leave he said again, "Must have been some dream."

She scrunched back against the headboard, wrapped her arms around her knees. What was going on, who was this man? Was he visiting Addie? No, he said he didn't know any Addie. Then how did she end up here? Did Addie drop her off at some strange person's house? But why would he do that?

Then it hit her. This was a joke of some sort. Yes, that was it. She remembered now: Digit had told Addie he could move in with him. This must be Digit's house and they sent in some friend of Digit's she didn't know to play a little trick on her. They were probably out in the kitchen right now laughing about it. Well, it wasn't funny. It wasn't funny at all.

When she stood up she saw she was in pajamas; she usually wore a nightgown. "Must be Digit's wife's," she thought, although she didn't remember getting into them. This was all very strange. It wouldn't be like Addie to undress her and put pajamas on her. She must have put them on herself.

She looked around for her clothes, and while there were woman's clothes folded neatly on a chair they weren't hers. In the closet was a robe, and it fit her perfectly.

She opened the door expecting to hear several voices but all she heard was the far off sounds of pots and pans. Someone was humming a melody she recognized. It was "New Morning," that song Addie had introduced her to. So, it was Addie. The part of her that wasn't angry was relieved.

As she followed the sounds she saw how nice the house was, and she passed a large dining room with sliding glass doors looking out onto a deck. She had never been to Digit's house before, and would never have thought he lived in such splendor.

She reached the kitchen and there was a man leaning over looking into a cabinet with his back to her. "Addie," she said, and before she could say any more, the man who had offered her coffee stood up and faced her.

"Should I be concerned?" he said, as he put the pan on the stove. "Really, Verona, if you're going to dream, can't you dream about me?"

And he smiled as he moved around her in the large, airy kitchen. "Ready for that coffee now? That robe looks good on you. Remember how you weren't going to buy it?"

Verona stood, speechless. The man walked over, pulled out a stool. "You really don't look well," he said. "Here, sit down."

And she needed to sit, and as she sat she saw on the wall a picture of this man, and three children, and her.

———————

"Verona," she heard a voice calling to her. "Verona, wake up, baby."

And Verona didn't think as she opened her eyes and looked into the face of the man with the beard and glasses. "Thank God," he said. "You fainted; I barely caught you."

She was on the floor and he cradled the back of her neck in his hands. "God, you scared me. You've got to start taking better care of yourself, start eating better," he said. "Remember the doctor said you've got to start taking iron supplements. You look better now. Let's walk into the living room."

And he helped her up and walked with her to the living room with his arm around her waist. She sat on the couch. Looking back at her were more photographs of her with this man, and of her with those children. She seemed to be having a good time in them. She looked at this man who looked back at her caringly. She wished she knew his name.

Seeing him, and seeing the photographs didn't awaken any feelings in her, however. This must be her life, her real life, she thought, but she felt no relief, no release in being here. She wished he was Addie.

"Don't think," the man was saying to her. "Let me get you a glass of water."

She gazed at the photographs when he left the room. None of them kindled any memories or yearnings. If she *had* had children, shouldn't she have an innate sense of loving them? But she felt nothing and the feeling frightened her.

Could it all have been a dream? This man knew her name, he called her Verona. But hadn't she picked out that name from the back of a boat? Had that been her real name all along? Waking up in this strange bedroom, she had the same feeling of being lost that she did when she came to on Nantucket. But that was several months ago. Or was it? It all seemed so real. Although this house was big, and obviously outfitted for comfort, she didn't want to be here. She wanted to go back to the island, and Sandy, and Addie, especially Addie. If only she could go back to sleep and wake up and be back where she wanted to be.

And as the man came back to her with a glass of water, she drifted off to sleep.

"Verona." Someone was calling her name. "Verona." She heard the sound from far away, as if she was in a dream.

"Verona." Who was calling her? "Verona, if you don't wake up now you'll be late for work."

She opened her eyes, cautiously. She looked at the ceiling and saw — that it was her ceiling! She pulled off the covers and looked and she was wearing her nightgown. She sat up, and there was the mirror and the window looking over the Lily Pond. "Verona." It was Sandy's voice, and then footsteps on the stairs. When Sandy entered the room Verona leapt from her bed and hugged her.

"Okay, okay," Sandy said. "Glad to see you, too. You'd better get moving."

And as Verona dressed she stole a cautious glance at the

mirror. Her hair was short, this wasn't a dream.

———————

As Verona bicycled to work she breathed in the fresh Nantucket air, glad to be alive amid the old houses and the people; glad to be back where the lighthouse called to her and the foghorn echoed its low lonely lament through the night. Whoever she was, she was staying. Her life was here, she knew it now more than ever, and the past, her past, was history.

She hoped.

When she saw Addie that afternoon, she rushed to him and kissed him. "Tell me you're real," she said.

"Oh, I'm real, all right, a real moron. The cops are fining me five hundred bucks for that bonfire. They went through the ashes and found my name on that old work manual. Beyond that, we all had to pitch in to bail Chuck out of jail. He was set up."

Verona didn't know what "set up" meant, nor did she care. She was glad she was back where she belonged. It was as if she had woken up for the first time on Nantucket all over again.

"It was Fred," Addie was saying. "Fred from the Steamship Authority. Chuck's sure of it. He kept bugging him to get him some cocaine, so Chuck finally landed him some, just to shut him up. The cops wouldn't tell him anything, but he figures Fred's some kind of a narc or something. He's got a court date next week."

Verona didn't understand any of it, nor did she want to try. She'd think about Chuck later; right now, she simply wanted to be with Addie. There were stirrings within her she hadn't felt before, stirrings that made her turn to Addie impulsively and kiss him again. Only this time, he kissed her back.

Chapter Forty-Three

CHUCK HAD a court date set for early October — he and the ten or so others rounded up by the police. "It was Fred," Chuck confirmed to Addie. "He was never from the Vineyard, and he'd never worked for the Steamship Authority. The cops put him in there."

"I'll bet his name's not really Fred either," Addie said.

"Quick thinking, honey," Chuck said. "No wonder you're such a success."

"I gave him a ride to his place once," Addie said. "Kept asking me the whole time if I could get him some blow."

"We should have known he was a phony," Chuck said. "I should have known the time he called me and I could hear him taking a piss while he was talking to me. Can you believe that? I mean, excuse yourself or something, but don't take the phone into the bathroom. Didn't he think I could hear it?"

"You gave him your phone number?"

"I was just trying to help out a lonely guy. He seemed harmless enough sitting there at the bar. He really fooled me."

"So," Addie said, "do you have a lawyer?"

"I'm representing myself."

"Only a fool represents himself," Addie said.

"We'll see how foolish I am."

———————

With the season winding down, Addie gave it everything he had on the tours that remained.

The summer traffic gone, he dawdled along Easy Street and its view of the harbor, slowed around the side streets of town to let his passengers take all the pictures and movies they wanted.

Driving out to 'Sconset, however, he had little to say. He daydreamed about Verona and the kiss they'd shared on the wharf. They needed a little alone time; there always seemed to be somebody else around whenever they were together. At the fourth milestone someone asked him where the beach was, which was good, because it snapped him out of it. He'd forgotten he was driving, not the best thing to do with a busload of tourists. It was like the times he tried doing two things at once — giving his spiel while thinking ahead to what he was going to say next — nearly short-circuiting his brain.

The market in 'Sconset was closed for the year, so there were no stops for ice cream, but he crisscrossed the village, going by all the little cottages that had been fishing shacks two hundred years before, the cottages that in summer were festooned with roses.

Back in town, although the pace of life had slowed, the delivery trucks were still out in force, dropping off the overnight mail and packages the growing year-round population required.

"Is it me, or does there seem to be an inordinate number of UPS trucks on the road?" he asked his passengers. He looked in his rearview mirror, and those who weren't asleep didn't have an answer.

But as he turned the next corner, there was a UPS truck on

the side of the road. "Hey, there's one," somebody said, and the chase was on.

Addie drove towards the airport, to where the new commercial district of the island was being developed, and, sure enough, there were UPS trucks galore. "I mean, this is a small island," Addie said. "Do you really think they're all delivering underwear, or lounge chairs?" His passengers were more alert now, waiting to find more UPS trucks.

"There's another one," someone called out as Addie headed back to town.

"And what's up with those brown shirts?" Addie asked. "Pretty incriminating if you ask me. If I didn't know any better, I'd think there's some kind of conspiracy … "

And then, as he turned the corner onto Main Street, he knew this tour, and any tips he'd hoped to collect, were history.

———————

A police cruiser, its red and blue lights flashing, blocked his path. Beyond the cruiser, a crowd of people, hundreds of them, rolling all the way down towards the docks, had taken over Main Street. The people were chanting something Addie couldn't make out at first, while a banner that stretched across the street proclaimed: "Lighthouses: the only traffic lights we need."

Addie opened his door. "I don't think we'll be moving for a while, folks. If you want to get out here, you can." He hopped off the bus and walked toward the crowd. A man with a bullhorn was on the steps of the Pacific National Bank, the historic brick symbol of whaling capitalism built at the top of Main Street. He led the crowd in the chant that Addie could now clearly understand: "No Bonere; no Bonere."

The crowd blocked traffic at every street that intersected with Main. When it blocked a fire engine that tried making its way through the mob, the police urged the firemen to turn the hoses on the people, but the firemen refused.

The man with the bullhorn then handed it over to a primly dressed woman who stood on the bank's top step. "Now hear this," she said, and the crowd beneath her roared. "There will be no more chipping away at our history, no more erosion of our values. Over the years we've seen our businesses leave town, the businesses that served our mothers and our grandmothers and our great-grandmothers. We can't live on T-shirts; we can't eat fancy jewelry. Look around you, look at the UPS trucks around town. Why does everything we need have to be mail-ordered?"

The crowd shouted back its approval. "Well, we've got news for you, Mr. Bonere: we may not be able to stop the steady change that wracks our island, but we can, and we will, preserve our historic integrity. There will never be a traffic light on this island! If we have to guard every street corner, man every sidewalk, we will!"

The crowd went nuts then. "No more Bonere, no more Bonere," they all shouted, although it soon was abbreviated into: "No mo' Boner, no mo' Boner."

Jason Bonere, of course, was nowhere to be seen; he was off-island, standing in the middle of the traffic rotary in Hyannis, waving a sign that said: "Jason — and the People — for State Rep." They'd find out later what his last name was, after they got used to his toothy grin and his child-like enthusiasm. It had worked on Nantucket, after all, where people had no problem ticking off Bonere on their ballots.

He was especially cheerful today as he waved and gave the thumbs up to the cars that circled him. The plans for the traffic light were finalized, and there was nothing anyone could do about it. He went beyond town politics and got quick state approval because he was putting it next to the elementary school; a necessary safety measure, he successfully argued, for the island's children. With the state on board, let them try to stop it now, he thought. Just let them try.

So even if he'd known about the rally, he wouldn't care. He was leaving the island. His house — the house that had been a cherished summer home to generations of Boneres; the house he and his cousins had inherited; the house he had gained title to through a shady land court lawyer — was already on the market.

The police tried breaking up the crowd, but no one would leave. The cops pulled out bullhorns of their own, which only made the crowd shout louder: "Rub out Bonere, rub out Bonere, rub out Bonere." And then a rookie cop made the mistake of firing a Taser at someone and the crowd got ugly.

The first thing to go was the police cruiser parked at the end of Main Street. A handful of people rocked it back and forth until they flipped it onto its side. Not satisfied with that, they flipped it again until it landed on its roof. The crowd let out a hearty cheer and the chase was on.

Loose cobbles were hefted from Main Street and thrown through the storefronts of the businesses that were perceived by the mob as tacky, or glitzy, or both. The cruiser near Addie's bus was the next to go, as the crowds flipped that, too, onto its roof like a dead turtle. The State Police had responded to the riot, but with only three of them on the island they thought it prudent to keep their distance. "We can get a chopper here in an hour," Sheriff Shank told the police chief.

"And what good would that do?" he wanted to know.

"We could drop tear gas on them."

"Oh, that would be great, just great," the chief said. "I can see the off-island headlines now: 'Island police attack residents.' No," he said, wiping his brow and exhaling deeply through his nose, "I think the only thing we can do is let this play itself out. They'll get tired of this."

"When?" a state cop asked.

"Soon, I hope," the chief said.

But the crowd rallied. When the windows of all the off-island businesses had been smashed, they grouped together in the center of Main Street and shouted: "We want Bonere, give us Bonere."

"I'll give him to them if they want," the chief said, hoisting his walkie-talkie. "Get Bonere over here," he radioed the dispatcher.

"He's off-island, Chief. Campaigning."

"Damn it," he said. "That Bonere's as useless as tits on a bull. I could've told him this island doesn't need a traffic light. And now look."

"Pretty amazing what'll get people riled up," the state cop said. "You'd think they were coming after their first borns or something."

"You haven't been here long, have you?" the chief said. "Traffic lights and neon — the two unmentionables. You could pave over the cobblestones or put aluminum siding on all the old houses in town before they'd let a traffic light go in. Still, I never expected this."

———

Addie, meanwhile, was just glad his bus had been ignored in the melee. The collective consciousness, it seemed, was only interested in off-island representations; except for the police cruisers, of course. "Digit was right," he said to himself as he watched the crowd pulse like a single organism. "They won't let it happen." And seeing the peoples' response made him happy. He was gladdened by their reaction to a seemingly inconsequential traffic light; he was proud to be an islander.

And then, at the bottom of Main Street, the crowd billowed like a building wave, and as the wave rolled up the cobblestones, Addie saw the crowd part to let a solitary figure through. He stood on the bumper of his bus for a better look. It was Senior

Chief Sally Nancy, she of the United States Coast Guard station on Nantucket; whose men braved the worst possible conditions at sea under her command; who had earned the admiration and respect of Nantucketers through her caring competence around the waterfront; who held court at the Atlantic Café and knew well the concerns of islanders, both young and old, and who could cut through bullshit with a bawdy but refined sense of humor.

Grabbing a bullhorn from a policeman, and striding purposefully up the bank steps, Chief Sally Nancy looked through her steely blue eyes at the crowd. Her small stature belied the force of her personality as the mob instantly hushed.

"Listen up," she bellowed through the bullhorn. "I know how you feel. I'm an islander, just like you. But this is no way to solve this situation. You can't undo the damage you've already done, but this little tantrum is over. This is not the way islanders behave. Look at you, acting no better than off-island vigilantes. The people who would resort to this display aren't the Nantucketers I know, the ones who give shelter to visitors stranded in a storm; the people who rush out in their boats to help search for a lost fisherman; the people who bring food to the sick, or comfort to the elderly; the people who are always willing to lend a hand without asking for anything in return."

The crowd stood still, and silent. For the first time since the rally started, Addie could hear the anti-traffic-light banner rustle in the wind.

"I can tell you this," Chief Sally Nancy continued, "that traffic light will never get the green light on this island, not if I have anything to do with it, and I have the weight and force of the U. S. Coast Guard behind me to back it up." The crowd let out a cheer, but before it could again go wild, she raised her arm: "Now go home, all of you. My men will clean up this mess."

And as the crowd dispersed, she strode down the steps, handed the bullhorn back to the cops, and rolled up her sleeves.

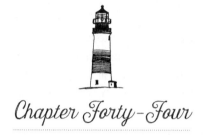

Chapter Forty-Four

THE NANTUCKET courthouse took up the second floor of the island's Town and County Building, a utilitarian brick edifice a clamshell's throw from Steamboat Wharf. On most days, court sessions were light, with the judge dealing with drunk drivers, or bar fights, or the occasional deer poacher.

On Chuck's court date, however, the court and second floor hallway were filled with alleged felons: Chuck and the ten or so others charged with trafficking in drugs, along with the usual holdovers from the past weekend's bar brawls, and about twenty people rounded up by the cops for disturbing the peace and breaking windows during the anti-traffic-light rally. A handful of others were charged with willful and malicious damage to public property: namely, flipping over police cruisers.

Addie, Verona, and Sandy had gotten to the courthouse early to lend moral support to Chuck. They could hear the traffic light people in the hallway as the "No more Bonere" chant was revived.

Judge Clive Portnoy saw the ruckus when he entered chambers. He said to court officer Myron Meese as he donned his robes: "What idiot scheduled all this for today? Isn't it enough to deal with this police sting without sorting through another mess on top of it? What are all these people here for anyway?"

"Disturbing the peace, your honor."

"Disturbing the peace? All of them?"

"And breaking windows, and creating a disturbance."

"They don't look like the usual hoodlums. There are people my age out there."

"Some of them flipped two police cruisers onto their roofs."

"Flipped police cruisers?"

"Yes, your honor. It was part of the protest."

"I don't care what they were protesting. Flipping over police cruisers is against the law, I don't care what jurisdiction you're in." The judge paused, looked up at his framed portrait on the wood-paneled wall. Only two more years, he thought. Only two more years until his retirement and blissful fishing in the Florida Keys.

"What were they protesting?"

"A traffic light, your honor."

"A traffic light?"

"Yes, sir. One of the selectmen got state approval to install a traffic light, and … "

"What idiot would want to install a traffic light? Didn't he know something like this would happen? There hasn't been an uproar like this since some other idiot tried to make people pay for fishing licenses. There are some things you just don't touch on Nantucket."

"No, your honor."

"No, what?"

"There are some things you just don't touch."

Judge Portnoy poured a cup of coffee. "Who was it?" he asked the court officer.

"Who was who, your honor?"

"Who's the moron behind the traffic light?"

"Bonere, your honor."

"Excuse me," the judge said, bristling.

"The selectman, Bonere, Jason Bonere."

The judge sighed, turned to the roses on his desk and inhaled. Good, these roses had a scent. He couldn't believe some roses had the scent bred out of them, just as he couldn't believe some people preferred white roses over red. He'd nearly run Meese out of chambers on his ear the day white roses appeared in his desktop vase. "You better get out there, Meese," the judge said as he gingerly rearranged his flowers. "Try and establish some order before we get things underway. What case are we trying first?"

"The drug felons, your honor."

"Alleged drug felons, Meese."

"Yes, your honor. There's also a charge of public nudity."

The judge turned, opened his mouth to say something, but shook his head instead. It wasn't the morning he had hoped for.

———

The police led Chuck and the other drug defendants into the first two rows of benches. From the back of the courtroom, the anti-traffic-light group was herded into whatever seats were available. Some of them had to stand against the back wall.

Addie, Verona, and Sandy looked over at Chuck, who flashed the "okay" sign and winked. Addie surveyed the rest of the courtroom and nudged Verona.

"Verona, look behind you. Isn't that Rebecca?"

Verona and Sandy both turned around. "It is Rebecca," Sandy said. "What's she doing here?"

"Maybe she's just an interested citizen," Addie said.

"Bullshit," Sandy whispered. "She's sitting with the people who got arrested."

Sandy got up, walked to where Rebecca sat and leaned over. Addie and Verona saw Sandy nod her head and then place her hand on Rebecca's shoulder.

"She was part of the rally," Sandy whispered when she returned. "Said, 'There'll never be a traffic light on this island while I'm still alive.' I can't believe the cops arrested her, though."

"She's feisty," Addie said.

"Oh, brother," Sandy said.

"All rise," said court officer Meese as Judge Portnoy entered through the door behind his bench.

"Now," the judge began, "it seems we have a group all charged with trafficking ... "

"Yes, sir, your honor," the district attorney said as he rose from his chair. "If your honor please ... "

"Enough. I understand the charges. All of these defendants allegedly supplied drugs to a police informant, is that the gist of it?"

"Yes, your honor. As a result of months of investigation ... "

"Enough," said the judge. "I understand they're all represented by one attorney."

"All except one, your honor."

"All except one." Judge Portnoy drummed his fingers. The fishing trip he'd had planned for the afternoon was looking doubtful. "And who might that be?"

"One Charles Finley, your honor."

"Charles Finley," the judge said looking down from the bench on the assembled defendants. Poor bastards, he thought. These weren't criminals. They looked like schoolboys, all except one who seemed more worldly than the others; who, dressed in his suit, emitted a certain charm, and who rose now without prompting.

"Your honor," Chuck said. "May I approach the bench?"

"And you, I presume ... "

"Charles Finley," Chuck said, stepping forward. "May I?"

The judge, resigned now to an afternoon in court, waved him forward. Chuck, accompanied by the district attorney, walked towards the judge and continued to the side of the bench. Judge Portnoy was provoked by the D.A.'s presumptiveness. "Get back down there," the judge said.

"Your honor, if I may have a word in private … " Chuck started to say.

"These are open proceedings," said the district attorney, who had followed Chuck and stood at his side. "There is no precedent … "

"Hush," said the judge. "Now, young man, you can speak quietly right here. I'll advise the court recorder that these comments, for now, will be off the record."

"Thank you, your honor," Chuck said flashing a hint of a smile. As he leaned in close to the judge's ear, the district attorney leaned forward as well. "Back off," the judge said to him, noticeably irritated now. "I'll hear what Mr. Finley has to say."

"I'm afraid there's been some kind of mistake, your honor," Chuck began.

"Oh, I'm sure there has," the judge said derisively. "Now let me get this straight: you're innocent, right?"

"Oh no, your honor, not based on these charges, anyway. I did procure drugs for their little stoolie, and I was naked when they arrested me." The judge leaned back in his chair. This couldn't be happening, he thought. But before he could order Chuck to GET AWAY FROM MY BENCH AND SIT DOWN THIS INSTANT, Chuck continued.

"You see, your honor, I'm doing a little investigating of my own. Allow me." And he reached into his suit jacket pocket and produced a leather folder that he flipped open for the judge to see.

"FBI?" the judge said. "Let me see that," and to the district attorney he said, "Why don't you take a seat?"

"But your honor … "

"SIT DOWN!"

"Go on," the judge said to Chuck.

"I'm undercover," Chuck whispered. "Been working this case the better part of two years. I couldn't tell the police when they arrested me because I've been under strict instructions not to divulge my true identity. I got caught up in this sweep as part of my surveillance activities."

"You don't say," the judge said.

Chuck moved even closer. "But I was moving in as all this went down, and now I've wrapped up my investigations. I don't have to be undercover any more."

"But isn't that dangerous?" the judge asked.

"Not with this case. She's not dangerous at all, at least not in a physical sense. But now, with all this," and he looked out at the courtroom, "it's time to bring her in."

"Will you need any assistance?" the judge asked.

"Oh, no, your honor. She has no idea. In fact she's in this courtroom as we speak."

"She is?"

"Yes, she is. Right over there."

The judge looked where he thought Chuck was looking and he looked squarely at Rebecca.

"You're here investigating Dr. Malone, aren't you?" the judge whispered to Chuck.

"Dr. Malone? She's dead, your honor. At least according to the Commonwealth of Massachusetts she is. Really now, you can't believe everything you read on those websites. You should get out more, do a little fishing." He leaned in closer still. "Just who are you looking at?"

And the judge nodded his head, surreptitiously he thought, in Rebecca's direction. He cupped his hand to his mouth. "The old lady," he said.

"What old lady?" Chuck said out loud. And the people in the courtroom then started to murmur and look around. "Order in the court," the judge said. "This is none of your business what's going on up here."

"The person's in the courtroom, your honor, but she's not that old lady. She's over there."

And Chuck turned and the judge saw him look at Verona.

"What's he doing?" Sandy asked Addie. "I don't like the looks of this."

"Oh, you know Chuck," Addie said. "Who knows what he's doing?"

"I don't think I know him at all," Sandy said. "Think about it: do you really know anything about Chuck? He talks a lot, he's friendly, but he's never really revealed anything about himself."

"Aren't all gay guys like that?" Addie said. "Who was he looking at anyway?"

Verona knew. Chuck was looking at her. It chilled her when his gaze fell in her direction. It was like he was looking right through her. He knows something, she thought, and her sense was that she wasn't going to like what he knew.

"I'd like to continue this discussion in my chambers," Judge Portnoy said to Chuck. To the packed courtroom he said: "This court will adjourn for," and he looked at the clock, "twenty minutes." The judge started to stand, but the court officer said nothing. "Mr. Meese," the judge said.

But Myron Meese didn't hear the judge because he was sleeping, his head thrown back in his chair, his mouth wide open.

"Mr. Meese," the judge said again, but Meese didn't budge.

"MR. MEESE!"

And without waking, Meese stood abruptly and said, "All rise."

"About time," the judge said as he jerked at his robes and led Chuck into his chambers.

"Now, Mr. Finley," he said as he slumped into his chair, "will you kindly tell me what is going on?"

"Be glad to, your honor," Chuck said. "For the past two years I've been investigating a woman adept in the ways of identity theft. She's been practicing her scams at various places around the country: in Florida, California, Rhode Island, you name it. She's good at it; never stayed in one place too long. As soon as we could trace her, start to move in, she'd be gone.

"While she was proficient at stealing social security numbers, credit cards and the like, she was equally skilled at concealing her own identity. She is a master of disguise, and has appeared at different times to be much older, or much younger, than she is. She has even posed as a man, which served her well in places like San Francisco and Provincetown.

"I've been working the east coast and was assigned to work undercover on Nantucket, not because there was anything to investigate here necessarily, but because I could slip in and out without attracting attention to myself. There are a lot of people here, as you know, your honor, who leave the island for the winter months, or who take vacations at odd times of the year, or are here sometimes for a week, sometimes for a weekend. The bus job was perfect for my assignment because there were so few expectations. If I needed a few days off, or a couple of weeks, there was never a problem doing so. I also had the winter off to go where I was needed. If I was assigned to a case in Texas in March and returned to the island with a tan, well, no one was going to ask me what I was up to.

"About a year ago we learned that our suspect had traveled to, of all places, Nantucket. Like so many others, she probably figured she could get lost here, but as so many have found out, it's harder to hide out on Nantucket than it is in Manhattan."

"Everybody knows everybody," the judge interjected.

"Exactly. Or there are people who make it their business to know everything about everybody. Which was also great about my cover: no one paid a second thought to me asking questions about what people did, who they were sleeping with, or where they went when they left the island. People thought I was just being nosy.

"The only thing that went wrong was Fred," Chuck continued, "our undercover snoop. I knew he was working his little scam for the police, and I tried like hell to avoid him, but he wouldn't leave me alone. If I had altered my Nantucket habits, or suddenly appeared to have found religion or something, all that work could have been blown. So you see, if I didn't buy him that little bag of coke … "

"Your suspect may have discerned you weren't acting like yourself," the judge said.

"And disappeared again. The agency agreed I couldn't take that chance, so I knew I was going to get arrested. I even made sure I was brought in right before her eyes, at a beach party. I called Fred to tell him I had some blow for him and let him know exactly where I was going to be."

The judge sat back in his chair, ruminating. "Wait a minute. What's this about public nudity?"

"All part of my cover, your honor. Our suspect would have expected me to behave that way, outlandish as it was."

"Good work, Mr. Finley, or should I call you something else?"

"You should call me Mr. Finley. I can't reveal my real name to you, or to anybody."

"Your suspect must have found easy pickings on Nantucket," the judge said.

"Quite the contrary. She laid low. In fact if headquarters hadn't alerted me to the fact that she was here, I probably wouldn't have known."

"Didn't you know what she looked like?"

"As I told you, she has a multitude of disguises. I'm assuming her appearance now is what she really looks like, or closely resembles it."

"But if she hasn't done anything here, how can you bring her in?"

"We have enough on her from her past crimes. I was able to lift some prints from a glass soda bottle she drank from and shipped it off to the lab. When I get word that it's a match, we've got her."

"And when will you get word?"

"It's coming today. That's why this court date was such an … inconvenience."

"On behalf of the police, I apologize, Mr. Finley. Wait a minute. Why would she be here?"

"She's got her own cover to consider, remember? Believe me, she thinks she's pulled it off, that no one suspects a thing. Besides, she's a friend of mine. Or thinks she is."

"You're devious, Mr. Finley."

"I'm afraid I have to be."

"But you pointed her out in the courtroom."

"What choice did I have? I couldn't blow my cover to the cops, and I couldn't chance being sent to jail by you, and I couldn't tell her, 'Oh, by the way, if you're thinking of supporting me by coming to the courthouse, think again.' As you can see, I had no choice. And I had to trust you to do the right thing."

The judge, bolstered by this statement, drew himself into a more upright position. "Should I have the police arrest her? She may try to escape."

"And give herself away? Not a chance. Besides, I could have been pointing at anybody. No, your honor, leave her to me.

"Now, about this little misunderstanding I have with the police … "

"I'll take care of it, Mr. Finley, or whatever your name is. Case closed."

"Thank you, your honor. And remember, what I've just told you is under federal jurisdiction — for your ears only. Leave the state police and island cops out of it. Your country appreciates your cooperation."

———————

Chuck left the judge's chambers, walked back into the courtroom, and calmly approached Addie in the hallway. The anti-traffic light people continued their chants. "Ready to go?" Chuck asked him.

"What the hell is going on, Chuck? What was that all about?"

"I can't tell you right now. Where's Sandy?"

"She's over there, getting a drink of water. She's really pissed at you."

"She ought to be. Where's Verona?"

"That's what I'd like to know. I thought she was going to the bathroom, but she's gone, she's not here anymore."

And without another word, Chuck headed for the stairs.

Chapter Forty-Five

SHAKEN, VERONA didn't know where to turn. She needed air, needed to get outside. Her mind reeled as she walked hurriedly from town and towards the Lily Pond, unaware of where her footsteps were taking her, unaware of the narrow streets, or the cars parked on the side streets, or the people passing by.

A sudden uneasiness gripped her. Was someone behind her? She did not want to turn to look, as if by looking someone would be following her, and so she kept walking. She had to keep moving; moving prevented her from thinking; moving stopped people from gaining on her.

And then she was outside Sandy's house, and there was her bike, and she hopped on it and rode away.

The wind that pushed against her, that collected and spun the few leaves that had fallen, was a minor irritant. In her state, she barely noticed it.

Plywood scarred the storefronts in town, some due to the aftereffects of the traffic light uprising; the others — the businesses untouched by the mob — were boarded up for more practical reasons. The weather reports were grim, as Chief Sally Nancy well knew when she'd addressed the crowd several days before. She'd been advised of the storm swirling off the Bahamas, and as she received updates and checked the computer models she feared the worst. Weather was upmost on most Nantucketers' minds, and she hoped they were paying attention to the predictions. Every boat in the harbor had to be hauled or tied down immediately.

"The wind is in from Africa," rightly sang Joni Mitchell. Hurricanes begin off the coast of Africa as low-pressure systems that follow the trade winds into the Atlantic. Nourished by the tropical ocean, and reinforced by wet, warm air, the low pressure gathers air from all directions and expands into a giant cylinder that feeds on itself as it rotates in a counterclockwise direction across the summer waters. The combination of humidity and warm water increases the area of low pressure, producing intense energy, and high winds, as the trade winds push the giant storm towards either the North or South Pole. As long as the hurricane is over a relatively warm ocean, and can feed on moist air, it will continue to circulate and grow.

Nantucket hadn't been hit with a big one in years, but it had been an unusually hot summer, and this particular storm, Chief Nancy knew, had catastrophic potential.

With all that had been going on lately, capped by Chuck's appearance in court, Addie and Sandy had no idea what was brewing in the Atlantic. Neither had seen a TV or listened to the radio in days, but when Sandy returned home after witnessing Chuck's finger-pointing display, there was a phone message from Ken.

"Where's Chuck?" he asked when she called him back. "He's not answering his cell."

"Damned if I know, and, to be honest, I don't care."

"I need him to help get these buses back to the lot," Ken said. "Have you seen Addie?"

"He was with me earlier, but I don't know where he is now."

"Look," Ken said. "Get down here right away. I could use your help battening down this office and getting all the buses moved out of here."

"What's going on?"

"There's a storm coming, fast. I want to get this place closed up and get the hell out of here. I don't know how much longer the boats will be running; if I have to, I'll fly."

"You're leaving the island?"

"And if you knew what was good for you, you'd be leaving too. Get down here as soon as you can, and if you see Addie get him down here too."

Sandy raced through her house, closed her windows. Verona wasn't in her room, and she called to her as she went from room to room. Must be with Addie, she thought. The poor thing could probably use a little consoling right now.

And as she sped down to the wharf her only thought was to murder Chuck. She didn't know what he was up to, but the look on Verona's face when he pointed at her was disturbing; she hated seeing Verona so upset, and she didn't want to figure out what Chuck's pointing at her had to do with it — not now. He better not be at the wharf, if he knew what was good for him.

"Give me a hand clearing this stuff out of the yard," Digit was saying to Addie. "We don't want anything blowing around out here."

After Chuck left the courthouse Addie ran back to Digit's to get his car and search for Verona. Verona was pale when she left the courtroom so suddenly; he thought she might be sick.

"Something's wrong with Verona," he said as he helped Digit stow scallop nets in his shanty. "I've got to go find her."

"I'd think Ken will be needing your help getting things squared away on the wharf after this," Digit said. "Verona can take care of herself."

"Why would Ken need my help? What are you talking about?"

"Haven't you heard?" Digit stopped what he was doing and looked at his friend. "A hurricane's coming. Tonight, this afternoon maybe."

Addie noticed that the wind had picked up, but that was nothing unusual; it was always windy on Nantucket. "How bad?" Addie asked.

"Bad," Digit said. "Real bad. A hundred-year storm, or worse. I've been tracking it all day. Where the hell have you been?"

"In court. We went to see how Chuck would make out."

Digit motioned for Addie to help him move some lumber away from his house. "I'm surprised they even had court today," he said. "How did he make out?"

"Chuck? I'm not sure. He talked to the judge privately for most of the time, and then it looked like he pointed to Verona. And then she got sick or something … "

"Tell me later," Digit said. "I can handle the rest of this. Get down to the wharf and help Ken. And then get your ass back here. I'm going to get what I can at the store, fill the tub with water, and board up as many windows as I can. Let's hope we can get everything done in time."

Addie drove towards the wharf in a daze. The other drivers he saw had crazed, wild-eyed looks, and a long line of cars was making its way to the boat. "What should I do?" he thought. He should help Ken, but he was worried about Verona. He only hoped Sandy would be at the wharf. She'd know where Verona was. She had to.

The cars were backed up for blocks leading to the wharves, so Addie made a U-turn and parked near the Lobster Trap restaurant. He ran to the bus office, where Ken was nailing plywood over the windows.

"Where's Sandy?" Addie asked him.

"At the lot. Chuck's on his way out there in my car to pick her up. Grab those keys and take that last bus out there, will you? I'll radio Sandy that you're on your way, and Chuck can give you both a ride.

"But if I were you I'd have him drive you right back here and get on the boat. The last one's leaving in a half hour."

———

The last person Sandy wanted to see was Chuck, but under the circumstances she supposed she had to. Ken was right, there was a wicked storm coming, she could feel it, and business had to be tended to.

And then she could kill Chuck.

She waited in her bus for him to pick her up and watched the treetops shudder in the sudden gusts of wind. The storm was picking up fast, and she could only hope that Verona was at home, that she'd seek haven there.

———

Pedaling with abandon, Verona headed away from town, away from the narrow streets, away from the questions and confusion of the courthouse. She wanted to escape the eyes she imagined were seeking her out, to ride away from this day. Although there was no one on the streets she sensed there were people pointing at her, telling each other they'd found her at last.

She had killed a man, she was sure of it now. Even though she had tried to ignore them, the visions became clearer each time they reappeared — a man's body beneath her; she standing above it.

Why had she gone to that courtroom? As soon as she entered, saw all the people, the eyes staring at her, she wanted to leave. Why had she put herself out there like that, on display before the whole island? What had happened to staying within her small circle of friends?

Because her small circle of friends was going to support Chuck and she tagged along without thinking. For months she had tried fooling herself with her non-thinking mantra, but she knew all along what she was afraid to admit — that the past couldn't be erased even if you couldn't remember it. Rather than running from it, she should have confronted it.

But now it was too late. Now they were on to her, for whatever she had done.

She sought cover, protection from the open air, from the flat fragile openness of the island. A trail led into the woods and she eagerly followed it, letting the trees enclose her, enfold her, embrace her. The wind that had been picking up as she rode through town now seemed confined to the treetops as it battled the highest branches and left the forest floor becalmed for the moment. As she rounded a bend a wisp of smoke rose from fallen pine needles. Forgetting her predicament for the moment, she paused to ensure there was no fire.

To her side, the earth moved, and moved again as a square of earth shifted and an opening was revealed. And then came a hand, and a head that expressed surprise at seeing her. "What are you doing here?" it asked as the body attached to it stepped up into the daylight.

Verona wondered why this person looked familiar to her.

"You're not going to tell anybody, are you?" he asked. She recognized him then; it was the man she'd come across in the woods months before. So much had happened since then. She wished now that she'd stayed here in the woods with him.

"Well?" he said to her. "Are you going to talk?"

"You're the man who lives here," she said to him.

"You know me?"

"I saw you leave here one day."

"And you didn't tell anyone?" His question wasn't threatening. It was just a question.

"I'd forgotten all about it," she answered honestly. "Are you hiding?"

"Hiding? I don't think so. People in town know me. I work. I just have to be selective who I let know about this place." He laughed. "The town doesn't look kindly on people who don't pay rent, or taxes.

"This is my home," he explained. "I built it from scraps I found at building sites, dragging it here after dark. It's the only way I can afford to stay here."

Verona wanted to ask him how he'd dug out the room in the first place, where he got the wood paneling, but thought better of it. All she could say was, "Oh." The wind was picking up. It rushed through the rows of trees like an invisible train, billowing Verona's skirt in its wake.

"You'd better find shelter," the man said to her. "There's a big storm coming."

"Can I stay with you?" Verona asked. She envisioned being swallowed safely by the ground, hidden from everyone.

"Afraid not," he said. "I've already got a lady friend coming. I was coming out to get more firewood." He looked at Verona, saw the sadness in her eyes. "There's not much room down there," he said. " Believe me, if she wasn't coming I'd ask you to stay."

As soon as he said this, Verona was glad he had company. She saw in his eyes what this man's intentions were. If she was going to live underground, she wanted to live there alone.

"Let me ask you," the man said to her. "What are you hiding from?"

The question froze her. "Look, don't get me wrong," he continued, "there's nothing wrong with hiding out. Half this island's hiding from something, but it's knowing what you're hiding from that counts. How else will you know where to hide?"

Verona had to leave, she had to keep moving. "Find somewhere fast," the man called to her as she pedaled away, "this storm's coming quickly. But as soon as it blows over, come on back. My bed's big enough for two."

———————

Verona wanted to head back to Sandy's, to the safety of her room, but she didn't know what, or who, would be waiting for her back in town. She had to get somewhere, though, she could sense the storm approaching.

She pedaled against the wind as she rode out to 'Sconset. A stream of cars passed her, all traveling in the opposite direction.

Police cruisers with their lights flashing were either encamped along the road, ensuring that people were headed towards town, or were blocking traffic heading out to 'Sconset. None of them were looking at the bike path.

When she reached the high point overlooking the cranberry bog at Bean Hill, she stopped for a second to catch her breath. As long as she was moving she didn't think of consequences, of Chuck pointing her out to the judge; of being found out; of someone knowing who she really was. It gave her no relief that the man in the woods didn't seem to care. He was right about one thing, though: she didn't know where to hide.

Squinting into the swirling wind she looked out over the cranberry bog and across the moors to Sankaty, whose blinking beacon beckoned. It seemed like such a long way away.

As she pushed off down the hill, the wind came at her with

a sideways force that nearly drove her off the bike path. She had to make the lighthouse — she could think there, she'd know what to do. It was the only place of solitude she could imagine.

Pedaling got harder as she passed the open plains of the golf courses along the Milestone Road. The wind seemed to be hitting her from all directions. She got off her bike and walked until she felt a lull and then she got back on and pedaled again.

When she saw the turnoff to the lighthouse she knew she wouldn't be able to make it. The wind was against her. There would be no solace at the light today.

Her options diminishing, she rode into 'Sconset as the wind hissed and moaned around her, the wind that seemed to have blown all the life out of the village. Needing to move, she continued on to Codfish Park, the small summer settlement that fronted the eastern shore and the open Atlantic. The next stop eastward, as Addie would inform his passengers when he reached this point on the tour, was Spain. Verona pedaled to the end of the road where the wild ocean confronted her. The wind, more violent now, battered the waves, forcing them to wildly crest and fall.

Pushed forward by the increasing wind, the ocean climbed quickly over the beach as if it was trying to grab her. In the distance, she heard, in counterpoint to the moaning, howling wind, a steady banging. Walking her bike toward the clatter she saw its source: an unsecured cottage door that flapped incessantly. Without thinking, taking what shelter she could, Verona raced through the door as it opened and threw her weight against it to close it and lock it.

There was no one there. The small house had a living room with sliding glass doors fronting the beach, a galley-type kitchen, and two little bedrooms. The wind seemed louder now that she was inside and when she could stand it and the roaring ocean no longer she went into a bedroom, lay down, and pulled the covers over her head.

Now that she had stopped moving, the day's events flooded her mind. The pressure drop preceding the storm sucked the air from the room and made her drowsy. Despite the rattling windows that shook furiously with every increasing blast of wind, and despite the thoughts that thundered inside her head, she fell asleep.

Chapter Forty-Six

CHUCK WAS smiling when he pulled into the lot. "The bastard," Sandy thought when she saw him, but her thoughts were interrupted by the radio.

"Sandy, come in. Sandy, this is Ken."

"You just caught me, Ken. That laughing bastard Chuck is here."

"Hang out there a minute. Addie's on his way with the last bus. He needs to catch a ride with you two."

Chuck was at the door of the bus as Ken was saying this, his expression now changed, his ever-present smile vanished. He looked serious, almost pained, Sandy thought — as if the bastard could feel pain.

"All right, Ken," she said into the microphone. "We'll wait for him."

"I'll be on the boat," Ken said. "I hope you'll all join me."

"Doubtful, Ken. Maybe laughing Charlie will do us all a favor and leave."

"Whatever that means," Ken said. "Good luck."

Hints of rain swirled in the wind as Chuck, hands in pockets, stood outside the door to Sandy's bus. She glared at him through the glass, turned away to look through her windshield. Chuck rapped lightly on the door.

"Come on, Sandy, I know you're pissed. Probably been calling me a bastard and worse than that. Let me talk to you. At least let me in. Hey, it's getting pretty windy out here, have you noticed? Look, if you don't want to talk I'll just leave." Chuck didn't know Addie was on his way out to the lot.

Sandy opened the bus door a crack. "How could you?" she said.

"I had no choice. There was no other way."

"I can't forgive what you did to Verona."

"Verona?"

"When you pointed her out in the courtroom, you asshole. Oh, why am I even talking to you?"

"I wasn't pointing at Verona," Chuck said. "I was looking at you."

Sandy opened her door. "Get in here, you idiot. It's starting to rain."

Chuck boarded the bus, sat behind Sandy. Unlike his usual garrulous self, Chuck now said nothing.

"All right," Sandy said. "Do you want to tell me what's going on? And it better be good."

"How do I say this delicately?"

"Chuck, will you cut the bullshit for once in your life? Just tell me what happened."

"That asshole, Fred," Chuck began. "How was I to know he was a narc? He kept pestering me, and pestering me. I just wanted to get him off my back, you know? So I got him a little blow."

"We know all that, Chuck. That's why we were in the courtroom."

"So I couldn't afford another conviction. I haven't exactly led a life of discretion, you know. I was arrested a couple of times, nothing big, a pot bust here, a reckless driving charge there. I couldn't take a chance I'd get off this time. If they wanted to make an example of me, they had plenty of ammunition."

"What does that have to do with … "

"So I told the judge I was with the FBI, and that I was undercover investigating this woman who was stealing people's credit cards and social security numbers. It was the first thing that popped into my head. I'd just seen a story about it on TV."

"And … ?"

"And so I kind of looked in your direction."

"You bastard, you lowlife. You'd finger me to save your own ass?"

"What choice did I have, Sandy?"

Sandy looked up at the roof of the bus and sighed. "So now the cops will be after me."

"Not a chance. I told him this was my investigation and it'd be his ass if he involved the cops in any way. And … he bought it. It was the best performance of my life. All off the top of my head."

"So that's it," Sandy said, not looking at him. "And you think that's the end of it. You implicate me … "

"I didn't implicate anybody. He thought I was talking about that old lady Rebecca at first. He has no idea who I was supposed to be looking at. Believe me, Sandy, you've got nothing to worry about."

"Seems to me I've got a lot to worry about."

"There's nothing to worry about. The judge thinks he's helping out the government by letting me handle this bogus investigation. He has no names. What are they going to do, come after every woman who was in that courtroom?"

"You didn't give him my name?"

"Of course not. The only name he has is mine, and that's going to be changing soon. It's time for a new life. I cleaned out my place last week and shipped it all to a friend in Mexico. There's no trace of me left on Nantucket, and good luck finding me."

"So you're leaving?"

"Right now. Let's go. I'm on that boat with Ken. This hurricane couldn't have come at a better time."

A vehicle with its headlights on drove into the lot and appeared to be headed right at them.

"What the hell is that?" Chuck said, alarmed.

"It's only Addie," Sandy said. "We're moving buses, remember? A little skittish, are we? Can't say you don't deserve it."

"I'll be glad when I get off this island. You can't trust anybody around here."

"Just one thing," Sandy said. "How did you convince the judge you were with the FBI?"

"Oh, that," he said, reaching into his back pocket. Sandy flipped open the leather case.

"It's you," she said. "Is it fake? It looks real."

"Oh, it's real, all right. It's my dad's. Look just like him, don't I? A regular chip off the old block. Good thing the judge didn't check out the date. My father's been retired for years.

"And man, will he ever be pissed if he finds out."

———

"Where's Verona?" was the first thing Sandy asked when the three of them piled into Ken's station wagon. The look on Addie's face told her all she needed to know.

"I thought you knew," he said. "Chuck, we have to go find her."

"No way, Jose," Chuck said as he headed down Old South Road towards town. "I'm getting on that boat. You guys can go look for her when I'm out of here."

"Well, step on it then," Addie said.

"I'm obeying the speed limit, man," Chuck said. "I'm not breaking any laws today."

"Oh, yeah," Addie remembered. "What the heck happened in court today? Why did you point at Verona?"

"I wasn't pointing at Verona? Why does everyone think that?"

"Then who were you pointing at?"

Chuck put both hands on the steering wheel, hunched his shoulders, stared straight through the windshield. "Look, I've got a lot on my mind right now," he said. "I've got to pay attention here. Can we cut the blab for a while? Do you mind? Sandy can fill you in later."

Addie looked at Sandy, whose look assured him things were going to be all right. "I'm just worried about her, that's all," Addie said.

Traffic near the wharves was brutal. Chuck hopped out when the cars were backed up near the old power plant. "Hasta la vista, kids," he said. "I'm a boat person now."

Even with what he'd told her, even with what he'd done in the courtroom that afternoon, Sandy was a little saddened to see him go. One more character was leaving the island, even if that character didn't always possess the best judgment. She watched him run jauntily past the lineup of cars. The rain was getting heavier now; Chuck picked up his pace, turned toward the wharf, and was gone.

Sandy slid over in her seat and got behind the wheel. "We'll go to my house first," she said to Addie. "Let's hope she's there. We've got some time, but not much, before this storm hits."

Chapter Forty-Seven

"How do we get out of this traffic jam?" Addie wanted to know.

"Just watch me."

The cars in front of her were going nowhere, so Sandy did the only thing she could do — she threw it in reverse. The car behind her didn't pay attention to the backup lights at first, but when Sandy started moving backwards, the driver hit his horn lightly. But when he saw she wasn't stopping he laid on the horn. With her foot off the gas, but without braking, and still moving slowly backwards, Sandy kept her hand on the wheel and stuck her head out the window. "I'm backing up," she said loudly, pointing in that direction with her thumb. The guy behind her then stuck his head out his window and barked, "Where do you think you're going?"

Braking now, but keeping Ken's car in reverse, Sandy said to the man, "Look, if you start to back up, the guy behind you will back up and I can get the hell out of here."

"Are you crazy?"

"All right then," Sandy said, taking her foot of the brake and onto the gas pedal and backing up slowly again. "As soon as I tap his bumper he'll get the message," she said to Addie.

As Sandy backed up, the man laid on his horn, prompting others to do the same. Before long, the air was filled with the irritating din of car horns combined with the noisy confusion generated by the coming storm, but Sandy kept backing up, pushing Ken's car against the bumper of the car behind her. "Back up, you moron," she said. "The guy behind you will get the message. I just need an inch or two."

And the guy behind her, after trying to hold his ground, relented at last and threw his car into reverse, yelling out his window to the car behind him, "Back up before she wrecks my bumper. Let's get her out of here."

And the few inches was all Sandy needed to pull a U-turn and head away from town, waving a 'thank you' to the man as she did. "Never hurts to be polite," she said.

Sandy drove up Coffin Street to Union Street and took the right towards Main Street.

"Hey, you're heading back toward town," Addie told her.

"I know what I'm doing."

Sandy was right. All the traffic was below Main Street, heading to the boats and the grocery store. She turned left up Main Street. The town's main thoroughfare, clogged with people and traffic in summer, was pretty much deserted, with only a few people wandering around. Addie could feel the wind as it tunneled up Main Street and pushed at the car. The boarded up storefronts gave the old town a desolate look, as if everyone had abandoned the island. Addie thought back to that tour when he was asked about evacuation plans. "How bad do you think this is going to get?" he asked Sandy.

"Bad," she said.

When they got to her house, after driving up Main Street past the historic homes built by whale oil merchants, ship builders, and candle manufacturers ("These old things made out of brick should do all right you'd think," Sandy said to Addie. "I'm not so sure about everything that's shingled"), a tree was already blown over in the Lily Pond. Addie and Sandy ran through the house calling for Verona. Sandy went outside and looked around back.

"Her bike's not here," she said. "Damn it. I was praying this wouldn't happen."

"Come on," Addie said. "We've got to go find her."

When they got in the car Addie said to Sandy: "I'm worried about her. What did Chuck tell you? Did it have anything to do with her leaving the courtroom?"

"No, it didn't," she said. "At least I don't think it did. I'm not sure what's up with her, but I'm worried about her too."

"So where do we look?" Addie asked her.

"The lighthouse," Sandy said. "Sankaty."

The cops were out in force, trying to get people to stay in their homes. At the island's central rotary, a state police cruiser was blocking traffic to 'Sconset.

"Road's closed," he told Sandy. "Go home."

"I'm trying to go home," Sandy said. "We live in 'Sconset."

"We're evacuating 'Sconset," he said. "Everyone's supposed to go to the high school. There's a shelter set up there."

"Look, I've got an elderly grandmother out there," Sandy said. "We've got to go get her."

"The fire department's out there picking people up. They've probably taken her to the high school already."

"They can't have checked every single house out there," Sandy insisted. "And I know her, she won't leave until she sees me."

The cop paused for a second. He wasn't a bad boy, Sandy could tell. "All right," he said. "I'm not supposed to do this, but get back into town as fast as you can."

"Don't worry, I will."

"Do you really have a grandmother out there?" Addie asked her as they sped down the Milestone Road.

"What do you think?"

"Well, I believed you."

———————

The wind had increased dramatically by the time they reached the lighthouse. Sandy and Addie could barely open the car doors and, once outside, the wind pummeled them so hard it was tough standing up.

There was no sign of Verona anywhere. They made the difficult trek to the light, hoping the door would be open and Verona would be inside, but the door was locked tight. The light, built so strongly of granite in 1850, seemed to sway in what was now a steady gale.

"Where is she?" Addie yelled into the wind that blew his words into the swirling air as soon as they left his mouth.

Sandy could only shake her head. They headed back to the car.

"Where else could she be?" Addie asked. "We've got to find her."

Sandy pushed her hair from her brow. "She's not here, obviously. I mean, her bike would be here, wouldn't it? She's probably back home."

Outside the rolled up car windows the wind screamed off the bluff. "Let's just head back," Sandy said, "and hope we make it."

"I feel that she's out here somewhere," Addie said. "Can't we look somewhere else while we're out here?"

"Where?" Sandy said, exasperated now.

"Let's take a quick ride through 'Sconset, see if we see her bike."

STEVE SHEPPARD

"Look, Addie, we haven't got time. What if she's home? We won't be doing anybody any good if we get stuck out here."

"Please, Sandy. Just a drive down Main Street. If you thought she came out here, she could be somewhere in the village."

"A quick look, and that's all."

Salt spray coated the windshield as Sandy drove back down the bluff and towards the village. Addie strained to see if Verona's bicycle was anywhere along the way. On 'Sconset's Main Street, tree branches still laden with summer leaves swayed heavily. "We've got to get out of here before a tree falls on us," Sandy said. Addie looked past the post office and to Gulley Road, the street leading to Codfish Park. "Sandy, ride through Codfish Park and then we'll head back."

"Are you nuts? The road's probably washed out by now."

"I've got a feeling," Addie said.

"I've got a feeling you're crazy," Sandy said, as she reluctantly headed down the road to Codfish Park.

The ocean was breaking high onto the beach, the waves rolling up over the sand and onto the roadway. To the left, where the road continued along the shore, the water had already encircled the few beach cottages that were there. Beyond that, the road was under water.

"That's it," Sandy said. "We're out of here."

And as she negotiated the three-point turn neither she nor Addie saw the bicycle, its tires halfway submerged, leaning against the beach cottage two houses down.

"Let's hope to hell we can get back to town," Sandy said as she drove up 'Sconset's Main Street. All Addie wished was that Verona was already back at Sandy's waiting for them.

———

She woke to what she thought was a scream, but as she sat up in bed she realized it was the wind that seemed to tear with

272

conscious rage at the outside of the little cottage. Verona wanted to leave, but as the cottage suddenly shuddered in the wind she knew there was no escape. She could only hope the worst of the storm had occurred and that the wind would eventually subside.

But, as she soon discovered, things would only get worse.

Chapter Forty-Eight

IT TOOK Sandy an hour to make a trip that usually took twenty-five minutes. On the way back to town the Milestone Road was deserted; even the cops had sought shelter. She plowed through deep puddles, hoping Ken's station wagon would make it, avoided downed tree limbs and fought against the raging wind that pushed and prodded the car.

In town, fallen elms blocked streets, their long-fingered limbs reaching across property lines; water pooled around house foundations, in some cases hiding the foundations altogether. "We'll be lucky if I have a home to go to," Sandy thought. But there it was, still standing.

The Lily Pond lived up to its name as rain saturated the low-lying wetlands, creating pools of water that were on the rise throughout the property. Sandy knew her basement would flood. If that was the extent of the damage, she could live with that.

Addie's heart fluttered in anticipation as he entered the house. "Is she here?" Sandy asked, as she pushed the bolt through the front door and began searching for candles. Addie walked quickly from room to room; by the time he reached Verona's bedroom he knew she wasn't there. Her bedroom seemed cold to him, even though it was still technically summer.

"There's nothing we can do now, but wait," Sandy said when he met her in the kitchen. "Verona's a smart girl; she's somewhere safe."

"But where can she be?"

"Maybe she's at your house."

Of course, Addie thought. Why hadn't he thought of that in the first place? "Where's your phone?" he asked Sandy.

"Right over there," she said, "but it won't do you any good. I've already tried it. The lines are dead."

Damn it, he thought. Why didn't he have a cell phone like everybody else? "You don't … "

"Cell phone? Nope. After seeing all those assholes all summer talking to themselves it pretty much put me off getting one."

And as Sandy got another candle lit, the power went out.

"That's it," she said to Addie. "All we can do now is hope for the best." And she pulled open a kitchen drawer and took out a deck of cards. "Cribbage?"

———

The storm intensified as it approached the island. Sandy and Addie felt the house shake as the wind and rain punished the shingles, rattled the windows. They did not know what was going on outside. Addie couldn't get Verona off his mind.

"If it helps, I'm thinking of her too," Sandy said to him softly.

———

In 'Sconset, the little cottage was besieged by the wind, waves, and rain. Verona clung to the bed, wishing it would end. It was all happening so quickly now; the day's events in the courtroom seemed like a week ago.

But Chuck had pointed at her. He knew something. What?

What did he know?

Had Chuck been on to her the whole time? Had he followed her to the island? Was he a cop? If so, why hadn't he arrested her?

As the storm shook the little cottage, Verona's thoughts turned to more immediate matters. She wished she hadn't come out here, wished she'd turned to Addie, or Sandy, instead of hopping on her bike. But her mind had been racing — she needed to move, to run away, to keep her thoughts at bay. The storm seemed now to be laughing at her, mocking her: who did she think she was?

She wished she knew; she wished she knew everything. If she did, perhaps she wouldn't be out here, alone.

———————

Addie couldn't concentrate on cribbage, didn't want to play a game, didn't want to be stuck in this house. He walked to the kitchen, paced back into the living room, picked up Sandy's old copy of *The Electric Kool-Aid Acid Test,* flipped through it in the candlelight, put it back down. "What are you doing?" Sandy said without looking at him.

"I can't sit still," he said. They both heard a crash from upstairs. "Shit," Sandy said. "Don't tell me a tree's fallen through the roof."

They ran upstairs and felt the wind rushing through Verona's room. But instead of a broken window it was merely a window that had opened. A gust of wind had knocked over the light on the bedside table. Nothing gave evidence of something crashing into the house.

Addie struggled to close the old window, finally got it locked. As they turned to leave the room, Addie saw the flicker of Sandy's candle reflected in the mirror.

"Wait," he said to her.

"What now?" she asked.

"Bring that candle back here for a minute; I think there's something written on the mirror."

Sandy's face appeared ghostly in the candle's shadow. When she held the candle up to the mirror, all they saw at first was the flickering yellow flame.

"Stand to the side," Addie said. "I'm sure there's something there."

"That's just dust," Sandy said.

"Let me see that candle," Addie said, but as he moved the flame back and forth in front of the mirror all he could see were remnants of streaks left behind by a polishing cloth. He must have imagined what he saw. He was sure he had seen the word: "Gone."

She couldn't be gone. When this storm was over he'd never leave her side.

In 'Sconset, the winds seemed to abate, the moaning storm to cease its relentless attack. Verona rose cautiously from the rickety bed, slowly got her bearings as if she was on a boat and needed to get her sea legs under her. She could hear slight wisps of wind now outside the cottage, as if the storm had tired and was moving on. She listened for the reassuring call of a gull but there was only silence.

Verona couldn't see the surge rolling in from the ocean, the great tidal upheaval that mounted and moved now towards the shore and the little cottage as the night took hold.

Chapter Forty-Nine

T HE LAST of the storm released its grip on the island the next morning. Its course had altered so that instead of making a predicted landfall between Martha's Vineyard and Nantucket, which would have been disastrous, it lessened in intensity and veered to the right before it reached Long Island. Still, it remained a Category 2 storm — a hurricane to remember.

Sandy's house had survived the onslaught, but water ponded around the foundation and Addie was knee deep as he surveyed the damage.

The brightening sky was white against the grey remnants of the neighborhood. Broken shingles and snapped boughs covered the ground. The treeline was jagged and haphazard, making the street resemble a horror movie set. Ken's car had been pushed sideways, its windows fogged with salt spray, and an eerie stillness was in the air.

There would be no driving or biking anywhere from here, Addie knew, and as soon as he was sure Sandy was fine he was off.

He expected the worst as he walked towards Digit's house,

but he was gladdened when the parts of the island he saw along the way had survived nature's hit. Tree limbs littered lawns and streets were pretty much impassable, but things could have been worse. As he passed the Homestead he saw a giant elm uprooted and leaning against the roof, the tree's root system surprisingly small and thin in the island's sandy soil. But the old building was still intact; a little roof damage, perhaps, but that was about it.

At Digit's house, barrels, lobster-pot buoys, bits and pieces of lumber, nylon netting, ladders, and red plastic gas cans were strewn about the property. Parts of the picket fence were either missing entirely, or had been knocked down by the wind, giving it a gap-toothed look.

But when Addie went looking for Digit, his friend wasn't there.

Which for some reason gave Addie an uneasy feeling about Verona.

———————

Addie set out immediately for his rental, hoping Verona was safely inside or that he would meet her along the way if she was out looking for him. He prayed. He quickened his pace as he passed islanders who stood outside their houses with surprised yet blank expressions, as if they had just completed a roller coaster ride but hadn't yet had time to grasp what had happened.

Wires were down and work crews were already out. Chainsaws could be heard in the distance; their intermittent sputters and barks the soundtrack of slow recovery.

He didn't notice the pickup truck that pulled alongside him. There had been no other cars on the road, not even police cars. "Hop in," Digit said through the rolled down passenger window. "If you're heading to your place, I've already been there."

"Is she … "

"No one's there, not even you. Where the hell've you been?"

"I was stranded at Sandy's." His heart sank; Verona wasn't where he'd hoped she'd be.

"We'll find her," Digit said, reading his mind.

"So she wasn't with you either?"

"No. And I worried all night about you. To top it off, I was stuck with Marsha and her new boyfriend because the road was blocked to his house. What could I do? I couldn't turn them out into the storm. What a pleasant evening we had."

"Really?"

"No."

"I'm worried about her, Digit."

"I know you are, but she's all right. I haven't heard of any casualties, and I've been out for a couple of hours already. Old North Wharf's gone, surprise, surprise, and Straight Wharf's all torn up — there's bricks piled up all over the place, like an earthquake. Brant Point's underwater all the way to the Jetties, and the steeple's blown off the Congregational Church.

"And it's a good thing they moved that lighthouse," he continued. "Sankaty lost at least twenty feet."

"Don't worry," Digit said when he saw Addie comprehend none of it. "We'll find her. We'll check the high school first and take it from there."

"Is it all right to drive?" Addie asked as he opened the passenger side door.

"Of course it's all right to drive."

"I mean, isn't there a state of emergency or something?"

"You've forgotten my bumper stickers," Digit reminded him. "I told you they'd come in handy."

Addie looked blankly through the windshield as Digit drove, not noticing the ripped off roofs, upended trees, or downed telephone poles along the way. *Oh, Verona, you need me now,* he thought. *I need you now.*

———

While islanders sorted through the rubble in the windless aftermath, the storm continued its push eastward, out to sea eventually, but not before kissing 'Sconset goodbye.

The lull Verona had sensed before nightfall was merely that — a lull that strengthened and magnified with seeming malice. The first wave hit as she lay fitfully on the metal cot. It wasn't a pounding, but a steady, insistent pressure that felt alarmingly alive. When the wave subsided, Verona heard a great whoosh!, like millions of scuttling crabs.

The next wave was not as benign. It was as though by receding it sought reinforcement, and it struck with unremitting fury.

———

At the high school, dazed occupants shuffled from the gym, many greeting family members with teary hugs. Digit said subdued hellos to people he knew as Addie passed among the rows of cots placed from one end of the gymnasium to the other. As if on the deck of a wave-tossed ship, he faltered with the awareness that she was not among those who remained. He stood unsteadily and scanned the room again and again, benumbed to what he saw until everything, the cots, the pushed back bleachers and the incongruous basketball hoops kaleidoscoped into a blur.

When Digit went looking for his friend it was as if Addie had shrunk: he barely saw him alone in a corner, his eyes downcast.

"She's not here, is she?" he said. Addie looked at him blankly.

"She's somewhere, Addie," Digit said, trying his best to sound reassuring. "I've asked the cops stationed here: there were no casualties, other than some guy who had a heart attack, but they said he would've had that anyway. Let's not mope around here — let's head out to 'Sconset. I just heard that Codfish Park took the brunt of this. The shoreline's gone."

281

Addie's mind shut down when he heard the words, "Codfish Park." He followed his friend submissively to the school parking lot, where cars calmly shuttled in and out, patience holding sway in the aftermath of calamity.

In 'Sconset, Digit parked on Main Street in the spot reserved in the summer for buses. A footbridge that traversed the road leading down to Codfish Park remained stalwart despite its rickety appearance, and several people were lined against the walkway's rail, watching the out of control ocean.

The swingset that had stood on the beach for decades was gone, but so was the beach. "Incredible," Addie heard someone say, and while there were other exclamations, he could only decipher unintelligible murmurings above the ocean's unhampered roar.

They all saw it then, as if unleashed from great barrier walls, the ocean rushing with force onto the beach. It swept and swelled under and around a little cottage to the left, rising again as it did so, and with giant arms of water pulled the building off its cinderblock foundation — as if it were a treasure to be claimed — and tugging, tugging, slowly carried the cottage back into the sea.

Caught in the swirling and energetic tide, the cottage bobbed and jerked as it was first swept outward and then swallowed by the ocean's force. Like a cork, it popped forcefully from its immersed state, breaking the surface and releasing white trails of spray across its rooftop. But then it was forced and compelled along the shore and further out to sea as the onlookers watched helplessly.

"Oh, my God," someone gasped, but most stood mute, spellbound.

The whole episode seemed so unreal that it at first transfixed Addie, but then he realized with certainty, as he had felt from the beginning of the storm, that this is where Verona had ended up, that she was here in Codfish Park, that he shouldn't have given up so easily when he was with Sandy and the ocean was merely lapping over the streets and beach.

He had to move. He walked slowly at first, then ran off the footbridge and onto the high road that overlooked the shore. He ran along the bluff, keeping his eyes on the cottage, trying not to think what his heart was telling him, that Verona was somehow involved, that he had been led here to witness this. Ahead was a path leading down to what was once the beach. Digit caught up to him as Addie clumsily started down the steep bank, side-stepping into the wind.

"Addie," Digit yelled. "What are you doing?"

"I've got to get down there."

"You aren't going anywhere, pal. Those waves will suck you out, sure as shit. You see what they did to that cottage."

"I've got to get to her."

"Her?"

"Verona … "

"Verona?" Her name was carried by the wind from Digit's lips and cast offshore.

"She's in there. I know it."

And they both watched as the little cottage was swept east along the shore, remaining miraculously intact for a couple of hundred yards or so, as though it was a modern day ark. But bits of its siding broke off, the roof began to lift, and the side heading into the waves ultimately caved, undermining the remaining walls until the entire thing collapsed into a floating wrack of lumber.

They heard the shocked murmurings from the people on the bridge as they, too, witnessed the devastation, but neither Addie nor Digit saw the bicycle that trailed behind, its handlebars riding above the waves until they finally, inexorably, went under.

The waves continued to mount and ride halfway up the bank, pummeling what was left of the cottage. "Let's get out of here," Digit said. Sirens sounded in the distance, the police coming to shoo everyone home. "No one was inside. There couldn't have been."

"I've got to make sure," Addie said in a whisper, his voice hoarse even though he had been quiet most of the morning. "You must know another way down there."

"Don't be crazy."

"Please, Digit." And Digit saw the desperation in his friend's eyes.

"Well, we could try heading down to Low Beach and see if we could backtrack … "

Digit avoided the cops and fire engines as he wended through the back streets of 'Sconset and down to Low Beach. He was able to drive the pickup onto the road heading to the sewer beds, but the rising and swelling ocean prevented further progress. "Might as well take our shoes off," Digit said. "We're going to get wet."

They walked back toward the wreckage along the newly carved shoreline, trudging through the soaked and sodden beach grass, at times having to scamper and crab back up the bank to escape the encroaching and determined waves.

They got as near as they could but were stopped by the pounding surf. All they saw was a pile of rubble rocked in and out on the tide, and what looked to be a metal framed bed flung to the side. Addie looked out into the ocean, trying to see anything in the waves, but the water crashed into and upon itself so fiercely and quickly that nothing was distinguishable except the dark maw of the elements.

Chapter Fifty

IT CAME back to her slowly yet insistently, an unfolding that wouldn't stop, and she yielded to it, letting the thoughts roll through her, giving in to the swirling images that months ago would have sent her running, or bicycling, as if by moving she could somehow escape her crowded mind.

But the flood rolling through her brain relaxed her like a drug, calmed her, and she comprehended it all as though it was a movie, and she was merely watching.

It was the shock of the second wave engulfing the cottage, she realized later, that triggered the awakening — the will to live, to escape, that snapped her from her dream.

She felt the force of the water pushing, pulling against the cottage, draining the atmosphere so that she inadvertently gulped as if she was indeed drowning. The walls and windows shook, and she was sure the cottage was about to collapse around her. Yet the cottage held, and as the pressure outside increased the door suddenly burst open and, pausing at first, she lunged towards it and out into the rising water. She fell but willed herself to stand. She was waist deep, drenched, and the merciless ocean tried pulling her back but she moved forward, forward, half-walking, half-swimming, until she was free of the watery grasp that carried off the cottage as consolation.

There were steps ahead, steps going up, and she stumbled up and away, away finally, from the demanding ocean below.

There were people nearby, standing on a bridge of some sort, some now coming toward her, crowding by her as her reverie continued to unfold; they were merely silhouettes, peripheral to her reality.

A couple approached, asked, "Are you all right?" and it was all right because her little movie had ended and she was back, the colors returning to everything around her.

They offered a ride and a blanket to wrap herself in. On the way to town, they passed the boat with 'Memories' written on its bow, water from the storm licking the hull as if it had just floated there. Verona had pedaled past the boat countless times, ignoring the quarterboard after the first time she'd noticed it, but now the words held new meaning.

When the people asked her where she wanted to go she knew exactly where — to a certain guest house in town.

———

"I can't believe you've come back today, of all days," said the woman who answered the door. "Still, I can't say I haven't been expecting you." She stopped, looked Verona in the eye. "You look different somehow."

"Cut my hair."

The woman nodded, satisfied. She invited Verona inside, went behind the front desk and took out the suitcase stowed there.

"I thought you'd forgotten," the woman said. "I was just about to take this to the police when the hurricane put a stop to everything. You left so abruptly, I figured something must have called you away. I thought of calling you, but you never did leave your address, and I wasn't about to go through your suitcase and snoop through your things — I respect my guests' privacy."

Good, Verona thought. Thank God for that.

"Have you been away this whole time?" the woman asked. Verona barely heard her, her mind continuing to fill, like an empty pitcher held under a free-flowing tap. She collected her wits and answered the question before too long a pause.

"Yes," she said honestly.

The woman handed her the suitcase, seemed to notice for the first time the blanket wrapped around her. "Are you all right? You look like you've been out in this storm all night. Do you need a place to stay?"

"I'm all right," Verona said. "I'm fine. And, thanks, but I do have a place to stay. Although ... I hope you don't mind ... but is there somewhere I could change? I'll gladly pay you for the ... "

She was about to say, "inconvenience," but the woman stopped her.

"Of course you can change. There's only a few people here, and they came specifically to be here during the storm. Can you beat that?"

Well, yes, I can, Verona thought.

The woman pulled a key from the rack. "This way," she said. "First door on the left, same room you had before. I'll let you carry your suitcase, though. It's kind of heavy. You must have done some shopping while you were here.

———

When the door closed behind her, Verona hefted the suitcase onto the bed, hesitantly undid the two latches that kept it shut. She put her hands on the suitcase lid, closed her eyes, took a deep breath, and opened it.

It was still there. She sank to her knees and quietly wept.

She had to gain her composure. She was only supposed to be here to change.

She knew now why her memory had gone, why it was easier to forget, although she felt relief at being back. She had to remember; it would have been horrible if she hadn't. Before she changed into the dry clothes her suitcase contained, she lifted the urn from within, held it with both hands.

"Oh, darling," she whispered. "I'm so sorry."

She put the urn back in the suitcase, looked through her things for the other important piece of her past — the letter — it was still there. And so was her wallet, and her credit cards, and her driver's license, all there, all telling her who she was, who she had been. The guest house owner told the truth; she hadn't gone through anything.

There was no joy in remembering, just a strange solemnity that settled in her gut. There were things she had to tend to, things she had to finish.

That she still remembered everything about her days as Verona, however, brought her an unexpected calm. Verona unlocked secrets she would never have discovered. It was as if she needed to be Verona, was fated to be Verona, and was now two people with two separate identities who had merged into one. What was it she had told Addie, *It's okay to let go of your past?*

She hoped she would never again forget her past, no matter how painful those recollections might be. The people who resided in her memory deserved no less.

She dressed, thanked the guest house owner, and stood on the top step before venturing to her next destination. Strange how the skies cleared so quickly after such a tempest. She let her mind replay the events that had taken her to Nantucket, allowed the suppressed thoughts to resurface.

Chapter Fifty-One

H ER FIRST trip to Nantucket had been an adventure, had in large part shaped the years that followed. Later, she and her husband honeymooned on Nantucket, and they returned, if not for annual pilgrimages, every other year at the least.

Had it been nearly two years since their last visit? She stopped, wasn't sure she wanted to remember … but it had happened … a memory she was certain would never be erased.

Ted enjoyed taking risks, found adventures wherever he happened to be, whether it was white-water rafting with his friends, or hang gliding, or, she smiled when she thought of it as she always had, bungee jumping. How ridiculous was that? But he loved it! She shared his happiness in his thrill seeking; it was one of the things that attracted her to him.

That what happened was so mundane, so non-death-defying, was something she had spent the year before her memory had vanished trying to come to grips with.

They had been stuck on the island. On the day of their departure, an unexpected storm came up, a wind-whipped beauty, and there were no boats, no planes, no way off. Ted wanted to explore in the wind and driving rain. She preferred, she told him, to hunker down in their island hideaway, to wait out the weather.

"Let's go out to your favorite spot," he'd said, "to the lighthouse; check out the erosion."

He loved taking photographs, a hobby he'd pursued from fast film to digital. When they arrived at Sankaty, he bounded from the car, rushed to the bluff, camera in hand. Leaning over the edge, disregarding the wind, he peered through his viewfinder at the crashing waves below. "It's spectacular," he yelled as she approached, and he turned again to snap away, his upper body poised over the bluff, his feet barely on the firmament.

She saw it then, a crack at one corner, a thin line in the earth that materialized and spread as if an earthquake had struck, and like an earthquake a large section of the bluff opened up, separated, and was gone.

In that second she imagined Ted still there, that the falling chunk of land hadn't carried him with it. It was too sudden, too absurd, too slapstick, to be true.

Afraid of the wind, or in respect of its power, she got down on her knees and crawled to the edge …

But it was before she had even met Ted, indeed before she had ever set foot on the island, that her connection to Nantucket had been cemented.

The letter arrived shortly after her twenty-first birthday, hand-delivered by an attorney's office she had never heard of. She thought she was in some kind of trouble, why else would a lawyer be writing her?

Or could it have been about her parents' estate, of which there was none, she, an only child, having to bear the costs, and the responsibilities, of settling their affairs some two years before? She was surprised they had even found her, this attorney's office from where — Brockton, Massachusetts? — in San Francisco. After her parents' death she assumed she had moved far enough away to never get another lawyer's letter.

She waited a day before opening it, wanted to call her mother, but her mother wasn't there to call anymore. Enough. It was her life now; she had dealt with attorneys' missives before. She opened the letter.

The crisp paper was folded neatly in thirds around another envelope. Below the attorney's return address was a salutation bearing her name and this message:

"This envelope is to be delivered to you on the occasion of your twenty-first birthday. It is our hope that it finds you well. If you have any questions concerning this letter, please be advised that we are bound by legal restrictions not to reveal any further information about this document. Sincerely ... "

Fine. The same legal mumbo-jumbo she had been forced to decipher after her parents died. She held the other envelope, partially yellowed with age, in her hands. What was this? Was it something to do with being adopted? But she'd known she was adopted for years, her parents had told her about it when she was twelve, probably to spare her the shock of something like this happening years later. She had always been thankful they had told her, been honest with her. She knew she was loved, was wanted, was indeed chosen, and that was all that had ever mattered.

Get on with it, she told herself, and she opened the second envelope.

When she did, a small key fell out. "What is this?" she said out loud. But there was only one way to find out, and she unfolded the enclosed piece of paper.

"To someone very special," the hand-written letter began.

There was no date, no return address.

"I hope you have had a happy life, filled with all the pleasures and discoveries of youth and adolescence." *Oh, there have been discoveries*, she thought, *more than you know*. She continued reading. "I hope that with each successive birthday you have grown to be self-assured, confident in your abilities, and true to your ideals and dreams. And now you are twenty-one, an adult.

"This letter is not written to disturb you in any way, or to disrupt the life you're leading.

"Consider me a friend, someone who cares deeply about your well-being. As I write this, I am old, and most likely will not be around when you receive this letter. For that reason, I saw no need to include a return address, nor to mention my name.

"I know your parents, they are kind and loving people, and I hope they are well. I know they have given you all that they can, and I am sure you realize that.

"I have enclosed a key to a safety deposit box located on the island of Nantucket, a special and magical place, one very dear to my heart. The box is at the Nantucket Savings Bank and is in your parents' names. Its contents are yours to do with as you wish."

And that was that. Nothing else was written. She read the letter again and again, searching for clues.

Who was this person? Her parents never mentioned anything about Nantucket, or about any relatives she may have had there. She'd heard of Nantucket, learned a bit about it in school, knew it had something to do with whales, or *Moby-Dick*, but that was all she knew. Her parents took her on vacation to Cape Cod a couple of times, but never to the island. Growing up in the land-locked town of Holbrook, in eastern Massachusetts, Nantucket could have been on the other side of the world.

She held the key. On it was inscribed a number: 21, the number of the box, she surmised. Was it a coincidence that she, too, was twenty-one, or was the box specifically chosen to mark this milestone in her life?

If Nantucket seemed far away when she lived in Massachusetts, it was a continent's length away now. It would be ridiculous to take such a trip, considering that she had little money, no savings. What could the box contain? A treasure map? Who was she kidding? Old postcards, probably.

Still, she had to go.

———

She had found work in the mailroom at IBM, a temporary job that turned full-time after a couple of months. She had a vacation coming to her in six months. She'd go then.

On the bus one day, a month before her planned trip back east, she saw a street sign she'd never noticed before: Nantucket Street. It made her feel good about going.

———

She flew to Boston and took a connecting flight from there to the island. She didn't know the island even had an airport, but it was a large enough plane, and the day was bright blue. The plane hugged the Massachusetts coast, and she could make out the arm-like profile of Cape Cod. The plane continued past the Cape, over open ocean, and she couldn't see land when the plane first began its descent. For a moment, she thought the plane had engine trouble. Why would it be going down over water? But suddenly there it was, a bit of land that took distinctive shape as the plane neared, a pork chop in the ocean.

She felt giddy when she got off the plane, as if she was on a real adventure. She had made no arrangements other than her flight, didn't know if the island even had taxis.

As she waited for her luggage, another passenger on the flight, a middle-aged woman, approached. "You're new to the island, aren't you?"

How did she know? "Yes," she said cautiously. Great. Was this island full of people looking to take advantage of someone?

"I could tell," the woman said, smiling. "I saw the look on your face as we approached, the wonder in your expression. Isn't it a marvelous sight, seeing the island for the first time?"

She had to agree that it was. "I'm going into town," the woman said. "Can I give you a ride?"

"Well … "

"Come on, I don't bite. Is someone meeting you here?"

She said nothing, but her look gave it away that there was no one to meet her.

"Grab your bag and let's go," the woman said. "You're going to love it here."

On the way to town, the woman told her she'd been on vacation herself, but was glad to be home. "The mainland's a nice place to visit, but I'd never want to live there," she laughed.

She said her name was Flossie, and that she rented out rooms if she was looking for a place to stay. "I have several young people living with me," she said, "some for the summer. Don't worry, I don't charge much. Young people with little money need a place to stay as much as the rich folks do. Are you headed anywhere in particular?"

She lied a little, said she had an appointment at the Nantucket Savings Bank.

"I hear they're looking for tellers, summer help," the woman said. "Good luck. I'm sure you'll do just fine. I'll drop you off at the corner of Main Street, the bank's just across the street."

The woman wrote down her address, told her to stop by if she was so inclined. "No pressure," the woman said. "I'm there if you need me."

She got out of the car on Main Street, and was immediately taken by the wide cobblestone street, the brick buildings that lined both sides, the elms that graced the sidewalks. It was like stepping back in time, what she imagined San Francisco may have looked like a hundred years before.

When she approached the bank, her heart skipped. She was here at last. What was in the box? It was a thought that had been haunting her for months: *what was in the box?* She couldn't imagine.

She came prepared. She had her parents' power of attorney if there were any questions, but there were none. She stood at the teller's window, offered her key, and the teller came back with a card for her to sign.

"It's been a long time," the teller said to her.

She looked at the teller quizzically. What was she saying?

"Your box," the teller said. "It's never been opened."

She tried looking at the signature card for a name, but the teller whisked it away, grabbed a ring of keys, and motioned for her to meet her at the safe. "You can leave your suitcase over there," the teller told her. "Don't worry, I'll keep my eye on it."

She followed the teller to the vault, and there it was, box 21! She inserted her key as instructed, the little door opened, and the box was handed to her.

"There are rooms right around the corner for privacy," the teller told her.

She held the box in her hands — it was light, hardly weighed a thing — went into the room, and closed the door. She tried to control her breathing. This was it, there really was a safe deposit box waiting for her. She opened the lid slowly, and —

Money! The box was filled with money! The bills were stacked neatly, separated into six piles. The band around each noted the amount: five thousand dollars! Six stacks of five thousand dollars each!

This couldn't be real. But the key had fit into box number 21. She put the money onto the table and looked to see if there was anything else inside, a note, something.

There was only one thing: wedged into the back of the box was a letter. Finally, she'd learn the truth.

But the letter wasn't in an envelope, and it wasn't addressed to her.

Chapter Fifty-Two

H ER HANDS trembling, she unfolded the letter carefully. It was on plain white lined paper, and like the letter she'd received six months before in San Francisco, there was no date, no return address.

"Dearest Rebecca," the letter began.

"I know I'm not supposed to contact you, but these years without you have been tortuous. My only hope is that you receive this letter. I have given it to a Nantucket fisherman I met in New Bedford, Clarence Hathaway, who promised he would deliver this to you.

"I should have never have left the island that day, but the captain was insistent, said I would surely be arrested, that it would threaten the safety of everybody on board. I was dazed, confused. Before I could think, we were underway.

"When we reached port, the captain insisted I have nothing to do with you, no contact then or in the future. He said you had already forgotten about me and that if I tried to reach you it would only hurt you.

"I believed him, Rebecca. I did not want to hurt you. I did

not want to hurt you any more than you'd already been hurt. I tried to forget you, thought I was doing the right thing.

"But I could not forget you, Rebecca, any more than I could forget how to breathe. Oh, Rebecca. How I miss you, how foolish I've been to listen to others and not to follow my heart.

"If you receive this letter, and have put me out of your heart, then destroy it and never think of me again.

"I am off now on a mission. The war is horrible, but being involved in this cause has, at times, distracted my thoughts from the terrible way we ended. I need to set things straight about what happened to your father. I need to let people know that I was there, but that it was an accident. My conscience won't leave me alone about this.

"You cannot write; I will not be allowed letters until I return, which I am told will be six months from now.

"I only ask this: if you still want to see me, meet me on Straight Wharf in seven months' time. I will send word to Hathaway upon my arrival and wait for you there. If you do not want to see me, tell him when he calls that I should be on my way.

"I can only pray, Rebecca, that you will want to see me. Who knows what this mission will bring, but know that I will return to Nantucket, no matter what. No matter what, Rebecca, I will be there.

"Gerald."

Chapter Fifty-Three

SHE TOOK the letter and ten thousand dollars of the money and put it in her purse. She left the rest in the safe deposit box.

She stayed at Flossie's that night, read the letter again. Even though she'd been living in San Francisco, had gotten accustomed to being on her own, had felt she was handling what life had thrown at her just fine, she now felt suddenly small, and alone, like the orphan she truly was.

The letter was disturbing, there was no doubting that. What kind of person would do this: leave her more money than she could imagine, while also confusing her and troubling her with this letter? Perhaps the letter wasn't meant for her, but she reread the original letter she had packed in her suitcase and there it was: "The contents are yours to do with as you wish."

She wished she had never come to Nantucket, never been confronted with the money, or the message, or the need to reexamine her life.

The next day, her mind clearer, she reassessed.

She kept the money in her purse as she walked around the

old town, letting the events of the day before settle in. She tried not to think as she breathed in the salt air and took in her surroundings. People smiled as she passed, and she began to focus not on the letter, or the letter that had been delivered before that, but on the sudden fortune that had come her way. Thirty thousand dollars! Was it real? She reached into her purse, thumbed the crisp bundle of bills, wondered what she had done to deserve this generous gift.

She wandered down to the wharves, sat on a bench where the boats came in and little blue buses lined up to take people on sightseeing tours of the island. She shook her head and had to smile. If she'd assumed the letter would reveal some secret about her past, that assumption was quickly blown apart. What did the letter mean? Who was Rebecca?

It must have been the Rebecca this Gerald had written to who'd left her the money. But why? Why would this stranger, a person she'd never heard of, choose her?

Her parents had no brothers or sisters, and there were no remaining relatives for her to turn to. She could only imagine that her parents knew about this secret, knew of this benefactor, and patiently waited for this sweet surprise on her twenty-first birthday. Why sure, they'd say, you had a rich aunt, but we all felt it was best to wait, not allow some future promise to taint your upbringing, not allow expectations to cloud your appreciation of the day-to-day joys of growing up.

The first letter had mentioned her parents, wished they were well. Of course they knew about this. They never mentioned it because their sudden illnesses overshadowed everything else, sapped any thoughts of the future, displaced any reminiscences of the past.

The second letter was a mistake, there could be no other explanation. Rebecca never meant to leave the letter behind. After all, it had been shoved into the back of the box; she'd had to dig it out. What had been written in the original letter? "I don't write to disturb you in any way."

Her thoughts, her assumptions, made her despondent. If only she knew who this Rebecca was, she'd be able to find some answers.

But she didn't even have a last name to go on. After all she'd been through in the past two years, she decided to let it drop, get on with her life, take the money and run.

Chapter Fifty-Four

SHE REMAINED on Nantucket two more days. She thought of asking Flossie if she had any idea who Rebecca might be, but then she'd have to answer more questions, tell her about the letter and where she'd found it. She'd be forced to go into her whole life story, and the retelling, in her current, confused state, would be too overwhelming. She didn't want to risk telling anyone about the money that was in the safe deposit box, fearing that she might have to give the money back, turn it over to some attorney for its rightful disposition.

She'd had enough of attorneys.

Besides, the other letter was old, older than the letter that told her to come to Nantucket. Whatever had happened had happened long before, there was nothing she could do to change anything now. Besides, she was glad it hadn't happened to her, glad it wasn't she who had received this horrible letter.

Reading the letter once more, she told herself that it ended happily, that Rebecca did meet Gerald, that they sailed off into the sunset.

Of course, she told herself. Why else would Rebecca have

crammed the letter into a safe deposit box and forgotten about it? Rebecca didn't need the letter anymore, its promise had been fulfilled.

It was a plausible enough explanation, the least troubling scenario, and she allowed herself the luxury of thinking it true.

———————

She returned the letter from Gerald to the safety deposit box, recounted the money that remained: it was still there, twenty thousand dollars! She felt suspicious counting it, she didn't know why, as if it wasn't rightfully hers.

But it was, the letter said it was.

She searched the signature card for a name when she signed out the box this time and there were two typewritten names at the top: her parents' names, no other. Again, there were no questions as to her proprietorship; having the key seemed proof enough.

She decided to leave the twenty thousand in the box, rather than risk carrying so much cash with her back to San Francisco. She'd return for it, it had been sitting there safely for who knows how long anyway.

She'd be back. She had plenty of money to travel now.

Chapter Fifty-Five

B Y THE time she met Ted, a promising sous-chef, she'd nearly
forgotten about the letter in the safe deposit box. As an en-
gagement present, she surprised him with a trip to Nantucket.

"You can't afford this," he'd said when he saw the tickets.
"Where did you get the money?"

"It was left to me," she told him firmly, deflecting further
discussion.

They stayed with Flossie, who remembered her, was glad to
see her back.

She was eager to return to the bank, make sure the money
was still there. She took Ted with her, wanted to see his face when
he saw the rest of her fortune. It would be their fortune now.

The teller recognized her, greeted her as though she'd never
left the island. With a puzzled Ted in tow, she went back to the
little room and opened the box.

"What's this?" he asked her.

"Ours," she said.

She took the money out, put them in piles on the small table, four little stacks of five thousand dollars each. "This ought

to help with a down payment on a house, don't you think?" she laughed. After a long embrace, she collected the money in her purse. She closed the lid to the box, and was about to take it back to the safe when she remembered the letter.

"Oh," she said, offhandedly. "There's this, too."

"What is it?" he asked.

"Just a letter. You can read it later."

She told the teller she wouldn't be needing the box any-more, and asked if there were any outstanding fees that needed to be paid.

The teller checked and said that the box had been paid in full. There were no payments due, in fact, for the next ten years. "You may as well hang onto it," the teller told her.

She didn't ask who had paid; she knew there wouldn't be an answer. "Best to let it rest," she said to herself.

———

On their honeymoon, Ted was determined to find out who Rebecca was, what the letter meant. They stayed this time not at Flossie's, but at the Jared Coffin House hotel in the center of town.

"You may have some kind of legacy here," he'd said to her. "If Rebecca is the same Rebecca who sent you that original letter, she's probably a relative. Why else would she leave you all that money? Aren't you curious? This is a small enough island that somebody should be able to tell you."

"I'm happy just to have the money," she told him. "I'm ner-vous about digging too deeply."

"What's there to be nervous about?" he'd said. "It's a mys-tery. Don't you want to know about your past?"

"I know all about my past," she told him. "Let's concentrate on the future."

"That woman might know; she's lived here all her life."

"What woman?"

"The woman we stayed with before, what was her name? Flossie? I'll bet it's as simple as asking her."

But Flossie wasn't around. She was off-island, they were told, visiting friends on the mainland. No, she wouldn't be back for another three weeks.

"Let's just enjoy our honeymoon," she said.

Chapter Fifty-Six

THEY RETURNED to the island two years later. They had begun building a life together in San Francisco, started a small restaurant, nothing fancy, but the customers were steady and loyal. Ted, by now an accomplished chef, taught her what he knew, and they worked in the kitchen as a team. The letters, and the mysteries they contained, were placed in a drawer with other memories.

Ted brought the letters with him on their visit, however. He sought out Flossie.

"Flossie passed away six months ago," he was told. He showed the letters to the person who delivered the news, a young man about his age. No, he had no idea who Rebecca was, or Gerald. Sorry.

She was oddly relieved when Ted told her about Flossie. Maybe they could just appreciate the island now for what it was, and not for any secret it might harbor.

Before they left the island, Ted asked the owner of the guest house where they were staying, a Mrs. Swain, if she might know. Mrs. Swain read the letters carefully, and as she read, she shook her head gently.

"Then you don't know who she is," he said.

"No, I've got a good idea who this might be," was her reply. "It has to be Rebecca Coffin."

And she told them the story of Rebecca Coffin's father, and his fall from the light. "It was so sad," Mrs. Swain said to them. "Although I didn't know her well, Rebecca was never the same after that. I don't think she ever left her house. I have no knowledge of this Gerald. Seems like he was at the lighthouse as well. I'd never heard that before." She thought for a moment, handed the letters back. "Oh, well, it's all in the past. I'd keep these to myself if I were you."

"Is Rebecca still … " Ted couldn't wait to ask.

"Alive?" answered Mrs. Swain. "Now that I couldn't tell you. She left the island years ago."

"Where?"

"I don't know. As I said, I didn't really know her; she was quite a few years older than I am, twenty years at least. I'd never heard mention there was a man in her life. Maybe they left the island together." She crossed her hands in front of her. "Are you related to her?"

"I'm not, but my wife could be. These are her letters."

Mrs. Swain looked at her as though she was trying to recognize her. "I'm afraid I can't help you any more than that," she said, not wanting to say what she believed: that Rebecca Coffin had most likely passed away, and that her passing was probably a blessing.

This girl, if she was indeed a relative, looked too fragile to tell.

Chapter Fifty-Seven

O N Verona's last debarkation, all these memories were with her, all the conversations, all the remembrances of the way the light shaded people's faces; of the sounds heard beyond conversations: of the people laughing as they rode past on bicycles; of dogs being walked by neighbors; of the birds chittering and tse-tse-ing in the trees and on the telephone lines; of the Town Clock's insistent tolling of the hours; of the distant waves at Surfside roaring their echo beyond the shore; of the wind: whistling, whipping, wending, willowing from every dawn and into the night that followed.

It had taken her a year to grieve, to come to terms with the death of her husband. She had brought his ashes with her to release into the wind near Sankaty.

She stayed in a guest house in town, paid cash for the room in advance. She told no one of her plans, didn't want the hassle of securing permits, or finding out that her plan would be restricted in any way. This was a private matter, she told herself. Nobody needed to know. She wanted to do this quickly, with no unnecessary disruptions.

She had brought the letters with her. She wanted to be rid of them, released from the burden of their cryptic messages. For the second time in her life, she was forced to start over, and she wondered how she'd find the strength. If she had to begin again, as she knew she must, she wanted nothing of the past to encumber her.

She would have her memories. That would be enough.

Before setting out on her private memorial service, she was prodded into conversation by the guest house owner, a talkative sort who wanted to know all about her.

Was this her first visit to the island; where was she from; had she come for a wedding?

What Verona said was said merely to stop the questions, to come up with a query to which this woman would have no answer, something innocuous to end the conversation.

"You wouldn't happen to know a Rebecca Coffin, would you?"

The question silenced the woman as though something offensive had been said.

But the woman smiled. "Rebecca Coffin? I never would have expected you to ask about her. I didn't think there was anyone who knew her, she's been gone so long."

Looking for an out, Verona unwittingly uncovered an opening. "You know her?" she asked, her heart inexplicably sinking.

"Yes, well, no, I don't know her," the woman said before brightening suddenly, "but my mother does. She lives at the Homestead, my mother, and she was just telling me the other day that an old Nantucketer, Rebecca Coffin as you said, had just moved into the Homestead herself. Now isn't that a coincidence?"

Verona almost sank to her knees. The woman kept talking but Verona couldn't hear, as if the woman was suddenly speaking underwater.

"I ... have ... to ... leave," Verona said, moving without

thinking towards the door. "I need air."

"Are you all right?" the woman asked her.

"I'll be fine. I just need to go outside for a while."

The woman stood speechless, her mouth caught open between words as Verona slowly stepped outside.

Thoughts raced through Verona's mind. This couldn't be happening. Rebecca was no more than a dream, had become almost a fictional character who, nevertheless, had complicated her life. She couldn't be real.

She turned and saw a bicycle in a rack by the side of the building. Feeling as if she was somebody else, Verona got on the bike and began pedaling, welcoming the breeze on her face, needing to feel the air to get her thoughts together.

It overwhelmed her as she rode through town, the whole series of events that had brought her to the island in the first place, the tragedy that had prompted her return. If only she hadn't received that first letter, a letter that had become a curse.

She rode, not knowing where she was going, unaware that her legs were pushing the bike forward. Rebecca was alive, she was real. It was too much to comprehend. She came here wanting to think only of Ted, but now she was forced to confront this unexpected, and unwelcome, news.

She had come to wrap things up, to put everything to rest. Her mind wasn't prepared for detours or deviations.

She rode on absent-mindedly, followed the winding curves of the Polpis Road, turning everything over in her mind. Rebecca Coffin. The name haunted her now. If only she had never heard it, if only she hadn't mentioned it to that woman.

She pushed hard at the pedals, hoping her exertions would relieve her troubled mind. But there was no relief.

Suddenly, there was Sankaty, an unignorable presence, a totemic icon that once offered hope but now represented despair. Seeing the light, she stopped, straddled the bike, and shook uncontrollably.

As if possessed, she turned and pedaled furiously back towards town. She knew what she needed to do, it came to her as if it was a message borne by the wind: she had to see Rebecca, face to face. There was no other solution. After all that had happened, after all the unresolved questions, after all the tears, she needed an answer.

In her haste she didn't see the patch of sand as she crossed onto the bike path. Her tires hit it at an angle and were swept from under her as if strings were attached to the spokes and someone yanked on them hard. She fell before she could react, her head hitting the sandy pavement — and a curtain closed on her consciousness.

"Are you all right?" It was a man's voice, somewhere off in the distance. "Are you all right?" the voice asked again, closer this time, as if a dial had been turned on a stereo.

Blurry legs came slowly into focus, followed by the tops of two sneakers. "White shoelaces," was her immediate thought. She lifted her head, groggily tried to take in her surroundings.

"Maybe you should lie still," the man said to her. She turned her head towards him, looked into the face of this man leaning over her. She didn't know why she thought it strange that he had a mustache. He looked at her with a concern that made her think for an instant that he knew her. She took a few moments to get her bearings, realized she was staring, studying him almost, trying to figure out if she should know him.

"You took quite a spill. I think I should call an ambulance."

"No, I'm all right," she said, pulling herself into a sitting position. Everything was clearer now, although her stomach felt queasy. She could easily have fallen off to sleep, but she concentrated on keeping her eyes open, determined not to lose consciousness.

"Are you sure?" he said. She saw the cell phone in his hand.

"Yes," she said determinedly, standing up now. He righted the bike for her; she held the handlebars for support. "I don't know if you should be riding," he said, looking into her eyes. "You could have a concussion."

"I'll be fine," she insisted. But she took his advice and walked the bike back towards town.

———————

She unconsciously moved ahead, felt like she was gliding, followed the flow of traffic as if it was a mechanical river. Unaware of her surroundings, gripping the bicycle like an energy source, as if her life depended on it, she meandered thoughtlessly to Main Street and then towards the water where the traffic ended and the docks began.

She saw the little blue buses lined up, and for some reason this comforted her; she wanted to watch them for a while; watch the people as they shuffled past; rest her eyes on the wash of colors that filled her senses. There was a bike rack that seemed to materialize out of thin air, meant for her, of course, and she stowed the bike, and here was a bench, and she took a seat, and the blankness descended.

Chapter Fifty-Eight

WHEELING HER suitcase that clacked on the brick sidewalk like a train on a miniature track, she walked now with purpose, her destination clear. She didn't notice the uprooted tree poised on the Homestead's roof, its snarling tangle of roots turned skyward, nor would it have deterred her had it fallen across the front door.

She lugged the suitcase up the front steps, rapped quickly on the door, opened it without waiting, and asked to see Rebecca.

People were bustling about, reestablishing order in the hurricane's wake, taking care of business. "She's upstairs," was the hasty reply. "In her room, first door to the left. You can leave your suitcase here if you like."

"That's okay, I've got something in here for her."

———

The door to Rebecca's room was open. Rebecca sat in a chair, her head bowed as if napping. Verona's sudden presence made her start. She lifted her head, and a shock of recognition flooded through her. She looked upon this girl who had surprised her at the lighthouse, saw her as if for the first time: a woman who looked drained, delicate, yet who looked back at her with an intensity that couldn't be ignored.

Rebecca slowly rose to step towards her, to hold her if she could, to comfort her, and, yes, gather comfort for herself. As Verona silently accepted her embrace, Rebecca understood why Verona had come.

The girl/woman knew.

Or thought she knew.

———

Verona opened her suitcase, found the letter she was looking for and put it in Rebecca's hands. Why she decided to first show Rebecca the letter from Gerald, rather than the original letter delivered when she was twenty-one, she would later blame on her confused feelings, on the streaming emotions that eclipsed rational thought. It was the letter that had troubled her most, the letter Ted had tried so hard to decipher. Without this letter there would be no knowledge of Rebecca, no discovery, no reason to be here.

The concern Verona had for Rebecca when she didn't know who she was — when Rebecca was merely an old lady with a sad story — was displaced now by a yearning need to know, a fervent craving for finality.

Rebecca recognized the letter, one she had tried so hard to forget, a letter she had packed away and assumed had been lost when she'd left Nantucket all those years ago. "Where did you get this?" she said in a whisper, not looking up.

"I found it."

"Did somebody give it to you?"

"No, I found it."

It was as if the words came from the mouth of a spoiled child. So, she was wrong. Clearly, this woman sitting across from her, a woman who sat primly now on her bed, was not who Rebecca thought she was. The rising excitement she'd felt just a moment before dropped in her stomach like an anchor. She was angry with this woman, angry with herself most of all, for allowing herself to believe …

Why did this woman want to hurt her?

Seeing the sorrow in Rebecca's eyes, Verona was all too aware she had made a mistake, a selfish, misguided act of retribution. She had shown this old woman the letter from Gerald to make herself feel better, to transfer the years of uncertainty, indeed the anguish over the loss of her husband, onto the person who she felt had teased her with unanswerable questions, taunted her for years with a mystery that couldn't be resolved.

She had gone too far, had brought misery with her childish impulsiveness.

She knelt at Rebecca's side, begged her forgiveness.

"Please, Rebecca. I've been through so much … "

Verona crawled to her suitcase, hefted the urn, held it in her lap. "These are my husband's ashes. He died a little over a year ago. I'd come here to scatter them at Sankaty."

Taken aback, Rebecca wondered what in God's name was going on.

"That's why I showed you that letter," Verona said, her voice breaking. "He was determined to find you." She laughed through her tears. "He drove me crazy looking for you, wondering who you were."

"Where did you get that letter?"

"In the box, the safe deposit box."

———

The letter dropped from Rebecca's hands. She remembered now. She thought she had taken everything out when she'd put in the money left to her by her father, the money that was her little secret, the money she'd find some purpose for in the future.

And she had found a purpose for it, had written Flossie to transfer ownership of the box ...

She looked at Verona. Could it be true?

Verona took the other letter from her suitcase, offered it to Rebecca. "This arrived when I turned twenty-one."

Shaking now, Rebecca said: "Come to me. Come here, child."

And she hugged Verona as tightly as she could, and wept.

———————

Confused, wiping away a tear herself, Verona pulled herself back, looked into Rebecca's eyes. "Why?" she asked. "Why me?"

Rebecca couldn't check the feelings of tenderness that enveloped her, no matter how hard she tried to suppress them; couldn't deny the upswell of happiness that surged through her. She studied Verona's face, not wanting to talk, not wanting to look away. She simply wanted to look at her. Why hadn't she known when Verona found her at the lighthouse that night, why hadn't she felt the connection then, not wasted these precious months?

Verona watched Rebecca's softened gaze, wondered what was going on. *Why isn't she telling me?* she thought.

"It is you who left me all that money," Verona said softly.

Rebecca nodded, remembered every detail: writing the letter, ensuring there would be no problems, no complications with either the delivery of the letter or access to the safe deposit box.

"If only you'd left me some way to thank you," Verona said now. "If I hadn't found that letter ... "

"From Gerald."

"From Gerald, I never would have known your name."

"But you know who I am."

"I know you're Rebecca, and that you left me the money, and that's all I know."

"But you saw me at the lighthouse."

"I didn't know who you were then."

"Who do you think I am now?"

"An aunt, a relative, a friend of my parents … " Verona's voice trailed off. She was weary, worn out from the exhausting and revelatory events of the past day. She peered anxiously at Rebecca, who wondered if she had the resolve to tell Verona the truth. "Then you don't know," Rebecca said to her.

"Know what?"

"Sit next to me," Rebecca said at last. "I only hope you'll be able to forgive me."

And before Verona was able to wrap her thoughts around these words, in walked Sandy.

———————

Sandy had done all she could to clean out her flooded basement. Needing a break, wanting to get away from the watery mess and breathe fresh air, she decided to check in with Rebecca, make sure she was all right.

On her way to the Homestead, she wondered about Verona, was worried that she hadn't heard from her, or heard about her by now from Addie. She'd check in with the police after her visit with Rebecca.

Amid the fallen limbs and uprooted trees she saw on her short walk, people were busily at work clearing the wreckage, inspecting the damage. The only talk in the air was that of the destruction that had been avoided, of the close call they had lived through. There were no whispers of people hurt, or missing, or swept away. This was good news. Bad news would have carried quickly, would have crackled through the atmosphere like raw electricity, its echoes a faint, but distinct, thunderclap.

She was surprised to hear Rebecca had a visitor, Irene most likely, but when she entered the room she stopped short at the sight of Verona. She went from shock to relief to exasperation in a second. Is this where she'd been all night, after all the worrying she'd done?

Before Sandy could speak, Verona was up and at her side. "Oh, Sandy," she said, reaching to hug her. "You won't believe the night I've just had."

"Tell me about it," Sandy said, her voice trailing as her eyes met Rebecca's. "Are you all right?" she said to her.

"I'm all right," Rebecca said flatly. "Now, if you don't mind, I've got a little unfinished business ... no, wait, I never thought I'd be able to say this."

Sandy and Verona both turned, neither of them prepared for what Rebecca said next.

"I'd like you to meet ... my niece."

Chapter Fifty-Nine

REBECCA BECKONED Verona with outstretched arms. "It's you," she said. "You know it's you."

Verona accepted Rebecca's embrace, too outdone to be overjoyed, too bewildered to comprehend what she'd just heard.

But after all she'd been through, after all the strange occurrences of the past year, there was no reason why it couldn't be true. The way her life had been going this news made as much sense as anything.

Her aunt. She looked at this woman she'd comforted at the light, this stranger who until now had only been someone she'd stumbled across, one of the people who came into her life as less than an acquaintance, one of the people you meet and then forget.

And now this woman claimed to be her aunt, her relative. If only her mother could be here.

Rebecca — the Rebecca of the letters and the money, the Rebecca who had confounded her for years, the Rebecca who had so intrigued her husband, the Rebecca that existed only in her thoughts, was now another Rebecca, a myth come to life.

And the myth was making claims too complicated to contemplate.

"I know it's hard to believe," Rebecca said, looking downward. "But it is. Only my niece would have received that letter."

"Perhaps I'd better go," Sandy said. Her words seemed to be spoken from another room.

"No, stay," they both said at once. "Please stay," Verona pleaded.

"I knew as soon as you entered my room," Rebecca continued. "I knew you'd come to see me about the letter."

———

In the seconds preceding her announcement, Rebecca vacillated between telling the truth or claiming to be, as Verona had ventured, an aunt, an eccentric relative.

She knew the lie, once told, could never be retrieved, but there was no other option — she couldn't bear to bring more pain, more confusion to her daughter. She had endured enough already. No, the truth in this instance would have served no one well.

And when Verona revealed her story, Rebecca knew she had made the right decision.

Chapter Sixty

"MY PARENTS never told me," Verona said, sinking into the armchair near Rebecca's bed. "They never mentioned I had a blood relative."

"Blame me for that," Rebecca said. "I thought it best that the family you had was the only family you should know. As soon as your parents adopted you, I stepped aside and asked them never to mention me to you. I didn't want to muddy the waters, or cause you confusion while you were growing up."

"Why?" Verona wanted to know.

"I wasn't what you'd call a responsible person. I was never much for family, anyway. I was too caught up in my own life; call it selfishness. No, you were better off with the family you had. Much better off."

"So you're really related to me?"

"Yes."

"On which side? I mean, my birth mother, or birth father?"

"On your mother's side."

"Are you her sister?"

"Let's just say we're related." It was the hardest thing Rebecca had ever had to say. Before Verona could ask another question, Rebecca hurriedly added: "And she loved you dearly."

"I know that," Verona said. "My parents made sure I knew it. They said she wasn't able to care for me; that she had chosen them."

"You were adopted?" Sandy asked.

God bless you, Sandy, Rebecca thought.

"Yes, they were wonderful people," Verona said, looking then at Rebecca, "as I'm sure you know."

Rebecca closed her eyes and nodded. She knew about it all too well. She hesitated before asking the next question. "And they are … ?"

"They died." Verona looked at the floor, then into Rebecca's eyes. "But now … there's you."

Rebecca had to turn away, pretended to cough. "Enough about me," she said hoarsely. "Tell me about yourself."

"I wouldn't know where to begin," Verona said wearily. She didn't want to talk. She still couldn't wrap her mind around Rebecca. Was she really her relative? "Tell me about my mother," she said.

Expecting this broadside, Rebecca's outward demeanor was calm. "Of course, my dear," she said calmly, "in due time. But, please, I never thought I'd ever see you. Tell me about your life."

Verona looked at Rebecca, at Sandy, at their expressions urging her on. It had been a wild ride, she had to admit, especially lately. It was all so inconceivable. She did need to talk about it; if only to sort things out for herself.

Too tired to fight, she began.

————

Sandy sat in silence as Verona slowly, cautiously, told her tale, finishing with her escape from the cottage and her regained sense of self. It was so unbelievable that Sandy from time to time wanted to say, "Stop," run that by me again," but she resisted these urges; as hard as it was not to interrupt, she remained a bystander, a witness, letting the words dance through her brain.

"I think we could all use a drink," Rebecca said at last, and she slowly rose and took a bottle from her bottom drawer.

Verona fell back onto Rebecca's bed, let it wash over her, the happiness, the sadness, the strange, surreal mystery of her life. She sat up and looked at Rebecca, and wondered if this truly was a dream.

And as Verona thought these thoughts she thought this too: this was not a time to think. Thinking would only complicate things right now.

Chapter Sixty-One

SANDY SHAMBLED home as if sleepwalking, fortunate there was little traffic about, for she looked neither left nor right, nor did she pause at side streets as the incomprehensible events played through her mind. It didn't seem real, but it was, an outcome that seemed strangely preordained, as if by reading Rebecca's journals she had elicited this result, had somehow willed Verona into her life to complete the story.

It was all so fantastic: Verona not knowing who she was, but then pulling her driver's license from her luggage to confirm it and ... what did she say her real name was?

Sandy's musings were interrupted by a pickup truck that slowed beside her, Digit calling her name from his rolled-down window. "Where've you been?" he said to her. "We went to your house and you weren't there. Are you okay? You look like you've seen a ghost."

"Who's we?" Sandy asked him.

"Santa Claus and I. Who do you think? Addie. Have you seen Verona? He's worried sick ... "

Addie. Forgotten about Addie.

"We've been out looking all morning," Digit went on. "Saw a house swept out to sea in 'Sconset. Did you hear about it? Unbelievable. Addie's at your house now, waiting for you, or for her. Have you seen her?"

"I have," Sandy said at last.

"Well, all right. I mean, is she all right?"

"She's fine. She's with Rebecca."

"Where the hell has she been? Addie's ready to go to the cops."

"It's a long story," Sandy said, walking around the front of the truck and climbing into the passenger seat. "Let's go see Addie."

Addie paced like a convict in solitary, feeling guilty that he hadn't searched harder for Verona before the storm. She couldn't have been in that cottage, please God, she couldn't have been.

She would have called out, wouldn't she, called for help? But no one would have heard her, he thought, tormenting himself, the wind and the roar of the ocean would have obliterated a human's fragile cries, especially Verona's.

Where the hell is Sandy?

His back turned to the street, he didn't hear the pickup approach, or its doors slam, or see Sandy moving quickly towards him.

"Addie," she said, startling him.

He saw the smile on Sandy's face, felt a relief he didn't know existed.

"She's all right," Sandy said. "She's had quite a night."

"Where is she?" he said weakly, hoping she wasn't going to say, "In the hospital."

"With Rebecca, at the Homestead."

"Let's go."

"No," she said, putting her arm around him. "She's exhausted, sleeping I'll bet. Trust me, she's all right." *And she doesn't need you confusing her right now,* Sandy thought. It would take at least a day or two to sort it all out.

"Let's go home, Addie," Digit said. "If Sandy says she's all right, she's all right. You've had a hell of a night yourself, we all have. Christ, I had to deal with Marsha and her new boyfriend."

"Go home," Sandy agreed. "I'm going to take a nap myself. I've done work enough for two days. She'll be back here later. I'll call you as soon as she does."

Seeing the worry on his face, Sandy was tempted to tell Addie and Digit the whole story, then they'd understand. But, no, this was something Verona had to tell Addie. It wasn't Sandy's place to repeat something as deeply personal as this; it would have been too much like gossip.

Still, she had to tell someone; she was bursting.

No, Sandy, she told herself, this was Verona's tale to tell. Or Rebecca's.

On her way upstairs, she lifted the phone, and a welcome dial tone emanated. The lines were up again.

No harm in calling Irene.

Chapter Sixty-Two

DIGIT WASN'T going to let Addie be alone, so, instead of driving to Addie's house, he drove home. Marsha's boyfriend's car was still there. "Man," he said. "I figured they'd be gone by now. What's she doing, moving back in?" He turned to his friend. "Do you mind if we go to your place? I can't stomach seeing them." He took Addie's non-response as a yes.

The power was out at Addie's rental, and besides a few shingles strewn around the yard the little house was intact. It seemed cold inside, however, a feeling that wasn't helped by all the boxes lying everywhere.

"I thought you'd thrown all this stuff out," Digit said. "You've still got crap at my place, too."

Addie said nothing, walked from one room to another. If Verona was fine, why couldn't he see her? He needed to touch her, be with her, hear her voice.

"Let's go to the Homestead," he said abruptly.

"Come on, Addie," Digit replied, "leave her alone. You heard Sandy, she's probably sleeping. Isn't it enough to know she's okay?"

"Staying here waiting is going to drive me crazy. How come Sandy gets to see her and I don't?"

"Now, aren't you something? What, are you married to her? You think you've got a right to see her? You can't wait an hour? I wish I had your problems. Let's go get something to eat. Anything will be better than hanging around here watching you mope."

"I'm not hungry."

"Well, I am. You got anything to eat here?"

"No."

"Didn't think so."

"You go ahead."

"No way, pal. I'm not leaving you alone, no matter how much of a pain in the ass you're turning into."

"Suit yourself."

"Come on. I'm starving. I promise you won't have to talk to anybody."

Addie shrugged. It was easier to acquiesce.

They both jumped when the phone rang. Addie looked at the telephone as though it was from outer space. It seemed as if he hadn't heard a telephone in years.

"What, you've still got an old dial phone?" Digit said. "You're probably the only guy on Nantucket whose phone is working."

No, Addie thought, there'd be one other person ...

"Sandy?" he said desperately into the receiver.

"No ... "

Addie caught his breath. It was the last voice he'd expected to hear. "Verona?"

"Yes. How are you?"

How was he? How the hell was she? "I'm great — now," he said, his voice rising unintentionally. He was nervous for some reason, walked as far as the phone cord reached in one direction before heading back in the other. "Can I see you?"

The pause on the other end of the line made him anxious. Why couldn't he be more discreet, have a little tact, give her some space? He stopped pacing, waited for a reply.

"I need a little time," she said.

Time? How much time?

"I'm sorry, Addie. That didn't sound right. I mean, later today, this evening. I need to rest. I just wanted to hear your voice, know that you were all right."

"I'm fine, but ... "

"I'm glad you're fine. Don't worry, when you hear about everything that's happened, I think you'll understand."

"Sure I will, but ... "

"Is Digit with you?"

"Yes, but ... "

"He's a good friend, Addie. Stay with him. I'll let you know when I'm ready."

"Sure," he said, wanting to say, "When?" but he knew better. He was old enough to know better.

He hoped.

Rebecca watched Verona sleep. After all the years, she was finally able to enjoy the simple pleasure of being with her daughter.

Her daughter. It was a word that held little meaning before this day, a word absent from the definition of her life. How glorious the word was now: daughter, a gift, a chance to make things right.

It was right not to have told her the truth. What benefit would it have brought? Imagine the shock! The truth in this instance would have made only one person feel better, and that person had relinquished her mother's role years and years before. No, it was best this way. What did it matter if her daughter thought she was her aunt? She could still love her like a daughter, that was all that mattered.

And now that she knew all that her daughter had endured, she wondered if she had enough love to comfort her.

She was glad Verona was sleeping. She could quietly revel in this moment, a day she never thought would happen, a day she never dreamed she'd be allowed to have.

From her chair she studied Verona's features as if gazing upon a newborn. There was a resemblance, she had to admit, although she couldn't say whether it was the shape of her ears, or the set of her nose. No, it was neither of those. What she recognized most was the determination her daughter possessed, even in sleep she could see it, the assuredness with which she carried herself. Her adoptive parents had done a fine job fostering these traits, and she was thankful.

She could sit like this forever, feeling a peace she could never have imagined. She vowed not to try and make up for lost time, to be content with what she had been given, to enjoy the harvest of their reunion, no matter how late that reunion had occurred.

She would take it slowly, give her daughter time to come to terms with this improbable discovery.

And if, with time, they should become close, well, who knew what truths the future might tell.

Chapter Sixty-Three

V ERONA STIRRED, stretched, opened her eyes into the pillow. She lifted her head, let her focus adjust on the smiling countenance of Rebecca. "How long have I been sleeping?" she asked.

"Not long. About two hours."

"And you've been sitting here this whole time?"

Rebecca nodded.

Verona pulled herself up, swiveled her feet over the side of the bed. "If only I had known sooner," she said.

Rebecca closed her eyes, nodded her head in assent. "It was what we thought was best," she said after a while, "for your parents to have you all to themselves, no strings, or long-lost relatives, attached. There was no sense confusing you."

"I'm confused now."

"I don't doubt it, after all you've been through." Rebecca looked out the window, needed to say something to fill the silence. "I left that money hoping I could do one nice thing for you, leave you some sort of legacy. I figured by the time you turned twenty-one it would be all right."

"You did. It was," Verona said, stifling a yawn, then yawning, "We have so much to talk about."

"Not now." (*God, not now,* Rebecca thought. *Enough's been said for one day — for a week!*) "There'll be time to talk. Your head must be swimming. Take a walk, get your bearings, breathe some fresh air, and for goodness sake, don't think. Go home to Sandy and see that young man you called earlier. What was his name?"

"Addie."

"Addie." Rebecca had never heard of a man called Addie before. Definitely not a Nantucket boy. "I'm sure he's itching to see you."

Verona put on her shoes, looked at her suitcase.

"Leave that here," Rebecca said. "You can deal with whatever you need to deal with tomorrow."

———

It did feel good to be outside again. Strange days, indeed, she thought as she slowly ambled along the sidewalk. She had lost so much, had almost lost herself, but she had gained ... a relative, an aunt? It couldn't be. She wished Ted was here to share this with her. He'd get a laugh out of this.

Stop it, Ver —, and she stopped, mid-stride. Verona. She still thought of herself as Verona, this other being, the one who had forged a new existence out of nothing. Verona. Now that was a question she needed to ask Rebecca: who had come up with her name, the name she had been accustomed to for all those years? Alice, a plain name, the name she had unquestionably answered to, the name that had defined her.

She liked Verona better. She was Verona now.

She thought of the lighthouse. "Sheila," she had called it, her mother's name, her adoptive mother's name, but her mother nonetheless. It made sense to her that she'd think of the light as

Sheila, a protective beacon watching over her in her state of un-knowing. Sheila, her mother, the one who comforted her, guided her, gave of herself unconditionally.

And now she had someone new in her life, and an answer at last to the mystery of the safe deposit box. She could never have the same feelings for Rebecca that she did for Sheila — how could she? — but she was willing to cultivate some sort of relationship with her. For better or worse, they had each other now.

She was lucky. Her parents, adoptive or not, had nurtured her, had given her an identity she cherished. She wouldn't have wanted it any other way. She couldn't imagine never knowing them, would feel cheated if she hadn't. The life she'd been given was the life she wanted.

For all the months she was determined not to remember her past, she realized now that she had been trying to get back from the start, her innermost being dropping hints, patiently urging her true self to reemerge. How fortunate that she did; what she had lost, no matter how freeing her other self seemed, was greater than anything her new life promised.

She understood the attraction of forgetting, of giving in, of allowing the painful memories to be washed from her mind, but now that she was back, she was thankful it hadn't consumed her. It was as though she had been part of a self-imposed cult, a cult of one, and she was glad she had finally snapped out of it.

Lost in her thoughts, Verona didn't realize she was once again on the docks. All was quiet by the water, and she strolled by the bench where she had awakened all those months before. Her awakening, she knew now, involved more than these past months — it had been constant throughout her life, a steady series of discoveries that she hoped would never end.

Chapter Sixty-Four

ADDIE AND Digit sat on stools at the drugstore lunch counter. Addie nursed a coffee while Digit scarfed a bagel with cream cheese, onion, tomato, and bacon.

"You needed to get out of the house," Digit reminded his friend between bites. "What were you going to do, sit by the phone all day?"

Addie twirled around on his stool, sat with his elbows propped on the lunch counter, watching the door.

"You think she's going to walk in here? I don't think she's ever even been here. Relax. She said she'd get back to you later. It's only been like an hour."

"I can't help but think something's happened to her," Addie said. "She sounded so different on the phone."

"You probably sounded different to her. That wasn't your usual storm we just got through."

Addie looked beyond the saltwater-frosted windows onto Main Street. People were beginning to mill about, greeting each other as they did in the off-season when they had the island to themselves again. Of all the shops on Main Street only two were open: the drugstore and the bookstore across the street.

Although his intentions seemed right at the time, he wished now that he hadn't been so casual in his relationship with Verona. His instincts to take it slowly may have come across as disinterest. If only he had been a little more honest about his feelings, Verona would have turned to him for comfort instead of taking off the way she had. Something had happened during the night to change her, he heard it in the way she talked to him. But no matter what had happened, he couldn't face losing her.

"Stop beating yourself up," Digit said without looking at him.

"What are you talking about?"

"I know you well enough to know what you're thinking. Will you stop worrying about her?"

"I'm worried she won't want to see me anymore."

"She wouldn't have called you if she didn't want to see you."

Digit paid the tab, spun on his stool. "I'm bound," he said. "Time to assess the damage at my house. Marsha and her boytoy ought to be gone by now; they'd better be. Come on, I'll drop you off at your place."

"No, go ahead. I think I'll stroll around town."

"Don't you want to be near your phone? You really ought to get a cell phone like everybody else."

"I'll get there soon enough."

"Don't go doing anything stupid."

"And what's that supposed to mean?"

"You know damn well what that's supposed to mean. Don't go looking for her, make a fool of yourself. She'll call you when she's ready."

"Hey, Digit."

"What?"

"You've got a bit of cream cheese on the corner of your mouth."

"Who gives a shit?"

Addie watched Digit lumber out the door, nod greetings to someone on the sidewalk, climb into his truck and head off.

Addie slid off his stool and walked to the Homestead.

————

"Seems like everyone wants to see Rebecca today," he was told when he knocked on the door. "Go on up, first door to the left."

Rebecca was in her chair when he entered the room. He looked around without greeting her.

"You could say hello," she said to him.

"Sorry, I … "

"I know who you're here to see. Well, she isn't here. If you'd have stayed put you'd probably have seen her by now."

He felt a little gladdened by this information, wanted to turn to leave, but hesitated. "So you made it through the storm okay."

"I've been through worse."

I'll bet you have, he thought, wondering how he could get the hell out without seeming too rude. "Well, if you're all right, I guess I'll … "

"Don't you want to know where she's gone?"

Of course he did. She knew he did.

Rebecca sized him up, wondered what her daughter saw in this man. He was good looking enough, but she didn't want her daughter charmed by someone who didn't have her best interests at heart.

"So, what's your story?" she asked him.

He didn't need to be interrogated right now. Just let me go, he thought, but he said, "I don't have a story."

"What good are you, then?" She was testing him, knowing his feelings for her daughter would be tested soon enough. "Everybody has a story."

"Well, I don't have one."

He wasn't trying to snow her, she had to give him that. Best to let him go. "She was going to Sandy's house," she said. "Go on, you don't need to hang around here any longer."

———

She's an odd bird, Addie thought as he hastened down the sidewalk, wondering why Verona had been there in the first place.

Any port in a storm, he supposed, trying to keep his excitement in check.

All he wanted to do was see her, smell her, be in her presence.

———

He tried to be cool when he entered Sandy's house, he desperately wanted to be cool, but when there was no one in the living room, or the kitchen, he couldn't help but call out, "Verona? Verona, are you here?"

"Who the hell's that?" came the voice from upstairs.

He ran up the steps, checked Verona's bedroom. Empty. "Sandy?" he said down the hallway.

"In here, you idiot. I told you I was going to take a nap."

Addie slowly opened the door to Sandy's bedroom. The curtains were drawn. Sandy was lying in bed. "And to what do I owe this honor?" she said, rising up on her elbows.

"I'm sorry, Sandy. Rebecca told me Verona was here."

"You're a sorry kind of guy, aren't you? Well, she's not here, not that I know of."

"Sorry about that."

"Stop saying you're sorry. If she's not with Rebecca, she must be at your place. Why didn't you just stay put?"

Why was everybody asking him that? He should have

stayed home. "She called me."

Sandy sat upright. "Did she tell you anything?"

"Only that she was all right. Why? Is there something I should know?"

"Oh, no, no."

"Can I use your phone? I'll call my place, see if she's there."

"Certainly. Be my guest."

"Thanks. Sorry I woke you."

"Stop saying you're sorry."

———————

He let the phone ring ten times, hung up, let it ring twenty. Shit.

He had to get home, but his rental was more than two miles away. He could call Digit, but he couldn't wait for him to get his ass over here.

He walked outside, saw Ken's car moored in a pool of water, but there, on the only high ground of the property, was Sandy's bus. The roads must be passable by now; if not, he'd find a way.

The key was in the ignition. The bus coughed a bit, but started eventually. He stuck to the main roads. If the cops stopped him, he'd say he had to get the bus back to the main lot.

He had to make a couple of detours due to downed limbs, but he made it home at last. He bolted from the bus, ran into his house. There was no one there, no sign of anyone being there after he and Digit had gone.

Now what did he do?

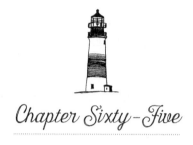

Chapter Sixty-Five

VERONA, SEEKING contentment, sat on the bench and stared at the boat that had given her her name. Like her, the boat, cradled in her slip, had weathered the storm.

She supposed she should move, head to Sandy's and collect herself, but it was so tranquil here, as if the persistent push of life returning to normal was on pause. The sounds of regenerated civilization were confined to the distance, hovering over the town, away from the wharves.

But she'd had enough solitude. She craved comfort, yearned for someone to talk to, someone to help her sort through the whole ridiculous mess. She wished she had a sister.

Who could she confide in? Sandy? Irene? She supposed she could, but she didn't feel close to either of them. She had kept both at bay, believing her quest for self-reliance would shield her, protect her, would somehow bring her a peace that no one else, because of the encumbrances of their lives, could understand.

She wished Addie was with her now. Despite her caution, he was the one she'd allowed in, given partial access to, the one to whom she had almost shared her state of unknowing.

She was glad now she hadn't. It would have complicated things too much, especially now. It was best he only knew her as she was.

Still, looking at the word stenciled on the stern before her, *Verona*, sweeping regally from left to right in gold script, she recalled the quote she'd chosen for her high school yearbook: "They do not love that do not show their love," from, oddly enough, *Two Gentlemen of Verona*, as though her name was predetermined. But her mind, freed from the restraints of its months-long suppression, rapidly brought forth another long-forgotten memorization, a quote she'd also considered as a teen-ager: "It is not in the stars to hold our destiny but in ourselves." What a laugh. She'd never been in control of her destiny.

A sudden stirring, then, a smooth commotion behind her, the quiet broken by a ship's whistle. The boat was coming in, back to business as usual.

She wandered over to the dock, watched as the deckhands hoisted the gangway in place. The boat looked beautiful to her, beckoning. She no longer feared what it once represented — a conveyance to an unwanted past. It was now a means to get away, a vehicle to put things in perspective.

She had the money, too, a credit card if need be. It was … back in Rebecca's room. In her haze, in her confusion, she had left everything behind.

She entered the ticket office, picked up a schedule. The boat would be back in less than three hours.

And she would be on it. She needed distance from every-thing, distance and open water to clear her mind.

Chapter Sixty-Six

Addie McDaniel, sojourner through life, collector of papers and paraphernalia pertaining only to him, steered Sandy's bus by wind-strewn branches, through stall-threatening puddles, over curbs concealed by storm-chased waters. With nowhere to turn, nowhere he could think of to look, he was taking the bus back to the Lily Pond.

He had waited by the phone, waited patiently, but after an hour he could wait no more. It was getting ridiculous, this chase. If she didn't need him, he didn't need her.

But he did need her.

If only he hadn't met her he'd be free right now, free to plan his escape. If Verona hadn't entered his life he wouldn't have doubts about what he should or shouldn't have done, wouldn't be worried about someone he barely knew, wouldn't have opened himself up to this yo-yo of emotions. If he could, he'd go to sleep and wake up as somebody else.

Now wouldn't that be an easy way out?

At the corner of Pleasant and Main, he was delayed by a utility truck making its slow advance up the cobblestones.

Across the street stood the Three Bricks, stalwart as ever, ready to be pointed out yet again on the next round of tours.

He supposed Ken would be back in the office tomorrow, prepared to finish out the season, get the buses lined up for hurricane tours — and he supposed he'd be there too.

He was about to turn left at the Civil War monument when he glimpsed someone stepping sprightly up the sidewalk. Something about the easy stride made him look again, and, it couldn't be …

He accelerated quickly ahead, pulled the bus sharply to the curb, and opened the door.

"Afternoon, ma'am," he said as casually as he could. "Need a lift?"

She stopped, looked up at the man in the driver's seat, and smiled as broadly as he'd ever seen her smile. She cocked her head to the side and said, "I don't accept rides from strangers."

"Nobody stranger than me," he said.

"Than 'I.' "

"You too? Then you'd better hop aboard."

And before she could take a step, he was out of his seat and into her arms.

Chapter Sixty-Seven

T HEY RAMBLED through the old town, the bus creaking along the cobblestones. She would tell him everything eventually, but for now it was pleasant to be a passenger, a relief to be taken for a ride. Neither of them spoke. There was too much to say.

He circled back to Main Street, parked outside the drugstore where he got sandwiches and coffees to go.

She hadn't realized how hungry she was, and she devoured her sandwich with relish as he drove.

She didn't ask where he was going. She was content letting him take over, thankful she didn't have to think, or reflect, or plan, or feel the need to sail away.

He headed away from town, turned right, and right again onto a dirt road that wound behind the airport and out, eventually, into a clearing where a wind-swept valley lay below. He kept to the high road until the road went no further. They were at the beach. They were alone.

As the waves rolled languidly to the shore, he guided her to the back of the bus, where he held her, and she held him, and they shared secrets until dawn.

Epilogue

SOMETIME IN March, Sandy received a postcard from Mexico. "Having wonderful time, wish you were him." It was signed Mr. Morocco. There was no return address.

The Atlantic Café was closed over the winter. The doors were locked, the sign removed, another era was gone.

Rebecca's journals and the old sea chest in the attic were donated, per her wishes, to the Nantucket Historical Association. An exhibition centering around the lonely life of a lighthouse keeper was planned.

The man who lived in the woods had his lodgings unearthed by a hunter one day. The ensuing brouhaha attracted news crews from Boston, whose stories centered on the high cost of island living and of one man's defiant, yet imaginative, response. The board of health, tired of the negative publicity, ordered his habitat dismantled, his underground dwelling filled in. Soon there were rumors that another illegal abode was taking shape deep in the moors, a tree house this time.

After losing his bid for state representative, Jason Bonere was last seen in a theme park in central Florida, demonstrating a proclivity for making balloon animals.

On the final day of the tour season, Addie topped off the tank, gave his tires some air. It was early autumn, the sun was setting sooner.

After dropping off his bus at the lot, he hopped into his old, beat-up Chevy, plopped a cassette into the deck, *New Morning*. "If Not for You," began playing.

He drove to the beach. Stars shimmered in the twilight. As the storied Nantucket astronomer and comet discoverer Maria Mitchell once wrote about her stellar observations, there was "not a breath of air, not a fringe of cloud, all clear, all beautiful."

He looked heavenward, made a wish, walked down the wooden steps to the sand.

He approached the woman sitting on the blanket, asked if he could join her, and, as one, the two of them scanned the steadfast constellations and the untold future they represented.

In Nantucket's domain,
Where seagulls play games,
And nothing is ever the
Same,
Perchance came a
Lady, or was it a girl?
Alone, and without a name.
You know, said she,
I'd rather be free,
Not shackled by some other past,
Grieving for things that might have been,
And wondering why love can't last.
'Round about then,
Or was it at ten?
Untidily crept a new tide,
Now all was known, and remembered again,
Despite all her wishes to hide.
Whatever! she said,
I'm here with my friend,
The better to feel
Heart's response.
Who is it who nears?
O, muse, do you hear
Refrains of my own renaissance?
Dreams of a child, once lost, now compel
Surrender to all that ends well.

As with any reputable tour bus monologue, much of the history mentioned in this book was gleaned from the archives of the Nantucket Historical Association, which has an excellent, and very navigable, website: nha.org. A visit to the NHA's research library on Fair Street, or to any of its properties, which includes the Whaling Museum on Broad Street, is an always-gratifying experience.

Another invaluable resource was Nathaniel Philbrick's definitive, *Away Off Shore: Nantucket Island and its People, 1602-1890*, originally published by Mill Hill Press in 1994 and reissued in 2011 by Penguin Books.

The Nantucket Atheneum, whose first librarian was the famed astronomer Maria Mitchell, has a vast collection of Nantucket books, along with a digital newspaper archive that can be viewed online at nantucketatheneum.org.

Nantucket Magazine, which last published in 2005, and is archived at both the Nantucket Historical Association and Nantucket Atheneum, was also referenced.

About the Author

FOR EIGHT years Steve Sheppard was editor of *Nantucket Magazine,* a respected quarterly dedicated to the history, people, and culture of the island. He was also an editor and reporter for the *Inquirer and Mirror* and *Nantucket Independent,* and a reporter for the *Patriot Ledger* of Quincy, MA. He has written for the *Boston Globe, Philadelphia Inquirer, Providence Journal, Cape Cod Life,* and *Sanctuary* magazine (the award-winning journal of Mass Audubon) among other publications.

He lives on Nantucket.